BONEYARD

D. M. DARROCH

ISBN 978-1-890797-25-6
Copyright © 2022 by D.M. Darroch

www.dmdarroch.com

Requests to publish work from this book should be sent to:
danelle@dmdarroch.com

Books by D.M. Darroch

Silvanus Saga

Canopy

Inventor-in-Training series

The Pirate's Booty

The Crystal Lair

Cyborgia

For young children

No, No, Nora

Nora and the Lake Monster

For Johnny O

The Present

I look at her.

I'm not sure which eye to focus on. Both together, they make my head hurt. Not a hurt like an alarm headache, but a sort of dizziness, like she's hypnotizing me, controlling me somehow. Except I'm more in control than I've ever been. Also, I'm not.

Her eyes are steady, unafraid, curious. She sits on the ground, legs curled beneath her like she's sprouted from the forest floor. Relaxed yet alert, her body is ready for anything, afraid of nothing. I am distinctly aware of her.

She is not beautiful like my Rajani. Not colorful and elfin. Not dangerous in that unpredictable way.

She is not delicate like Ami. Not gentle or timid. Not nurturing and tender.

And yet, there's something about her.

I see her.

All this time, I'm sizing her up. She's doing the same.

She sees me.

I decide to face it all. And I tell her everything.

Chapter One

It's always the last job that gets you.

If you worked the Hill long enough and paid attention, you would know about the slingers who were planning to quit, done with the after-curfew deals, about to go straight. The ones who were going to do one last job, one last sale, one last pick up. Those who stayed in the game one deal too long. The slingers that disappeared.

If you paid attention, you'd know when it was time to quit the business. You convinced yourself you differed from those other slingers. The ones who got caught.

One last job. I only needed one more job to top up my savings and have enough crypto to pay for my trip home. One last collection. Then I'd return to the shallows, get myself a little float. One last walk on the dark side of First City. Then I would put the dust slinging behind me, pick up a kelp fork, and take care of my mother. One last visit to Rajani before I joined the kelp farmers. I would make Ami proud. One last deal, and I'd be free.

I was late for the pick up. I cut across the central park to reach the hill where Rajani and the other dustrats lived.

Concrete covered the entire park; its inhospitable surface prevented rough sleeping. I tightened the drawstrings of my sweatshirt to cover my nose; the light-transmitting pavement reeked of chemicals. Prompted by my neural mesh, the sidewalk glowed on as I walked past, dotting a path through the darkness.

The message packets had been spliced into the automated curfew alert. I hadn't recognized the coded signature, which in retrospect should have been a clue, but the money was decent. The sender had arranged a pick up at Rajani's, and I figured, if they were in business with her, they'd pay as promised. She'd been slinging dust a long time, had bought my stash when I'd turned up in First City. It was Rajani who had taught me the street value of a bottle of Axon pills after I'd escaped from care with the clothes on my back and whatever I could fit into a pillowcase. She showed me how to survive on the Hill and had introduced me to the slingers and dusters who'd become my people. I had moved on from slinging and I was collecting now, bringing cash from the slingers to their suppliers. Though I'd moved beyond Rajani, I kept her close. I'd miss her when I went north. Even though she rejected my romantic advances—either she didn't like men or she didn't like me or the dust was all the lover she'd ever need—she was family to me.

She was sexy as hell, and because a part of me still hoped for a thing with her, my judgment was off. I didn't know the supplier who'd sent the message, which was unusual. Collections were usually a routine thing. I picked up payments from the same slingers, delivered them to the same dead drops. A few hours later, my crypto account filled. Occasionally, my mesh would get a transmission, additional pick ups or requests for a communication with a specific slinger. I'd never consider heading into the streets after curfew to collect for some unknown supplier.

But then, I'd never received a transmission from a strange supplier. And this one knew Rajani. She avoided the shadiest of suppliers. If this one was paying for a collection from Rajani, they were probably legit. I could ask Rajani when I got there. It would be fine. Besides, it gave me an excuse to see her before I went north. Remember, the money was decent. I needed a little more to pad my bank account. It would be my very last job. The very last one. No more after that.

Jogging around the corner at 13th, I pulled the hood of my black sweatshirt off my head. I shook out my bleached hair and dug my fingers into my sweat-tickled scalp. The air was humid and cloying and my jeans and sweatshirt, the uniform of the after-curfew collector, stuck to my skin. Soon, I'd be in the shallows again, feeling the gentle breeze off the water, dangling my feet from a float into kelp-filled waters. I could break curfew one more time, make a collection one more time. Maybe Rajani would let me kiss her, just once, my going-away gift.

Rajani's hole was five blocks down on H Street. And it was literally a hole; a set of steps below the street led to her door. Bars covered her windows on the outside, sheets of paper covered her windows on the inside. I'd known her three months before she'd trusted me enough to tell me where she lived. I always thought it helped that I wasn't a duster; she knew I wouldn't steal her stash. No, I'd had plenty of those Axon pills when I was in care, when they were testing their drugs on me. No way I'd choose to snort the powder from those pills, not that I judged anyone else's choices. After all, those choices were paying my way back home.

When I got there, H Street was empty. That should have tipped me off. I was overeager to see Rajani; maybe that's why I ignored so many warning signs. The optical fibers on the street had burned out; First City had never replaced them, not as long as I'd lived there. Cost-cutting measures or maybe the city leaders didn't want to know, not exactly, what happened there. As long as the throwaways kept to themselves, the city left them alone. Except tonight, no one was on the street. I wondered if a patrol had come through earlier and scattered the dustrats to their holes? Even the stairways to the underground apartments were clear of rough sleepers. Where had they all gone?

My scalp prickled, and I pulled the hood back over my head. I crept along the street, throwing glances to my left and to my right. I spun around and looked behind me. Whistling lightly under my breath, I picked up my pace. I didn't run though. Didn't want to appear weak or scared. Not here. Not ever. I stuck my hands into my pockets and hunched forward. I was minding my business. Last job. Good money. Then out of here.

Light bled from Rajani's window, tinted yellow from the papers across the glass. I stumped down the concrete steps to her door and raised my fist to knock. The door drifted open on its own. Rajani wouldn't have left her door open. She'd paid too much for her air processor. "In and out, quick! Door closed!" I could almost hear her voice in the silent night. Yet I kept going. Stupidly, blindly, working for that payday.

"Hey, Rajani! Queen Rani! Why's your door wide open? It's me, Lazlo!"

I stepped into the room. The air processor hummed in the corner, sucking in heavy oxygen air, pumping out a lighter vapor. I shut the door behind me. The ceiling light cast a harsh glare on the room. A battered beige sofa snugged against one wall, duct tape and chewing gum holding the stuffing inside. Rajani's discarded clothing, all bright reds, oranges, and yellows, coated the scuffed and water-damaged parquet flooring. A plywood table in the middle of the small room held a box of tiny plastic bags, three scrip bottles of Axon tablets, and a stack of glorious, old school, untraceable cash.

I pocketed the cash: that's what they had sent me to collect. The supplier would smuggle it out to Canada, wire it back to Cascadia, append it to the financial accounts wired into their networks. It would go out untraceable and return legit. And sometime tomorrow I'd get my payday, a boost in the cryptobank coded into my neural mesh, and I'd go north.

The bags, the pills—those were Rajani's trade. I left them alone. She scored those pills, crushed them into the dust that was so potent, even when cut with lesser substances, that hooked a duster the first time they snorted it, sent them dissociating into beautiful, multicolored worlds with no rough living, no enforced curfews, no PAP alarms, all the light air you could breathe. And no Axon Pharma. The irony: dusters became dependent on Axon Pharma's pills to escape Axon Pharma.

That dust she was slinging? Those pills were Axon Pharma's solution to the mental illness, what we called *yiyuzheng*, the illness that caused the insiders in their light air high rises and their air processed offices to off themselves. The mental illness that was the unforeseen side effect of Axon Pharma's own neural mesh technology. But *yiyuzheng* was an insider illness. We outsiders didn't live long enough to suffer from it. Didn't stop them from testing those pills on the throwaways though, the lost kids of the outsiders. The kids like me who'd been stolen from their families and sent to care.

That dust Rajani was slinging, those pills she was crushing, had made me who I was today: a runaway dust slinger with an overactive dendrite disorder.

And those dendrites were on fire now. I squeezed my hands against my head, the agony unshakable. An alarm was sounding, shooting tiny darts of energy through my mesh, knocking me to my knees. I curled up on the dusty floor among Rajani's clothing and squeezed my eyes tight, willing the alarm to stop. Tears pricked in my eyes, crept beneath my eyelids, and dripped down my face. I wiped them away quickly and forced my eyes open.

Rajani's dark eyes stared back at me; her lifeless body stretched across the bathroom threshold at the end of the hallway. Multicolored braids pooled around her head, shimmering garishly in the bright light, and her lively brown face had faded to a dull gray.

I crawled painfully toward her and placed my hand against her wrist, against her neck. Her skin was still warm, but she had no pulse.

"Rajani? Wake up, Rajani!" I slapped her face again and again. White dust powdered her upper lip and her tiny nose. She'd tested the supply; maybe she'd taken too much? But dust didn't kill you, did it? Long-term dusters vanished into ever-longer states of dissociation until, one day, they never returned. Couldn't tell reality from fantasy. They didn't go out like this; Axon dust didn't kill them. Did it? How long had Rajani been using?

She wasn't breathing. I didn't know what to do, but I couldn't just sit there staring. That was Rajani lying there, my first friend in the city, my almost lover. I wiped the dust from her nose, crouched over her, put my mouth on hers, and blew. Pushed on her chest a few times. Blew again. I pushed on her chest again.

And finally, my heart understood what my brain already knew. Rajani was dead. Alive, she'd never have let me close like that.

I lay on the floor beside her. The alarm was shooting currents of energy through my mesh, slicing through my brain. The signal enveloped me, crushing my brain. I buried my head in my hands, cringing from the physical pain, yet unable to avoid seeing the body of my friend. She had a slender frame and thin hands and feet that were constantly moving and dancing. Her vibrant pink and blue and yellow braids extended her body and punctuated her words and emotions when they were swinging free. Her facial piercings, nose, lip, eyebrow, gleamed and shimmered with every one of her myriad facial expressions. Every bit of Rajani lay still, silenced forever.

Nausea overwhelmed me, and I rolled away from Rajani's body and vomited. Pulses throbbed against my skull, and I knew I had to run. This was a full PAP alarm, "Preserve And Protect"; its purpose was to lower the resistance of people in a specific area, making them easier to arrest. It would soon knock me out. If the police found me hovering over a dead body, well, that wouldn't be an optimal outcome.

I gritted my teeth and forced myself to stand. Stumbling toward the door, I saw those three scrip bottles on the table. No way I could leave those here. If some rough sleeping duster got their hands on those, they'd surf the neural gray zone so deep and hard they'd never come back. Besides, I could trade or sell them, add a bit more crypto to my bank for the journey north.

I'd never steal from Rajani, not when she was alive. It might sound cold, but she was dead. I could do nothing now to help her. If it had gone the other way—me lying dead on the floor and her alive and staring at my stash—I knew she wouldn't have thought twice.

I grabbed those three bottles and jammed them into my pockets. The alarm in my head hammered, and I knew I couldn't fight it much longer. I forced my body to the door, dragging one heavy leg behind the other. Drawing that inside air into my lungs, I put all the energy I had into my two arms, hauled my hood over my head, yanked open the door. Ascending a mountain couldn't have been harder than climbing those three steps to the street. I was close to being in the clear when the fog rolled over my mind and all went blessedly numb.

Stinging in my nose, acrid fumes, and I was awake again. A glaring beam of light in my face, shadows around me, the pounding never having stopped, and a voice: "Wakey, wakey sleepy head."

Rough hands grabbed my arm and pulled me up. I slumped forward, my body not yet mobile, and my face stung from an open-handed slap. My vision cleared. Facing me was a respirator mask, neural-blocking helmet, and PAP body armor emblazoned with the joint Axon/Cascadia logo. The *hundan* wearing it was bigger than anyone raised on kelp, textured food product, and nutrient water. An insider.

"Check the pockets," he said.

The hands holding me patted me down and tossed the three scrip bottles to Respirator Mask. "What have we here?" Hands waved the wad of cash.

I was having trouble staying vertical. The alarm continued looping over the network, far longer than I was sure was legit. But as long as patrols wore neural-blocking helmets, they'd continue to break the Cascadia law on humane alarm limits.

"This where you live, Rat?" said Respirator Mask, walking down the steps to Rajani's apartment.

My head rolled to the side. The fog was creeping in again. I opened my mouth to answer, but only drool came out.

"Freaking duster's totally out of it," said Hands.

"Got a dee-bee in here. Probably his slinger."

My arms were yanked behind me, cold metal squeezed my wrists. I was being arrested, but it barely registered through my haze.

"Looks like this is your last trip paid by Axon, Rat," said Hands. "Unless you count your next trip—to jail."

I wanted to tell them I wasn't a dustrat or a thief; I hadn't killed Rajani. It wouldn't have changed anything. I was in the neighborhood; I looked the part, and they caught me with the goods. They had me in cuffs; why didn't they shut off the alarm? One thing I knew for sure: I was in trouble. Well and truly in trouble.

Chapter Two

❧

The next two days thundered past, the neural hangover brought on by the PAP alarm worse than any I'd ever experienced. Two days of a screaming headache, nausea, and vomiting, and when I came out of it, I'd been charged with drug trafficking and negligent homicide. My chances of an acquittal were slim to none: I'd taken both the money and the drugs, and my fingerprints and DNA were all over Rajani's place.

I sat in an aluminum oxynitride cell for two months. The unbreakable transparent ceramic isolated me from physical human contact while making my every movement visible to the guards and the other prisoners locked in their see-through cages. At first, I was shy about washing or using the toilet. That modesty disappeared, fast.

I recognized many others, dusters and slingers from the Hill, arrested the same night I was. A long line of down-trodden throwaways stretched from one wall to the other, packed into ten-by-ten boxes. The bodies changed frequently as their cases were processed. Jail time for some, lucky if they were rough sleepers. A week or two free of the heavy air. But that light air came at a cost if they were dusters. Withdrawal sent them into dark dissociations, the complete opposite of the colorful daydreams they experienced when they were using.

I rotted in my cell for a long time, waiting for my judgment. The tired face of my court-appointed lawyer flickered from a screen outside my cage at the worst imaginable times. He even startled me when I was taking a leak once. My attorney video-visited me a couple times a day at first, less and less frequently as my case dragged on.

The last time my lawyer's careworn face appeared on screen was a few minutes before a guard hauled me out of the cell. The lawyer looked down, not into the camera, as he read my sentence: ten years lockup in Coulee Correctional. Still avoiding the camera, he said I was lucky my birthday wasn't for another month. I'd spend the first year of my sentence in juvenile lockup. If I'd been eighteen at the time of my offense, my dual charges would have sent me straight to adult prison for double the time. I had the feeling he read that bit as well.

Lucky. That was the word he used.

Coulee Correctional was an antiquated, male-only prison. Most Cascadian prisons accepted all genders; gender-neutral incarceration was the norm. But not Coulee, oh no. No female company for old Lazlo. How was that lucky? They'd imprison me for ten years in the windblown desert of eastern Cascadia, separated from First City and the shallows by the vast sweeper forest. Lucky, he said.

Ten years! A quarter of an outsider's life expectancy. Lucky.

Even if the processed inside air awarded me a few more years, Ami would still be outside, slowly dying. Lucky.

I didn't have ten years to waste.

"I'm innocent!"

The cuffs snapped around my wrists. The guard was a wall, beefy and stoic. No point in struggling against him, but I would not make it easy for him, either. I went limp, all dead weight. It seemed like a good idea until he pulled a black metallic device from his belt. A transparent screen showed one flashing green dot. He grinned at me, pressed a button on the side, and a needle pierced through my brain, a quick, deep jab. I heard myself grunt in a less than human way.

"We're not going to have any trouble, are we inmate?" The guard hauled me to my feet by my elbow.

My lips struggled to form words. All I could muster was a low hum and some drool. It was the first time I'd seen a PAP tracker, but it wouldn't be my last. Before I actually laid eyes on one, I'd assumed they were blunt tools of control, central alarms used to sweep the Hill. The gadgets were standard issue for patrols and correctional officers, but I hadn't realized they could pinpoint the location of one person. Or direct a PAP alarm to one specific neural mesh.

The guard frogmarched me through the hive of holding cells, out the back of the building, and packed me into a long, automated transport. Several other prisoners sat in the transport already. I met their eyes, gave nothing away. A few stared stonily forward, like me. Show no emotion, except maybe anger. Certainly not fear. And definitely no tears, not like the boy weeping in the corner.

"They get you for?" asked the boy next to me.

"Innocent," I shot back.

"Yeah. Me too." He laughed but asked no more questions.

A couple more prisoners joined us; all together there were fifteen of us. No adults, except for the two guards. They climbed in last, waving their trackers at us. They didn't have to say anything. From the looks passing between prisoners, I figured we'd all gotten a personal introduction to what that shiny device could do. Still, one of those *hundans* thought it necessary to say: "No funny stuff, any of you."

The transport doors slipped shut with a pneumatic hiss and the external ventilators closed. The internal air processors clicked on to protect the corrections officers, those lifelong insiders, from the heavy atmosphere. Didn't want them aging too fast, not them. We prisoners knew how little we were worth. Cascadia would never waste energy for light air on us. But then, the best air I'd ever breathed had been in lockup.

A blast of light, carbonated air tickled my nose, and I scratched it, my cuffed wrists clinking. A whirring mechanical sound echoed through the metal chamber, likely the solar arrays positioning themselves. With a rough jerk, the transport began moving.

We swayed left as the transport rounded a curve, our packed bodies holding each other in place. Banking right and left, we were quickly on the transway, the wide, paved road used primarily by self-driving transports. The transport gears ratcheted higher, and the speed forced my body back into the seat.

The Coulee correctional facility was 500 miles away on the other side of Cascadia. Though Coulee was almost directly east of First City, we would have to drive nearly half the total distance south toward the border of Nocal to skirt around the sweeper forest. The forest marked the border between eastern and western Cascadia. Within the next decade, scientists expected the transway, the only land connection between both halves, to be overtaken by the sweepers. When that happened, many believed Cascadia would split into two nations like Nocal and Bahia Sur had fifty years ago.

Cascadia sent its convicts to eastern prisons like the one in Coulee. Most crimes were committed on the western side, a simple equation since most Cascadians lived there. Centuries of wild grass fires, drought, and baking sun had sent the easterners below ground. I wasn't entirely sure how they made their living, but I suspected many of them guarded prisoners from the west.

My seatmate nudged against me with his shoulder. "He's going to puke."

I glanced at the boy across from us, riding backwards. His skin was clammy and pale, his eyes clamped shut.

While I was being transported to care after they tore me from Ami's arms, I'd thrown up. I was twelve, and I'd never ridden in an autonomous transport or any other solar-powered vehicle. Up to that point, I'd only ever rowed boats built from discarded parts. I'd never even been on a kelping vessel. Speeding in a rocketing metal silo with no windows to the outside world, no fresh ocean air in my lungs, scared and missing my mother—of course I'd been sick. The speeding transport had forced me backward, and when I vomited, the vomit had flown backwards, coating me in my puke. Worse than traveling to prison for ten years would be arriving covered in someone else's puke.

"Uh? Guards?" said the boy seated beside me.

One guard had fallen asleep. The other looked back over his shoulder. "What?"

"This guy's going to throw up."

"Not my problem." He turned back around.

"Do something!"

The guard ignored him.

"You useless, lazy—*hundan!*" My seatmate curled into himself, moaning. "Stop the PAP! Please!"

Without turning, the guard waved the tracker in the air. "Say you're sorry."

"Sorry... sorry!" My seatmate shuddered. "Stop the PAP... now... please!" He passed out, his head hanging forward.

"Anyone else?" Meeting with silence, the guard dropped his arm. "Quick learners."

The sick boy was not improving. If he heaved, vomit would land on me and my unconscious seatmate, and that would make me puke too. I thought I might try to pulse him, sending a calming image from my neural mesh to his.

I closed my eyes, imagining fresh ocean air, sunshine, and Ami's mint tea. It had settled my stomach when I was young, and I pinned the homey image in my mind; I pictured the nauseous prisoner across the aisle, shot the image at him, a pinprick into his neural mesh.

I wasn't sure it would work on a total stranger, but I could think of nothing else to do. If I didn't try something, my seatmate and I were going to be covered in puke. I'd tried this before, pulsed thoughts at Rajani when she was having a bad trip. I'd massaged her neural mesh often in the two years I'd known her. The other times I'd gotten through to someone else's mesh were mostly accidental, like when I got to Big Danson, the kid who'd bullied me when I'd been in care.

The very first time I was lying on the floor, Big Danson sitting on my stomach, holding me down, burping in my face. His breath stank of the rehydrated protein product—"Now with more poultry flavor!"—we'd had for dinner. He was heavy, and I was having difficulty catching my breath. I wanted to get him off me. It was when he drooled a stream of saliva from his mouth, taunting me that he'd drip it on my face, that I lashed out. I squeezed my eyes shut, imagining myself sticking him with Appei's kelp fork. I'd hold him down and force salt water down his throat. When I opened my eyes, he was coughing, choking almost. He had rolled sideways off me and was gasping for air, his face pale and stricken.

At that moment, Miz Hazel had intervened and punished

me for bullying Big Danson. The beating she gave me barely registered. I was a little kid raised on Ami's bedtime stories. Of course, I became convinced that I had magical powers. My destiny wasn't to grow up in that care home, locked away with the other throwaways. And I kept practicing. Of course, now I know there's no magic involved, simply an undocumented side effect of the Axon pills. But at age twelve, the belief in magic gave me the faith and confidence I needed to escape.

I concentrated on stomach-calming thoughts, sticking them with my mind into the nauseous prisoner's mesh, like Ami's tiny sewing pins into one of her overstuffed pincushions. The sound and odor of retching hadn't begun, so I kept going until my seatmate stirred.

"Ow, my head." His arm brushed mine. "Hey, you sleeping?"

I opened my eyes and looked at him, but he wasn't talking to me. The prisoner across the aisle was snoring.

Chapter Three

The steel can rocketed along the transway toward Second City. I watched the sleeping boy for about an hour until a different whirring noise indicated that something had changed. My seatmate noticed it too.

"You hear that?" he said.

"Yeah. What is it?"

"Switching to cell. Too dark for the solar arrays."

"It's still daylight—"

"Sweeper forest." He said it with a bored tone. Like it should be obvious. Like he was an expert.

"You seen it?"

He shifted in his seat. "Close up? Nope. Read about it, though." A second passed. "You?"

I shook my head.

Climate scientists had engineered the sweeper forest centuries ago. Together with the kelp fields and the geological capture sites, the forest sequestered the excess carbon that had caused the earth's change. Science halted the global warming, but not until after we had already done extensive damage to the planet. The fix that finally arrived, a forest that could clean the air, was now causing damage of its own.

The sweeper forest cleaned the carbon from the air, held it in its mass of roots and bark like dirt under a vast rug. At the same time, it exhaled oxygen. Lots of oxygen.

Here we were, driving beneath a scientific marvel, Cascadia's signature contribution to humankind, and we would not see it. No windows in this metal can. I imagined what the sweepers looked like. How different would they be from the sideways-leaning windswept and salt-kissed trees near the shallows? Were they honestly all that much taller than the trees on the green roofs of First City? If I didn't see them now, driving beneath them, I'd have to wait another ten years until I had a chance. A decade stuck in the Coulee wasteland.

In my mind, I soared above our float in the shallows and glided over the shoreline trees. I was a seabird, one of those plain sand-colored ones that dives deep into the water and steals from the deck of floats. Then I was in First City again, no longer a bird, and Rajani was there, laughing at me, her multicolored braids dancing about her head.

My seatmate shifted, and Rajani disappeared from my thoughts. The transport was slowing, stopping.

"Coulee?" I asked.

"Nope." He sniffed. "We've covered 300 miles, maybe a little more. Not even close."

Lucky me, sitting beside such an authority.

The other boys were stirring, chatting amongst themselves and having the same conversation.

One guard stood and waved his PAP gadget. We were immediately quiet.

"I need ten volunteers," he said.

Momentary silence until one boy piped up, "What for?"

"Obstacle on the transway. Need some of you to clear it."

My seatmate nudged me and whispered, "Guess we're the road crew now."

Another boy asked, "What's in it for us?"

"Five seconds. Decide who's going out there, or I haul out the ten ugliest *hundans* I see."

I swallowed. Ten years. Might be my only chance.

"I'll go."

The guard nodded at me. "Nine more."

"What you doing?" said my seatmate.

"Seeing the sweeper forest."

I pushed past him and walked to the front of the transport. A guard unlocked my wrists, and I rubbed them, massaging away the memory of the hard metal. I stood alone for a minute before a tall, brown prisoner stepped forward.

"Chance to get some air."

The other prisoners sat silently, eyes cast down. The tall boy sized me up.

"Five, four, three, two," said the guard. "You, you, you—" He pointed and clicked the tracker at each poor *hundan*, sending a short trigger to their neural mesh as he selected them.

Forced labor and a headache. A simple threat would have been enough. He knew that, but these guards enjoyed watching suffering.

The air processors clicked off, and the doors slid open. Ten unshackled prisoners stepped onto the dark and empty transway. Unlike the eight-lane transways in the west that connected First City and Second City, the transway through the forest was narrow, with barely enough space to accommodate one transport each way. The light from the transport's interior cast a murky glow on the ground to reveal a road buckled by roots and dirty with pine needles. One guard remained inside, monitoring the remaining prisoners, while the other followed us out of the vehicle. The door slid shut behind us, cutting off the light.

"What the—"

"We supposed to work in the dark?"

"Can't see!"

"Shut up! Give me a sec!"

The guard fumbled with his flashlight. It was midday, but standing under the sweeper trees, it might have been midnight on H Street, only darker. In a flash, the city kid in me disappeared, the collector who avoided the lights after curfew. The light was what I wanted now. I needed to see where I was. I stared into blackness, listened to the breathing of the others, and tried to ignore the goosebumps running up and down my arms.

A memory of Ami came to me, her warm and sleepy scent as she cuddled me after a nightmare. I squeezed my eyes tight, and then opened them slowly, adjusting my vision to the gloom. The prisoners stood huddled together, a shadowy crew of gray figures. The guard's light finally flicked on and he motioned with it toward the obstacle: a pile of dead wood had fallen across the transway. Some of the downed branches were as wide around as my torso; others were even wider.

The guard stood facing us, his back braced against the transport. As he panned the light from left to right, I could barely detect the sides of the road. Massive upright cylindrical shapes edged the transway; Rajani's entire 600 square foot apartment would fit inside the cylinders, and it was impossible to see far beyond them. The dark gray tree trunks, because I realized suddenly that I was looking at the sweeper trees, disappeared into the murky air above our heads. "Get moving," said the guard, his voice breaking slightly.

"What's got him so worried?" said someone.

Someone else mocked, "Awww, he's scared of the dark.".

I waited for a sadistic pap, but none came. The flashlight beam wavered and strengthened.

We spread out across the transway. The branches were large and heavy, and required a minimum of three boys working together to drag one to the road's edge. I teamed up with a short, bulky kid and the tall boy who'd volunteered with me. Slowly, our ten bodies bent and lifted and hauled branches a few feet, dropped them, gathered our strength, and hauled them a few feet more.

"We need more than ten prisoners," I said. "We'll be here all day."

"Work harder," said the guard. His flashlight was no longer illuminating our work area; he was pointing the light deep into the forest, a pathetic yellow glow that barely pierced the gloom. In fact, he wasn't even watching us.

"*Hundan*," said the short kid. "Lazy *hundan*."

I expected to watch him twitch in pain when the guard papped him with the tracker, but he seemed not to have heard, distracted as he was with his bizarre examination of the forest.

"Think he'd notice if we took off right now?" said the tall boy.

His question hung unanswered in the thick air. We were all thinking the same thing. Nowhere to go.

Eventually, there were only two branches left, the biggest ones. I didn't know how long it had taken to clear the transway, but we were tired and sweating in the heavy, moist air. That was when the flashlight flickered out. The guard cursed and whacked the flashlight a few times. The light blinked on again temporarily and then died.

"Hurry, you *hundans*!" He sounded almost panicky.

"Coward," I said, bold now that he couldn't see where to aim the neural jab.

He turned his back to us, those he was responsible for

watching and controlling. Ten prisoners in the dark. One distracted guard. We could easily take him, knock him out, get our hands on the tracker. Get those transport doors open, take out the other guard.

And that's where my plan stopped. Transports weren't driven; they were programmed. This one's destination was the prison in Coulee. To change it, we'd need a password. If the guards had one, unlikely as that was, it would be mere hours until Coulee noticed we hadn't arrived at our destination. I didn't have time to think through our options because the transport door abruptly slid open.

"Aren't you *hundans* done yet?" The second guard yelled from inside the transport.

"Just finished," said the first guard, shining his flashlight on us as we dumped the last branch. "Next time, you're out there." He shoved his way in, not caring that we were all still outside.

One after another, we presented our wrists to be cuffed, and returned to our seats. Could we have escaped? Had I missed my only chance? Ten years yawned into the distance, stretching from this moment in the sweeper forest until the end of my sentence in Coulee.

My seatmate moved his knees to the side, and I climbed over him. "Was it worth it?"

I shrugged, staring out the open door, the transway briefly visible. A shadow scuttled through the beam and was gone. The doors slipped shut, and the transport sped forward, pushing me back into my seat again.

Chapter Four

The next time the transport slowed, there was no doubt we'd arrived at Coulee Correctional. Our bodies shifted from side to side as the vehicle banked tightly around a corner. I lurched forward as we crept down a steep grade. A rough grating sounded outside the transport, followed by something heavy grinding open, and we were rolling forward again, ever downward.

The prisoners surrounding me nudged each other, laughing nervously. My brain drifted away, and I was floating on my back in the kelp fields, cool saltwater supporting me, a warm breeze kissing my cheeks.

"Hey bro, where'd you go?" said my seatmate, his voice bringing me back to myself.

"No worries." It had been a while since I'd experienced a random dissociation, one of the side effects of the Axon pills. Axon Corp had formulated them to provide "gentle escapes from reality". They marketed the little pills to insiders for the "reduction of anxiety and stress". Thing was, I hadn't used the stuff since right after I'd run from care, when Rajani showed me what those pills—crushed, cut, and snorted—

could do to a brain. The lack of control had terrified me, and I'd never used again. Made me an ideal slinger and collector, because I never touched the stash.

Though I was handcuffed, surrounded by convicted strangers and two sadistic guards, being hauled blindly to prison far away from home, this wasn't the scariest thing that had ever happened to me. Why had my brain gone to that neural gray zone where the dustrats lived? Not good. Not good at all.

I needed to be in control of my mind. If my brain dusted out randomly, what chance did I have to escape?

I had to practice again. I vowed to strengthen my mind and regain control of my mesh. My brain was a muscle and if I exercised it, lifting heavier and heavier thoughts, pulsing them farther and farther, I wouldn't lose control again.

The transport doors slid open.

"Home sweet home, you little *shashus*," said a guard.

"Freaking *hundan*," said the boy beside me. "I'm no killer. I'm in for shoplifting."

"Thought you were innocent."

"Shut up." He pushed into the aisle behind the others, holding their wrists to be unlocked before they stepped off the transport.

My conviction would make me *shashu* in the eyes of the others. No difference in their eyes between murder, involuntary manslaughter, negligent homicide; they all resulted in the death of another person. If Rajani had died two months later, I would have been sent down with some seriously dangerous convicts.

I remained seated, let the other prisoners fight amongst themselves for the honor of being first to disembark the transport. What was the rush? I had ten years to see the inside of prison. It wouldn't make a difference when I got out. The tall boy who'd helped me clear the transway waited as well. The other prisoners cleared out, leaving us alone in the transport. I stood and walked up to him. His lazy eyes watched me.

I nodded my chin at him. "Lazlo," I said.

"Cesar."

I stepped off the transport, Cesar right behind me. The transport idled in a tunnel carved into rock. Rough and jagged, the ceiling was a space blasted out of solid granite. Light-transmitting concrete walls glowed yellow and sloped deeper into the tunnel. The other prisoners stood in a noisy clump, feeling the rough walls, kicking at the floor, and looking around.

"We underground?" said Cesar.

"Looks like."

A warning tingle tickled inside my head before a short alert jolted my brain. I gritted my teeth and looked around, searching for the guard who'd triggered it. Behind us, the transport doors closed. The vehicle reversed out of the tunnel, driving the transport guards back to the city. The alert stopped, and a transmission began. We stood silently in the narrow space as we each received the transmission.

<u>Walk down the tunnel, single file. No talking.</u>

We obeyed. The desire to avoid pain can make even the most stubborn *hundan* compliant. For a fat minute, anyway. Shoes pounding on stone, the whisper of pant legs, the sound of breathing. You'd never have known we were a group of throwaways and petty criminals. Well, not to hear us anyway. The fact that we were in prison might have given us away.

The rough ground was lit intermittently with optical fibers, dark where the native rock interrupted the glow. One prisoner in front of me tripped and went down with a curse.

The deeper we walked, the more the cavern walls pressed in. My heart roared in my ears. The only sound louder than its red thrumming was my breathing. Gray fog was rolling in over my brain and I clenched and unclenched my fists, fighting for air and space and calm. I stumbled to the side of the tunnel, leaned into the rough, cold rock, and closed my eyes. Footsteps shuffled past and bodies brushed by me. I breathed deeply and inhaled the cool air that smelled of antiseptic and lime with a light undertone of mildew.

Turning around, I pressed my cheek against the rock. The hard, jutting surface dug into my skin, grounding me. I forced the fog back. I would not lose control. Not twice in ten minutes. Not again. The prisoners' footfalls echoed through the cavern, more distant now as they walked away from me. I opened my eyes and watched as the lights flickered off ahead of me, a low gleam glowing around a bend in the wall as the boys moved forward. A lone light on the ground beside me remained lit, triggered by my neural mesh. I suspected the prison guards knew I was here, alone, standing still. My brain mesh made monitoring easy.

<u>Keep moving, prisoner.</u>

Drawing the cool air into my lungs, I continued down the tunnel, lights blinking on as I approached, blinking off as I passed. The tunnel straightened and a gust of wind hit me. High above the floor, ancient metal fans spun and rattled. The other riders were small specks at the end of the tunnel. One by one, they disappeared behind a blue door.

The sole remaining human in the tunnel, I was no longer claustrophobic. Solitary. A tunnel hermit. I was the only person in the world. Suddenly, I was frightened, right back in the transport that took me to the care home. I was twelve years old again, Appei gone silent and Ami left behind. Ami was all alone, but I didn't want to leave her. They stole me away; why hadn't she stopped them? I had tried to fight them, but they were too strong. I was a kid, a weak, throwaway kid.

Did she know where I was? What they'd done to me in care? She didn't know I was in Coulee. How would she?

My fear that ten years in prison had stolen my future was only slightly less paralyzing than the fear that I might have a future, but one without Ami in it. I'd survived without a family for too long. I'd worked too hard to get back to the shallows. Rajani had been a sort of substitute family. Anyone who'd known us together would testify that I'd never have harmed her. I'd lost her too, and now I'd lost ten years, paying for something I hadn't done.

I'd been so close to my homecoming, to seeing Ami again, my crypto bank ready to take me there in style. But Cascadia had taken that too. I was paying with my time and my hard-earned crypto for something I hadn't done. Ten years and my life's savings.

Being alone in this dark hole seemed final and hopeless and terrifying.

I could let the neural gray zone take me. The fog hovered there, waiting to smooth everything out, erase all the bad feelings. Erase everything Cascadia had done to me. Make me feel okay that they'd stolen my mother, my childhood, and these next ten years. I could let the residue of the Axon pills, the results of the lab-rat testing they'd done on my childhood brain, take me far away. My mind could stay there forever and forget the truth.

Honestly, I was tempted. It would have been easy. I'd be twenty-eight when they finally let me out. Long past Ami's expiration date. There might still be a chance to find a partner and have a kid before my mesh tracked off. Standing alone in that tunnel, dim concrete lighting the way to my future, mildew and moisture in my nostrils, it would have been easy to let the fog take me.

Except for the bitterness in my mouth, the seething in my heart, the fiery anger pulsing through me. My love for Ami had gotten me this far. My hatred for Cascadia and Axon would take me the rest of the way. I planned to escape this place or die trying.

I ran the rest of the way through the tunnel, my heart racing in my throat, goosebumps raised across my skin, and when I got to that blue door, I yanked it open and hurled my body inside.

Chapter Five

❧

I stood in a large circular room. The whitewashed stone walls stretched to an arched ceiling high above the polished cement floor. Blue doors labeled with one letter each circled the room. A transparent pod hung from the ceiling; guards sat in front of monitors inside the suspended cage.

<u>Prisoner, go directly to door J.</u>

I looked up into the guard pod. One of them was transmitting, but who? They stared straight ahead, transfixed by the monitors, trackers resting beside them. They didn't look at their prisoners or interact with them. No need to touch them or breathe the same air as them. I was less than a prisoner, less than a human. I was a little green dot on their screens.

"Hey, you there! Guards!" Reckless wild energy took me. Nothing left to lose. "Look at me!" A jolt deep inside my head, controlling, pulsing, forcing me to the ground in a painful ball. Through the jolting pain, I kept watching the guard pod, looking for something resembling human emotion. I didn't expect any of them to care about me; I wasn't that stupid. But I wanted to annoy someone, get some kind of rise out of them. Small and cowering on the floor, I tried again. "*Hundans!*" I screamed. The jolt intensified, but nothing changed. No facial movements that betrayed anger or disapproval. Not the merest flicker of irritation, like when you swat a fly from your arm. I was a tiny green dot, easily controlled by the press of a button.

<u>Prisoner, go directly to door J.</u>

The transmission interrupted the PAP alarm. I stood and stomped to the door, silently flipping off the guards in their ceramic pod. I flung open door J, revealing a large changing room. My fellow travelers were getting undressed, dumping their discarded clothing into a wheeled bin. Other boys I didn't recognize were there as well, dressed in yellow coveralls, "Coulee Correctional Facility" emblazoned across their backs.

"Where you been?" Cesar stood shirtless near the door as I walked in.

I shrugged. "Thought I'd step out for a smoke."

"Clothes off, in the bins," said a coverall-wearing prisoner, maybe sixteen or seventeen years old. "Showers through that hall. You get clean coveralls when you're done."

"Who are you then?" I asked him. "You guards?"

The boy scoffed. "We're juvvies. Prisoners, like you."

"So you got no." Cesar winked at me. "Don't much feel like giving you my rags."

"Yeah Cesar, now you mention it, I don't much feel like having a shower."

The coverall boy sighed and shrugged his shoulders. "Up to you. You'll figure it out." He pushed the bin along the hallway, collecting clothing from other prisoners.

Cesar looked at me. I didn't want to back down either, but my skin was sticky with dried sweat. A hot shower and a clean head of hair would wash away the long, stale ride and forced transway labor.

"Might as well." I pulled my t-shirt over my head.

"What you think happens if we don't?"

"They'll pap us. What else?"

Cesar grimaced, then kicked off his shoes and unbuttoned his pants.

Being naked in front of the other prisoners was uncomfortable. I'd sat in a transparent cell for months in First City awaiting my judgment, but there'd been walls between me and the others. Here, skin was everywhere. Dark, darker, light, lighter, every shade in between. I wasn't the skinniest boy, but I had nothing on some of them. At least I wasn't one of the hairless few. They'd have it rough until they started looking like men. Nothing to do but brazen it out. I strutted naked to one of the uniformed kids, dumped my old clothes into his bin, and walked down the corridor to where the shower heads jutted out of the wall. A sensor in the ceiling found my mesh and water streamed from the shower head, lukewarm and smelling rotten.

"Ugh!" I grabbed my nose.

"Sulfur." A freckled kid beside me scrubbed his pits. "Won't hurt you. Just smells like death."

"Shower quick. Water don't last." It was my former seatmate, pulling on a pair of yellow coveralls.

"Here." Freckles tossed me a jug of soap. I squeezed out what I needed, then threw it toward Cesar, who'd stepped under his own shower head farther down the line.

The suds, smelling of something caustic yet clean, cut through the sweat and grime on my arms and legs. I lathered my scalp and scrubbed my face, carefully washing the piercings in my left ear and lower lip. All my piercings, like my tattoo, were courtesy of Rajani, the first one traded for a hit of Axon dust, the others free of charge once we'd become friends. Long ago, I'd pawned the ear jewelry for my trip north. I still wore my lip ring, and I was glad I hadn't sold it: it used to belong to Rajani. It was all I had left of her, unless you counted the holes she'd made in my body and the tat on my leg.

The water shut off before I'd finished rinsing my hair. A coverall tossed me a towel, scratchy and thin with over laundering. "You'll get used to it," he said, but I didn't know whether he meant the brief shower or the towel. Maybe he meant the whole thing. Prison. "Shavers in the next room."

Toweling off, I grabbed a coverall off the pile and measured it against my body. It was too big, so I tossed it to the floor and scrounged through several more before I found one that would fit.

"Hey, you're making a mess." Towel Boy glared at me. "Pick those up."

"Make me."

No PAP, no power. And he was smaller than me. I could take him, easy. The next room had a wall of mirrored ceramic. The face staring back was thin and brown, not great looking, but not ugly either. Cheekbones weren't bad. Brown eyes, thick black eyebrows like Appei, thin lips like Ami. I grimaced at myself. I could look mean if I wanted. Scruffy neck beard growing; a couple months in First City jail had given it time. I picked up one of the electric razors and mowed the scraggly hairs.

Rajani's ring glinted in my narrow nose. The slight bump on the bridge hinted I might have broken it once, but I hadn't. It made me look tough, and I liked that. Black roots were showing in my bleached blond hair. The ends were dry and broken; I would have had it bleached again and trimmed by Rajani before I'd gone north. If only. I looked at the razor. Maybe I could buzz the ends, clean it up a little.

I remembered her, my dead friend. Rajani had stood over

me as I sat in the wooden chair in her kitchen. My petite friend had asked me to slouch; she couldn't see the top of my head. I wasn't tall, but to her I was. Her slender fingers combed through my hair, tickling my scalp just before the bleach stung and brought tears to my eyes. Rajani had teased me every time. "Look at Harish, big man, crying when I color his hair!" I loved to make her giggle, to watch as the pink kissed her cheeks.

I knew she'd never have been mine. She made that perfectly clear the one time I'd lost myself. I'd grabbed her and kissed her. She slapped me away, angry at me for trying something with her. I'd been ashamed, but it hadn't ended my infatuation. She'd told me it would never be. She'd said she preferred girls, though I'd never seen her with anyone. Later, I realized it wasn't girls she wanted, but Axon dust. She was a slinger and a dustrat, still functioning, but for how much longer? I knew she would never return my love. We would only ever be friends. But your brain can't turn off your heart, and she had sucked me in. The only way out for me had been to leave, earn my crypto and continue north to the shallows, leaving Rajani and my hopeless longing behind—

—the razor on my head sliced off long, bleached hanks. Behind one ear to the back. From the crown to the jawline. Hair that I'd been growing for years, ever since I'd escaped from care. Hair I'd been growing the entire time I'd lived in First City, ever since I'd first met Rajani. I shaved away my emotions, the instincts that weakened me. My need for Rajani had drawn me to her place that night, against my better judgment. I razed the feelings along with the hair; it fell to my shoulders and slipped to the cold cement floor.

The face in the mirror blurred, grew indistinct, and the razor kept buzzing, the hair kept falling. A hand gripped my wrist and pulled the razor back.

"What are you doing, Lazlo?" Cesar stared at me.

I scrubbed the tears from my eyes and scowled at myself in the mirror. A crazed prisoner gazed back: one half of my head was newly bald, the other long, badly bleached, and dripping wet. The two halves of Lazlo Khosravi, convicted *shashu*. I grinned. This was the new me.

Chapter Six

W e shuffled two by two into transparent cells. Home sweet see-through home. Cesar and I became cell-mates because we were standing together. I don't know how he felt about it, but it was fine by me. Him? Someone else? Who cared? At least he'd volunteered to clear the transway this morning. Had that only been this morning? Seemed like last week. Cesar had been the only other one besides me to step up. I didn't know if he had courage or was simply crazy, like me—it was okay either way. At least he'd be interesting. Interesting was the quality I was looking for in a cellmate. Being *shashu* and having ten years to burn meant I'd outlast all the juvvies I'd arrived with. I'd have more than a few cell-mates during my decade in a cage. Might as well start with a lively one.

Ten years in prison. Ten years ago, I'd been seven, nearly eight. Appei still lived with us on our float. Those were happy days, full of routine and safety. Our mornings began early with the rising of the sun. It streamed through the skylights, and my eyes would open on Ami, boiling water for morning tea. How I loved her flower tea, brewed with the dried blooms of the tiny, happy plants she nurtured in the cracks of the deck, old water bottles, and rusted pots. Each of us had a special tea cup: Appei's large, cracked and tea stained ceramic, Ami's ancient china with a delicate flower painting, its handle broken and glued a thousand times. My cup was a child's: a small, dented, blue aluminum cup that burned my hands if I picked it up too soon after Ami poured the water.

Ami sprinkled the tiny flowers into my cup with her long graceful fingers. Next, she wrapped her hand in a threadbare towel and tipped the pot, the angrily bubbling water streaming into my cup. Careful not to touch the metal, I'd watch the little dry yellow bumps swell and soften, feel the floral steam rise to warm and wet my face. I'd blow the whorls of vapor off the cup's rim until they disappeared into the morning air. Only then was it safe to touch the cup, and I would, holding it between two eager hands before closing my eyes and sipping the morning tea grown by my mother's nurturing hands.

Since then, my father had gone silent. I'd been a lab rat in care, become a dust slinger, then a collector, and now I was in prison. A lot can happen in ten years. Was Ami still brewing flower tea in the mornings? Would she pour tea into my blue cup when I got out of prison? Would it still be there?

Like my early days in the shallows, my days in Coulee settled into a predictable pattern. Unlike my life on the float, there was neither flower tea nor safety.

Awake at six, breakfast a half hour later. Digital school for everyone; boring subjects chosen to mold us into boring little citizens of Cascadia. We wasted our mornings reading and writing, not allowed to speak Chinglish, the hybrid slang most outsiders spoke, a mixture of English, Chinese, and Spanish, the dominant languages of previous Cascadians. Chinglish was inclusive, a street language that set us apart from the wealthy insiders. It wasn't only how we talked with each other; it was our identity.

Afternoons were for civics, mind-numbing memorization of laws and duties, another feeble attempt to get us to forget where we came from and where we'd return to. Didn't matter how many civics lessons or writing exercises I did, I'd stop being an insider as soon as my sentence was up.

When I aged out of school in a month, I'd take a job pushing a broom or running laundry or working in the cafeteria, fully reaching the potential for a throwaway. Then I'd move to adult corrections and get to practice that glorious career for the rest of my sentence.

Our free time was particularly scintillating. We could download any digibook from the vast prison library to our neural mesh to wile away our time. Our choices ranged from more civics to the history of Cascadia. No digibooks about mechanics, engineering, or science in the entire place. Certainly no fictional stories about imaginary people or faraway places. We throwaways shouldn't have an imagination or use our brains. That's what had gotten us into trouble in the first place. There were decks of cards, pulpy and ancient. Some juvvies invented games and taught them to new prisoners when they arrived, but most of the boys stacked the cards instead, competing to see who could build the tallest or most complicated structure.

Some prisoners lifted weights, mostly the older boys who'd aged out of school and would go to adult prison to finish out their sentences. I'd be one of them soon enough. I was an average build and should have lifted with them—my safety among hardened adult criminals would be at risk. But the only thing more boring than spending my free time reading civics was weight lifting.

My idea of entertainment was far more amusing than any of the approved activities. I was exercising other muscles.

For the first week, I kept to myself, easy enough to do given my chosen hairstyle. Most of the juvvies left me my space; only Cesar spent time with me, but then he didn't have a choice. We lived together. In those free hours, I watched and listened. The weight lifters were, as you'd expect, strong and not worth the trouble of messing with. Plenty of other prisoners to practice on.

I silently followed the card games, learned which prisoners were beefing with each other, dropped a word in this one's ear about that one, tiny untruths about what they had said. Then I sat back and watched the arguments develop, the fist fights start, the PAP alarms send the offenders to the ground. My life seemed better when someone else's was worse. I kept pulling the strings on my puppets, easing my boredom.

Sometimes I waited until a few boys were racing each other, building their card towers. A simple rush past one of them could stir up the air just enough to topple a tower. Occasionally, my efforts failed, and I'd have to think of something else to make the time pass. Usually though, the *hundan* whose building went down would get mad, start talking trash to the others, and before you knew it, you had yourself a nice fight. It was easy to mess with the other prisoners, and if it didn't make me any happier, at least it brought the others low with me.

One evening, following a spectacular card fight and multiple pappings, I lay relaxing on my mattress. The warning bedtime transmission had sounded—five minutes to finish bathroom routines—and I watched boys hurry to their cages for the night. Cesar walked in, his hair still wet from a shower.

Inmates, cells will close in five, four, three, two, one.

The ceramic panel slid shut, and Cesar sat, his bed creaking beneath his weight. He leaned forward, elbows on his knees, looking at his feet. He sighed deeply and then looked up and scowled at me.

"What?"

"You're a real *hundan*."

"Hmm? I don't speak Chinglish."

I grinned, but he didn't return the smile.

"We're not as stupid as you think."

"What are you talking about?"

He rolled his eyes and cursed under his breath. "Think."

I rolled up to a seated position and brazened it out.

"Your stupid little head games," he said. "Everyone knows what you're doing."

"I'm having some fun."

"Fun? Is that what it is? Bringing down paps on other juvvies?"

"I've done nothing to you. Don't know why you're so—"

"Just so you know, I'm moving tomorrow. Chan's getting out, so I'm moving into his space."

"With Daniels? He stinks!"

"Yeah, he don't smell great, but you're a piece of *goushi*. I don't want your evil stink on me no more."

"Cesar. Seriously. You can't possibly want to move in with Daniels."

Cesar threw himself back on his mattress, arms crossed over his chest.

"Seriously?"

Cesar rolled over on his side, turning his back to me. Cesar and I weren't super close, not friends, but I'd gotten used to him sleeping in the room every night. I hadn't connected with any of the others. They'd avoided me and I'd kind of encouraged it. I enjoyed being edgy, making them all uneasy.

"Lazlo, you're trouble. Everyone hates you."

My mouth went dry and my heart beat faster. I didn't like

the other prisoners, but I'd never considered they might hate me, not until Cesar said it.

"Enjoy living with Daniels. I hope you suffocate on his b.o." I lay back down on my bed.

The lights dimmed, and the transparent cages darkened all at once. A deep breath came from Cesar's side of the cell.

"I don't hate you, Lazlo. I feel sorry for you."

I lay still, watching the slumbering prisoners through the cell wall until the lights turned on again the next morning.

Pity is the worst kind of insult.

Chapter Seven

I nmate, present yourself at door P.

The transmission interrupted me mid-bite. The yellow food-product was more gelatinous than usual this morning and, sitting alone, I had no one to distract me from it. Cesar had woken, wrapped his few items in a bedsheet, and left our cell without saying goodbye. He might have thought I was asleep; I'd lain still, my back turned toward him. But I preferred to imagine him snubbing me cruelly. I held the hurt, polished it to a glittering hard shine, swallowed it down. A gleaming stone of bitterness clattering deep within me.

Long aluminum tables stretched across the cement floor of the cafeteria. Boys clustered around them, eating and joking, shoving each other playfully. A couple of prisoners hovered at the far end of my table, actively ignoring me. Tipping my head sideways so my non-shaved half would hide my face, I disappeared into my neural mesh. I tried to remember how I'd done it with Big Danson, pulsed a thought at him, gotten even and gotten away. Images raced through my mind: pill bottles and money, kelp and seabirds, Ami and Appei, Rajani, nothing I could use.

Inmate, present yourself at door P.

I lifted my head and looked around the cafeteria. No one was getting up and making their way to the exit. The transmission couldn't possibly be meant for me. They'd never summoned me before, not even papped me since the first day I'd arrived. I'd been extremely careful not to do anything that would bring attention to me. Well, except for the hair.

A tingling began behind my ear, and then a sharp burst hit, piercing straight through my forehead and out the back of my skull. A tear welled up and I exhaled through the pain.

Inmate, present yourself at door P.

Yup, they definitely were trying to get my attention. One alarm blast and I'd have a dull throbbing behind my eyes for the rest of the day. I stood, dumped the residue of my sorry meal in the incinerator receptacle, and left the cafeteria through the blue door that led to the circular central room.

Monitored by the guards in the hanging pod, I walked across the room from door C of the cafeteria to door P. I ran my hand along the curved stone wall, moving slowly as I neared the door. I'd been a resident of Coulee Correctional's juvvie wing for a month, yet I'd only been behind doors C, D, F, J, and K: cafeteria, cell, classrooms, bathroom, and rec room. Door M led to the weight room. Why was I being summoned to door P?

I grabbed door P's handle. Locked. I glanced up at the guards in their transparent room.

"Hey! Anyone wanna help me--"

Something clanked, possibly a lock sliding open, and I tugged again. The door opened, and I stepped through. The corridor was the same as every other: the walls a mixture of rough stone and light transmitting concrete, the floors a whitewashed hardened slurry. I walked on until I saw another door, slightly ajar. I peeked in.

"Come in! Come in!" boomed a voice. The resonant bass belonged paradoxically to a slight, dark-skinned man seated behind a digipanel of green dots. His brown eyes smiled at me hugely behind thick glasses. He waved at a chair. "Sit, please."

I tossed my head, sending my hair over my shoulder, and threw myself into the chair. I slumped down and thrust my legs outward, crossed my arms, and scowled.

The man turned his monitor, letting me read it, and then swiped a long finger across the digipanel. My name appeared on the screen on top of a page of tiny, illegible text. "Lazlo Khosravi. Age 17. Originally from the shallows, orphaned and sent to care at age 12—"

"My mother's alive," I said, even though I knew I was wasting my breath. The Cascadian authorities told this lie whenever they needed new lab rats. Appei had gone silent, leaving Ami to raise me alone. We'd gotten by for nearly two years: her sewing and my odd jobs had put food on our table. That is, until the authorities had grabbed me, shuttled me off to care and illegal drug testing, and implanted insider's mesh in my brain.

"—Ran from care at age 15—"

"Wrong. Ran at 13." Miz Hazel must have waited two years to report my escape to the authorities. Two extra years of government payments for a kid no longer living in her shack. That sounded about right.

"—Whereabouts unknown until arrest at age 17 for drug dealing and—hmmm. Seems like you were a fortunate young man." The man peered at me over his glasses.

"I'm innocent." Nothing fortunate in my situation. I tightened my mouth, glared at the man.

He removed his glasses, pinched the bridge of his nose

and blinked twice, putting the glasses on again. "But you think you're the victim, don't you?"

I said nothing.

"Ten years, one of those spent in the juvenile facility, the other nine on the other side with the adult offenders. If you'd been 18 at the time of conviction, the judge would have doubled your time."

I said nothing.

"Law says I gotta keep you here for a year. Which—you know—I've done that before. Plenty of other young men, similar situation. Difference with you, though, you're a sneaky pain in my behind."

I said nothing.

He slammed a clenched fist on his desk, and I startled but stayed silent.

"You think I don't know what you've been doing? Stirring up trouble?" He shook his head, smiled. This time, the smile didn't reach his brown eyes. "I've been the warden here since long before your mama hatched you. Yeah, do the math on that. Inside air. I'm downright old. Don't think I haven't seen your kind before. Smart. Manipulative. One kid like you can turn my school—"

"Did you just call this prison a school?"

"—Can turn my school from a place of order and rehabilitation into hell on earth. And yes, Mr. Khosravi, I called it a school. It's my duty to teach the young men in my care how to contribute positively to our Cascadian society."

I snorted and spat at the floor, daring him to hit me with a PAP alarm.

He watched me calmly and cleared his throat.

"I've seen your kind before. Unwilling or unable to change. We could wait another month, maybe two, see if you settle in. But we both know you won't. We'll be wasting each other's time. In the meantime, you'll be corrupting the other students with your attitude. But I'll give you a last chance. Just to be sure I'm not wrong about you." He leaned across the desk, fixed me with a look. "Do you accept that your actions have brought you to this place? Will you change your behavior?"

I sneered into his self-righteous face. "I'm innocent."

He nodded and settled back in his chair. "As I thought. We're agreed. Neither of us want you here. I've given this some thought, and there's one thing I could do. Technically, you have to volunteer."

What was this? He was giving me a choice? Was this another trick in Cascadia's grand scheme to screw Lazlo Khosravi? I was curious, and it showed.

"Oh, you like the sound of that." The warden chuckled and folded his hands. "I thought you might. But you've got to decide now. I've got a crew headed out early in the morning, only one spot left."

"Headed where?"

"The Line. It's hard work. Outside. You'd be the only juvenile. But if you volunteer, Cascadia will expunge five years from your sentence."

I stared at the warden. Five years off my decade-long sentence? It was too good to believe.

"Why me?"

"I told you. I don't want you here. Easy as that."

"What's the catch?"

"You heard the outside part, right?"

I scoffed. I'd lived outside up to now. That made no difference to me.

"Okay, not going to lie to you. You'd be doing me a favor."

I rocked back in my chair, stretched my hands behind my head. I would make the *hundan* beg.

"Cascadia gives me no choice. Court sent you here for a minimum of twelve months until you're nearly 19. If you'd been convicted at 18, you'd have gone directly to adult lockup. You come in as a kid, your minimum is a year in juvenile. I don't want you here now. I sure don't want you here another year."

"But five years off? For a little work?"

"Outside."

"Yeah, I got that. What else?"

"No hot showers or flush toilets. No more warm meals or carbonized air."

I bobbed my knee. Waited.

"No school."

"Nope. You're not telling me everything." *Hundan,* I'm a street kid. You can't pull a fast one on me.

The warden sighed and removed his glasses. He blew on the lenses and wiped them against his shirt. After he'd put them on again, he said, "Cascadia needs warm bodies to work the Line. Law says we can't make anyone do it, not even convicts. Hard job like that, cons only volunteer if they've got a reason. So we halve the sentence of anyone who volunteers. Juveniles are normally disallowed from participating, but I think, need being what it is, Cascadia will allow it."

"And that's it?"

"I want you out of my school. That's it." His eyes searched my face. "So, what do you think? Sound like something you want to do?"

Outside, fresh air, five years instead of ten. Physical labor, but so what? Kelp farming was hard work, and this whole time I'd been dreaming of working the water the way Appei had. I didn't want to rot in a cage for ten years. I was an outsider anyway, not afraid of a shorter lifespan so long as I spent my years living. Five years sooner to return to the shallows. Time enough to meet a woman and make a life. I wanted a family while I had time; I didn't want to go silent before my child was grown, like Appei had. Like Ami would soon. Five years would make a big difference in finding Ami before she went silent.

"Well?" said the warden.

I stood and reached out my hand. The warden raised his eyebrows before meeting my hand with his own.

"Five years off my sentence. You've got yourself a deal."

Chapter Eight

My mind seething with possibilities, I barely realized I'd left the warden's office. First thing tomorrow, this prison would be a memory. I was bound for some place called the Line. Hard work, outside, subtract five years. That's all I'd heard, all I cared about. Five years.

I passed through the central annex, so excited about a future that didn't include walls, I didn't glance at the guards hanging from the ceiling. Muscle memory led me through door F to the classroom.

Five years was still a long time. I'd been in care five years ago. I refused to rot for five years, either in a cage or on this so-called Line. Not going to happen. Especially not for a crime I hadn't committed. I hadn't killed Rajani. *Shashu?* Murderer? That wasn't me. I had killed no one; I never would.

Ami's face came to me: her soft brown eyes and serious gaze. She could always tell when I'd done something I wasn't proud of. When I pulled the neighbor girl's hair, when I sucker punched the neighbor boy, when I cut the flowers off Ami's plants in a fit of rage, when I threw rocks at the little brown birds resting on the water. One look from my mother, and I confessed. It was a compulsion, every time. And now, I pictured Ami's face in my mind, and we both knew I wasn't responsible for Rajani, not directly.

But I hadn't helped her.

I had been a dustslinger, selling Axon poison to any *hundan* with the habit to need it and the old school cash to pay for it. Yes, I had done that. They'd never caught me slinging—that night at Rajani's I'd only been collecting, no matter what my record said—but I had slung dust when I arrived in First City. Ami wouldn't be proud.

I would tell Ami that I'd had to do it. When I saw her again, I'd confess everything. I'd been thirteen when I ran from care. I'd needed the money, and I had nothing else to sell. What other choice did I have?

I'd had to run; if I'd stayed, Miz Hazel would have discovered I was no longer taking the Axon pills. I knew I had to stop once I realized what they were doing to me.

Like many outsiders, Ami and Appei didn't register my birth, so no hospital had implanted the mesh in my infant brain. The Cascadian authorities remedied that oversight. First, they stole me from the shallows and shipped me off in a transport. Then they stole my hair while I slept the sleep of the drugged. I woke with a wound on the back of my skull, voices and alarms inside my head.

I was confused, scared, and bald. Hearing voices. More than a hundred miles from home. They replaced my home on the float with an overcrowded shack in Second City, replaced my loving Ami with a cold stranger. Miz Hazel said the pills were vitamins. Said they'd help me heal.

The red A stamped on those tablets—how I grew to hate it. Morning, noon, night, I choked down the hard, dry pills. My wound healed and my hair grew black and prickly. But the sensations in my brain got worse. I became increasingly sensitive to the automated transmissions. Area alarms were more and more painful. Not long after, the regular automated transmissions and information bursts sent me to my knees in agony. I began experiencing tingling in my head moments before an alert sounded.

I thought I was insane the first time I grayed out. The rain was coming down hard, and I was carrying a mop to the bathroom. The toilet was on the brink of overflowing, a routine occurrence among Second City houses when the rain was heavy. I was readying a pail to catch the water from the bowl before it spilled on to the floor when a weather report began transmitting. In my mind, I was no longer in the bathroom but on the float with Ami and Appei, sipping tea and watching a storm roll in across the water. Before I could hug my dream parents, I was in Miz Hazel's bathroom again, toilet and salt water mixing around my ankles while she yelled at me, the lazy throwaway, to clean the mess. But for once, my head didn't hurt.

I grayed out more and more, dissociating for longer stretches of time. I was disappearing into my head without control. After I lost three hours one afternoon, I cheeked the pills and hid them. I never took them again.

Once, I thought about asking the other kids if weird things were happening to them, but I never did. Except for Big Danson, they were younger and trusted Miz Hazel. They were young enough to consider her a mother figure, not having an angel like my Ami at home. They wouldn't have kept my secret. And Big Danson was in temporary care while his mother finished a 12-month sentence in jail. They hadn't stolen him from his mother, not like me. He hadn't arrived at Miz Hazel's with new hardware in his brain. He wasn't taking the pills.

I waited and waited for Ami to find me. She never did.

By the time I turned thirteen, I realized Cascadia had

hidden me well. They needed lab rats and a Shallows kid like me, son of a kelp farmer, was an easy steal. It would be up to me to escape and find my way home.

I didn't realize how far away home was or how much it would cost to get there.

Sliding into my seat at the back of the room, I waited while the digiscreen scanned my mesh and launched the day's modules. I'd be out of this prison in less than 24 hours; I didn't plan to waste one second more on the mind-numbing language and civics classes. But there was nowhere else to be, not unless I wanted to spend my last day with a PAP-induced headache. So I sat still, seeming to play nice, while I watched the other juvvies and thought about how I might entertain myself.

Sinking down in my chair, I stretched my legs under the table, just far enough to kick the back of the boy's chair in front of me. Not such a hard kick as to be noticeable by the trackers, but enough to annoy the person sitting in the chair.

"What the?" He flipped his head around. I pretended to be engrossed in the fascinating lesson on my digiscreen. "Quit it, Lazlo."

I ignored him, flipped the page on my screen. He sighed loudly and turned back around. So, of course, I shoved my foot against his chair again. And again. And again. He suffered silently for a while, and I was about to give up. One more kick was all it took for my payoff. He jumped to his feet and knocked his chair over backward with a clatter.

"Leave my chair alone, you *hundan!*" he screamed, and I grinned as the PAP jolt took him down to the ground.

Everyone spun around then; I watched their reactions from the corner of my eye as I innocently completed a quiz on the proper way to address a Person of Authority. Spoiler alert: You don't talk to a POA unless they've addressed you first.

"Lazlo's usual games."

It was Cesar, distancing himself from me. As if moving out and abandoning me hadn't been enough. So it really shouldn't come as any surprise when I got even with him as he passed my table. A dumb trick that he should have seen coming, which made it doubly funny when he fell for it. Pun intended. He strode past me and all I had to do was stick out my foot, only the tip of my shoe actually, and he stumbled over it. He didn't even fall, only tripped a bit, jammed up against the prisoner in front of him. It wasn't my fault that the juvvie he tripped into was a hothead and shoved him against the wall. I didn't tell Cesar to take a swing at him. That the two of them got papped was kind of hilarious, actually.

If Cesar wasn't with me, he was against me. His own fault.

I strode out the door, making an enormous deal out of stepping over Cesar, curled on the floor and groaning. He grabbed my ankle as I passed.

"Apologize."

I kicked his hand free and kept walking. "Make me."

IN THE CAFETERIA, I grabbed a handful of protein sticks and some dehydrated food product packages and sat at my usual loner table. The salty sticks were too hard to bite into if you wanted to keep your teeth. I sucked on the end, moistening it with my saliva before gnawing it to a pulp. My jaws quickly tired, and honestly, I wasn't even that hungry. I shoved the food into my coverall pockets and thrummed my fingers on the table, looking around me. Everything was the color of dirt and whitewash, the color of tedium and despair. All the *hundans* seated around me in their little groups—they could have it. I didn't want to be one of them, belong to one of their stupid gangs. I was going outside, to the Line, five years closer to freedom.

Bored the same dumb faces in the same dumb yellow coveralls, I left the cafeteria and headed to the bathroom. Alone in the stall, I reached into my pockets for the dehydrated food product. I thought I might loosen the toilet pipe and jam the packets in there. Create a huge flood for the next *hundan* who flushed. It would be hilarious, but I didn't know when my prank would hit, and I couldn't hang around the bathroom all afternoon waiting. Not exactly inconspicuous. I shoved the packets back in my pocket and left the stall.

As I was washing my hands, someone entered the bathroom. I glanced into the mirror and saw the juvvie whose chair I'd kicked. He opened the door to the stall I'd just been in, and I regretted not booby trapping the toilet. A second boy walked in and stood right behind me. It was the goon who'd throttled Cesar. He bumped into my back and shoved me against the sink.

"Hey guy. You mind?" I pushed him off me.

Two more prisoners entered the bathroom. Some *hundans* I'd turned against each other during a card game or something. I didn't remember. Looked like they were buddies now. The toilet flushed and the boy came out of the stall, stood beside me at the sink, and washed his hands.

"We're sick of you, Lazlo."

"Look like I care?"

The goon behind me forced my head under the faucet, then grabbed me by the hair and tugged my head up, spinning me around. He held me while the other juvvies took turns punching me in the stomach. The goon tossed me to the ground, and I curled into a ball, protecting myself from the boot kicking that followed, a beating delivered by the prisoner whose chair I'd nudged.

Through the entire thing, no one was papped. I kept waiting for something to happen that would stop the fight. Surely the guards were monitoring their trackers. Surely, they could see what was happening in here with all the bodies surrounding me. I mean, if they papped someone for tossing a chair or shoving another prisoner, they must know I was under assault. I lay on the hard stone floor, taking my licks, no sound escaping me other than the grunts and stifled moans you might expect when someone's getting the crap beaten out of him.

One more person entered the bathroom, and I was relieved to see it was Cesar.

"Cesar... help..." The gang stopped wailing on me when Cesar appeared. They actually stepped away from me.

Cesar crouched beside me, a look of concern on his face. "How you doing there, Lazlo? Looks like the guys beat you good."

I sniffed, holding tears back. No way would I cry in front of these *hundans*, but his kindness surprised me.

"Yeah." I tried to smile. "Guess I sort of deserved it."

"Yeah. You think?" He pushed my hair behind my ear. "Lucky you. No one hit you in the face."

I groaned. "Think I might have a busted rib."

"That's too bad, Lazlo. At least they didn't mess up your face." He grinned, the concern replaced by something else, something dark. "They left that for me."

He gripped Rajani's ring and yanked it from my lip.

After it was done, after they'd left, after I checked the bruises on my torso, after I'd staunched the bleeding from my torn lip, after the searing pain had diffused to a throbbing reminder, I booby trapped every damn toilet in that bathroom. Enjoy the flood, *hundans*.

Chapter Nine

❧

Inmate, awaken and proceed to the atrium.

The door to my cell clicked open, and the floor glowed, lighting my way out of the prison dormitory as the other inmates slept. I'd spent the few dark hours I had before needing to rise fitfully tossing and turning, unable to sleep, my body aching from the beating. My chest was purple and bruised, but it didn't hurt to breathe, so that was a good sign. Perhaps the *hundans* who'd ganged up on me hadn't busted my ribs after all. My lip was hot and swollen, dried blood caked on my wound. Not exactly attractive, but it made me look tougher than I felt.

I peed in the corner urinal before pulling on my coveralls and tying my boots. The main bathroom was off limits now, a punishment imposed on the entire prison ward following the cascading flood I'd caused. Made zero difference to me. I was out of here. Good riddance!

The blue door to the atrium clicked open as I arrived and I stomped through, glancing one last time at the guard station. One man sat alone up there; he must be the night staff, skeleton crew, whatever. A door across the atrium opened and a uniformed guard stepped out.

"Lazlo Khosravi." A statement, not a question.

I nodded.

"Hands."

I glanced up again as I stretched out my arms. The guard in the aluminum oxynitride booth was watching. He saluted me ironically as the other guard cuffed me, hands behind my back. "Let's go."

Double middle fingers welled up in my mind and I pulsed the image at the guard behind the ceramic windows. His face clouded over, confused as I penetrated his mind. Surprised that my pulse had connected, I stumbled through the prison exit and into the subterranean tunnel.

"Off to the Line are you, Khosravi?"

"Yup."

"Either you're braver or more stupid than you look. And you don't look brave."

"*Hundan*," I said, lingering over the curse. But the guard only laughed.

"Warden must have really wanted to get rid of you. Passing up a full year of subsidies to get you out of lockup. He usually holds on to the juvvies as long as he can. Easy money. But not you, huh? You're a real tough guy, are you? A real wise one?"

I wished the guard would shut up. My bruises hurt, and I wasn't in the mood to be poked at.

"You know what's out there, right? On the Line?"

My lip itched, but with back-cuffed hands, I couldn't scratch it. I bit my lip and quickly regretted it as I tasted blood and wetness trickled down my chin. Great, I'd cracked the scab.

"You couldn't pay me enough to do that job. Guess most

people feel the same, which is why cons do it. So why'd you volunteer?"

The tickle of the blood was annoying me, worse than the itch had. I turned my head sideways, wiping my face with my shoulder, and ripped the scab clean off.

"You know the warden played you, right?"

The guard's eyes glinted. He was enjoying this, taunting me. I sucked my lip, the blood salty and warm. Ignored him, not going to show any interest. But what was he talking about?

He scoffed. "You don't know. Cons on the Line get paid. But not you, wise guy. Volunteer as a minor, you get time off, but Cascadia doesn't have to pay you."

I couldn't help it. I reacted, jerking against the restraints, anger clearly written all over my face.

The guard laughed, an ugly, sneering sound. "If you'd waited a couple months warden would have to pay and offer a reduced sentence. Ho! He got you good! Man's a master—doesn't pay to be on his bad side, boy."

Frustrated anger colored my cheeks, emotion billowing out of me in every direction. The injustice—they'd stolen my savings, zeroed my crypto to pay for my false imprisonment in Coulee. Now that I was no longer in the prison, working for them—for free—they should have paid me. I wouldn't get my savings back. I wouldn't earn anything for my work. The warden had swindled me worse than any Hill duster had ever done. And me, so cocky and sure that I'd gotten one over on him. I was blind, deaf, and dumb; not able to think, see, or speak. I was furious.

I wrapped all that bitterness and self-hatred—how could I be so stupid, such an easy mark—and I hurled it from me. I pulsed the violence at the guard, dumped it from my mesh. If I was lucky, I'd black out his vision for a moment and send him sprawling across the rocky pathway. But with no focus, no control over my emotions, my thoughts flew harmlessly around the tunnel.

At the parking strip near the end of the tunnel, a compact heliovan idled, a six-seater by the looks of it.

"Full van?" The guard greeted the heliovan driver.

"Yeah, a couple from the adult lock up. This the kid?" The driver, a light-skinned man with the thickest handlebar mustache I'd ever seen, looked me up and down, frowning. "What'd you do to your hair, son? Looks of that face, you ain't too popular with the kids in juvvie."

"Won't be much better where he's headed," said the guard.

The driver threw the guard a disapproving look, and a burst of gratitude coursed through me.

"Should I clip him in?" said the guard.

"I've got it," said the driver.

"Don't let his age fool you. This one's a criminal. Nasty one."

The driver pointed toward the front cab. A PAP tracker lay on the floor strewn among a case of water bottles. "Not my first trip to the Line."

"Okay, guess you know what you're doing." The guard uncuffed my wrists.

"Sit anywhere you want, son," said the driver.

I climbed in and chose a seat in the van's rear. Unlike the transport that had brought me to the facility, the heliovan had aluminum oxynitride windows. I'd be able to see where we were traveling. I hadn't been outside for three entire months. Traveling during the daytime, able to look outside, soon to be outside—I almost forgot how I'd been tricked. Almost. An adventure was coming and I couldn't wait.

"Hands on the bar," said the driver.

A long metal bar stretched across the back of the seat

ahead of me. Handcuffs dangled from the bar, and he clipped me in.

"Not worried about you, son, but the adult prisoners. Safer for everyone this way." He balanced on the edge of the seat in front of me and reached into his pocket. Shaking out a tissue, he said, "Mind if I—"

He dabbed at my face, gently wiping away the blood, pressing against my injured lip until I winced.

"Sorry son. Pressure will make the bleeding stop." His eyes probed mine. "How old are you, then?"

"Seventeen."

He shook his head. "Criminal. Damn criminal. Not you, son. That *hundan* warden of yours. Sending a kid to the Line. I don't care what you done. No place for a kid, the Line."

"I can take care of myself."

"I don't doubt that. Bet you've had to be tough. No kinda world out there." He crumpled up the bloody tissue and pocketed it, then leaned forward, his voice growing earnest. "Listen to me now. You watch your back. You hear? It ain't the crew you gotta worry about; Nelson's crew sticks together pretty much. Keep your mouth shut, do what you're told, you'll make it out okay. But keep your eyes open."

A low hum traveled through the cracked window and became louder, resolved into voices.

"Here they come," said the driver.

The other side of the cavernous space glowed as the sound grew louder, the neural mesh of the approaching men triggering the lights as they walked. I hadn't noticed another tunnel when the transport had dropped us off months ago, but it made sense. The adult prison, the larger part of Coulee Correctional Facility, shared the same carbon sequestrating structure as the juvenile detention facility.

The driver walked to the heliovan's cab, and then gave me one last look before he climbed in. He drew a deep breath and shook his head. "Seventeen." He swung the bulletproof door closed, safeguarding himself in the impenetrable driver's pod. The lock engaged with a click, and though I could see the back of his head, I was alone.

The voices boomed through the cavern and bodies emerged from around the stone wall. Five handcuffed and shackled men wearing yellow coveralls like mine shambled forward in a line. Two guards followed them out of the tunnel and strode toward the heliovan. One guard unfastened their ankles and led them to the van while the other stood watch, thumb poised over a PAP tracker.

"Hey, there's a weird-looking kid here," said the first prisoner, a short stocky man probably in his twenties with the worst acne scars I'd ever seen. "Where's the other half your hair, *hundan?*"

I stared him down. A little smack talk didn't scare me. Wouldn't get a rise out of me.

The guard shoved him into the front seat, left side, shackled him. A huge dark-skinned man was the next to climb in, sweating and panting after the walk down the tunnel. "Yo, Munch. Check out the freak," said Acne Scars. The big man glanced at me and collapsed into the right front seat. "Nothin I ain't seen before." Cuffing him, the guard called for the next prisoner, a tall, muscular man, about the same age as Acne Scars. Acne Scars called him Sook and directed his attention to me.

By the time he'd pointed me out to Faisal, a man with close-set eyes and a buzz cut who would have fit right in with the kelp farmers in the shallows, I knew Acne Scar was an idiot, but a scary idiot. The seat beside me was empty, so I waited for his last announcement, but Acne Scar ignored the last man who climbed in.

He was tall and lean. He seemed a little older than me, but not much. I glanced at him, trying not to be obvious, because he seemed familiar. Apparently, he had no hangups about staring, because he was looking at me intensely, not aggressively, rather like his eyes had gotten stuck. He had that semi-glazed look of a duster who was in-between sniffs. I told myself I'd seen him on the Hill or he reminded me of someone there.

He didn't duck so much as slouch bonelessly when he walked to the last seat. Swinging around so he could keep staring at me, he held his wrists to be locked to the seat bars. He was weirding me out with his intensity, so I glared back at him.

The van lurched forward and moved up the slope to daylight. We were eyeball to eyeball, and I wasn't about to blink first.

He said, "Rajani."

Chapter Ten

❧

The wind left me like I'd been sucker punched in the gut.

I blinked. "What?"

"Where I know you from. You're friends with Rajani."

And then it hit me who he was. His given name was something old-millennium, like Jason or Michael or Robert. On the Hill he'd gone by Dusty, and to have a nickname like that in a community where four out of five people were a slinger or a rat says something. He was gray-brown like dust: his hair a light brown, his skin tanned a light brown. Only his eyes stood out, bright blue against all that dust. But Rajani and the other slingers hadn't dubbed him Dusty because of his coloring. Rather, he was a dustrat who threw himself into the life with gusto. He wasn't that old, but he'd chased the neural gray zone so long and hard part of his brain stayed there. He spent half his days on the Hill spouting nonsense, seeing vapor.

Many rats were older outsiders, close to going silent and trying to escape their final years. Others were throwaway kids, tossed to the streets after they'd aged out, hooked on the Axon pills they could not afford. Dusty could have been one of those, except for the ready paper he was always eager to spend. Either he was a grade A street hustler, unlikely considering how stoned he usually was, or he was some insider's kid who'd gone slumming on the Hill once and liked what he'd found.

But if he was an insider's kid, what was he doing in Coulee?

"It's Dusty, right?"

"Yeah. What's your name again?"

"Lazlo."

"No, that's not it."

"Lazlo Khosravi. That's my name. Always has been."

"No. It's um…" He screwed up his face comically. "Um… no, don't tell me."

"Lazlo."

"Shhh. Quiet. I almost had it. Um—" His blue eyes shot open, and he grinned hugely, revealing a wide gap between his front teeth. "Harry! That's it!"

"No."

"Sure it is. Rajani calls you Harry. Too bad what happened to her." He waggled his head from side to side, a ridiculous caricature of Rajani, and sang out in a high-pitched voice. "Harree. Come here Harree, my lovely."

Faisal turned and looked at me and Dusty, snorted, then turned back.

"Harish," I muttered.

"Say again?"

"Harish. She calls me Harish."

He hooted and beamed. "See! I knew it!"

"That's not my name."

"Whatever Harry."

"*Hundan*, the name's Lazlo."

"Lazlo, Harry—difference does it make?"

"Harry gets you bloodied the second these cuffs are off."

"Okay, okay. Chill, dude. Just messing."

Dude? Who even said that? He was an insider for sure. Done with him, I looked out my window. The heliovan was exiting the tunnel to a pink sky. I hadn't seen a sunrise in three months and I wanted to enjoy it, but the annoying con beside me started talking again.

"So what'd you think of prison?"

"What?"

"Was it all you had hoped for?"

Ahead of me, Faisal barked out a laugh.

Dusty watched me eagerly like we were at a party or something, making small talk.

"You serious?"

"Long ride dude. Passing the time."

I stared out at the flat, brown expanse spreading in all directions. Rocks and dirt, that's all I could see. How far was the drive to the Line? I didn't even know what the Line was, yet I'd volunteered. Five years off my sentence, and I grabbed at it like a chump. Thought I was so smart, but that *hundan* warden—

"So, in case it's not obvious, I'm in for *hezui*." The con was still talking. "Yeah, I'm a duster. Pretty easy collar." He said it like an insider bragging about his career at some insider meet and greet. "Got me a year. A little boring in the clink, though. Thought I'd try something different for the second half."

Sook said to Faisal, "You believe this guy?"

Faisal shook his head and chuckled.

"Lazlo. Yoo hoo."

I turned my back to the chatty prisoner, but he wasn't taking the hint.

"What you in for? Hey. Lazlo."

I stared harder out the window. Didn't he know he was

making himself a target? These men were serious thugs, not some stupid dusters on the Hill. I leaned my head against the window, closed my eyes, pretended to be asleep.

"Harree—come here, Harree!"

The handcuffs cut into my wrists painfully when I spun around and made to punch the idiot. I bit my lip hard to stop from crying out and the bleeding started again.

"Yo, Lazlo. You're leaking."

"Shut up."

"What, too good to talk to me? *Hezui* not tough enough for you?"

I was innocent. But these cons sitting around us, listening to Dusty's foolishness and watching me doing nothing to shut it down? The target had been on my back since I stepped into the heliovan and this stupid insider—he was only serving a year, fewer months now, since he volunteered, plus crypto he didn't need—was painting that target bright red for these *hundans*.

Faisal was listening. Sook too. I wondered if the two men in the front could hear. Mostly, I worried about Acne Scar. I knew cons liked to gossip. Not much else to do. And I knew that Dusty with his insider ways and frequent dustouts would be entertainment for bored cons. I didn't intend to join him as the prison punching bag. I suspected slingers and collectors would be easy pickings on the Line, just a step above a rat, a *hezui*.

I took another look at the four cons sitting ahead of us. How many more would be on the Line? They were all far larger and stronger than me. If any of them took a swing at me, I didn't stand a chance. The only way I would establish some cred, buy myself some time until I could run, was to admit to the one thing I hadn't done.

"*Shashu*."

Dusty whistled. "Dude, for real? Who'd you kill?"

He shouted it; of course he did. And what had I expected? He announced it to the entire heliovan. No amount of bumping along the road or engine noise had muffled his voice. I imagined Dusty's voice bouncing around the inside of the van and piercing through the bulletproof window to the driver's pod. If he hadn't needed his full attention on the road, the driver would have turned around and taken back every nice thing he'd done and kind word he'd said to me.

None of the cons turned or looked, and that's how I knew they'd all heard.

Of course, if I told Dusty I was a killer, the next question would be who my victim was. But while it had been easy to lie about killing someone, I couldn't bring myself to say her name. It wasn't true, of course it wasn't, but claiming to have caused her death would abuse her memory.

"Shut it."

But Dusty kept at it, wheedling and cajoling like one of the little kids at Miz Hazel's. I tried to change the subject.

"How long you been at Coulee?"

"About three months. You?"

"Same." I figured they had arrested Dusty around the same time as me. The Hill had been quiet that night, as though the cops had swept for dusters before I'd arrived.

"So who was it? What'd he do to you? How'd you kill him?"

I shook my head, glared at him. Shut up already.

"Dude, come on. Is he from the Hill? Do I know him?"

"How should I know?"

"So he is from the Hill—" I could almost look through those light eyes into his brain and watch the blue-tinted cogs and wheels spin. "He's a slinger. No reason to kill a rat."

I tried to stare him down, but my eyes flickered.

"Someone didn't pay up. You muscled him." I imagined smoke coming out of his ears as his little-used brain gears spun and spun. "You're a collector. You killed one of your slingers."

This freaking *hundan*. The closer he stumbled to the truth, the less able I was to bluff my way out.

"I'm telling you nothing. Give it up Sharabi." A mistake, cursing him in Rajani's language, but it tumbled out somehow.

His wide eyes glowed. "Rajani calls me that."

Not trusting my face and what it might reveal about me, I turned toward my window again.

"Wait, you collected from Rajani. I heard that, no—"

I pressed my forehead against the window frame. The metal casing burrowed into my skin and I welcomed the pressure, wished I could force it deeper into my skull. Anything to take my mind off this other harsher, sharper sensation piercing through me. I saw Rajani again, lying motionless on the floor. My despair became real along with anger at whoever did that to her, anger at the cops who'd pinned it on me, bone-crushing sadness that Rajani no longer breathed this world's heavy air. And then I was angry at Dusty, this stranger I barely knew who dared to think I could have harmed a hair on Rajani's beautiful braided head.

I wasn't aware that I'd pulsed him, not until he said, his voice lowered, "Wow, dude. I see it clearly."

Chapter Eleven

❧

Five years ago when I escaped from care, I had slipped out of my bedroom in the dead of night. The other kids in my room had all fallen asleep, and I crept out carrying a change of clothes and my collection of cheeked pills stuffed into a pillowcase. I heard Miz Hazel's air processor behind her closed door and assumed she was asleep too. Stepping carefully to avoid the squeaky floorboards, I made my way to the kitchen. I was already hungry, thinking about my walk home.

The fridge light illuminated when I opened the door. The top shelf held cans of Miz Hazel's fermented grain beverage, strictly off-limits to us kids. Several bowls of reconstituted food product, poultry flavor from the looks of it, sat ready for our breakfast.

"I'm telling Miz Hazel."

Big Danson's face glowed yellow in the light from the fridge. He stood scowling in the doorway, fists clenched.

And I don't know what happened. Desperate to see Ami again, I thought of home. I was miserable, close to tears, but

I also wanted to shove Big Danson hard. All those thoughts came together at once, and he stumbled backward as though I had actually shoved him.

His lip quivered, and he looked about to cry before running from the kitchen.

I thought he might wake Miz Hazel, so I reached into the fridge to grab anything resembling food and got out of there as quick as I could. She had stacked protein bars on the bottom shelf, which I thought was odd because they didn't need to be cold, but they were better than chicken-flavored food product, so I grabbed a handful. Hidden behind them, something else that didn't need refrigeration, were bottles and bottles of Axon Corp pills.

I don't know why I stole them. I'd like to say it was because I wanted to spare the other kids the dissociation and gray outs I'd been having. But something inside my thirteen-year-old brain told me the pills would be useful.

And when I reached First City, they were.

I'd done the same thing to Dusty, shoved him away without realizing it. But rather than showing fear, he watched me with naked adoration.

"How'd you do that? You did that, right?" He leaned forward, speaking low, suddenly aware that we weren't alone in the heliovan.

"Do what?"

"Nice try." He grinned at me. "I know a dustout when I feel one. How'd you put me in Rajani's apartment?"

"Don't know what you're talking about."

"More than that, dude. I was sad. Really freaking down. How'd you make me feel that way?"

My lip quivered, and I looked away. Not gonna cry in front of this duster.

"That's freaking sick, Lazlo. Like, you were in my head.

And yeah, what happened to Rajani, you know, she didn't deserve, you know, to die. You didn't do it, right?"

"*Hundan*, shut up about it already!"

"They got you good. *Shashu* is what, like twenty years or something?"

"Ten." I shrugged. "Juvvie conviction."

"Solid," Dusty nodded. "Lucky, that. Well, I mean, you're wrongly serving time for a crime you didn't commit. But, you know, even with all that, it could have been worse, right?"

I gulped, couldn't speak. Nothing lucky about any of this. Words of wisdom from a stupid *hezui* rat with less than a year to burn and some inside father to pad his crypto account.

"Dude, you and me? Our kind—we're like less than human. I mean, we're not. But when Cascadia gets their hands on us, we get what we get. And here in Coulee, dusters and slingers, we're at the bottom of the hierarchy. I'm not saying it's fair or legit or anything, just, you know, we got no chance either way. And, I mean, ten years. At least it's not twenty."

And with that he gloriously, finally, thankfully, shut his mouth. I shoved my feelings down, buried them beneath fantasies of the shallows, and turned my attention to the window.

The heliovan was ancient, carefully maintained by the driver, but old nonetheless. Its springs groaned as we jolted along the rough road; vehicles like this didn't travel the transway. Its solar shield scraped across the roof, creakily adjusting to the angle of the sun. The sky stretched bright and blue in all directions, cloudless like I'd rarely experienced in the shallows or First City. The heliovan's tires kicked up dust and pebbles as it drove, its shocks bottoming out as we plunged into a pothole.

My eyes devoured the terrain. Low-growing sagebrush mixed with colorful wildflowers, brightening a vast brown expanse. Ancient dry creek beds wove through the expanse, accented by giant boulders in ochre, umber, and golden hues. The air blowing through my open window was hot, unlike the moist, clammy heaviness of the cities. This warmth sucked the moisture from my skin, drying my perspiration almost before I sweat it out.

I wiggled on the hard vinyl seat, searching unsuccessfully for a comfortable position. I could feel every bone in my butt as we rumbled along. Leaning forward, I rested my head on my shackled hands and watched the low-growing vegetation rush by.

"All the lovely colors. Come with me into the tunnel. Don't drown, don't drown," said Dusty.

Rolling my head to the other side, I watched him. He rested comfortably, the back of his skull leaning against his window, his legs stretched across the seat. At first, it seemed like he was staring at me, but soon I realized he wasn't seeing me. He was surfing the neural gray zone, fully immersed in whatever was happening between his two ears. Random hallucinations were a standard effect of long-term dust abuse.

"That's right, push off the sides and swim. Swim with me through the tunnel. See the rainbow? No, the fish won't bite you," he said.

"That's some trip he's on," Sook said to no one.

"Trust me! Trust me! Swim!"

"How long's this trip? Anyone know?" said Faisal.

"Dunno. A hundred miles. Two hundred maybe?"

"At this speed, we'll be lucky to get there by nightfall."

"Nah, Faisal. Won't take that long."

"Unicorns! Unicorns!"

"Someone shut that *hundan* up!" shouted Acne Scars. "We really gotta listen to that the whole way? Faisal, lean around, punch him."

"How you expect me to do that, Maduro? My hands are locked, just like yours."

"Hey you, kid with the hair."

I lifted my head, locked eyes with the idiot. Maduro. "Name's Lazlo."

"Okay, whatever. Kick that duster, would ya?"

"Unicorns and flowers! Swim!" said Dusty.

I sat back in my seat, stretched my legs out into the aisle, propped them on Dusty's seat, watching Maduro the entire time. "Nope."

Faisal settled back expectantly, waiting for the show to begin.

Maduro's eyes narrowed. "Do it."

I sniffed, yawned, didn't break eye contact.

"Kick him. Or take the consequences."

I had no love for Dusty. He was annoying and entitled, and had no sense of self-preservation. The driver was driving, paying no attention to us, but even if he weren't distracted, I had no fear that he'd pap me if I kicked Dusty. But I would not obey some loser con *hundan*. Never. And threats? They only made me want to piss him off more.

"I'm flying! I'm flying!"

"Kick. Him."

"No."

"Better do it, guy," said Munch.

The van bumped into a hole and bottomed out. Maduro and I kept staring at each other.

"What the? You weird *hundan*—with your freaky hair and blood running down your face. You don't know who you're dealing with!" He was losing his cool. I was having some fun.

I crossed my legs and settled back comfortably. If my hands had been free, I would have thrown them behind my head, pretended I couldn't care less.

"Oh yeah? Who's that?"

Maduro sputtered, said, "I tell you to kick the duster, you kick the duster, you hear me?"

"I got ears, *hundan*."

"What you call me?"

"You got ears, *hundan*?"

"Little weirdo! I'm your worst nightmare!"

"That's debatable."

Sook threw me a look of warning.

"Little *hundan* don't even know the hell he called down on himself!"

My logical half warned me to back down, apologize, and kick Dusty. My other half, my weird hair half—well, that was the half that made life interesting.

"Hareeeeeeee—" sang Dusty, and I couldn't help it. The entire situation was ridiculous.

I laughed, that hysterical hiccuping and snorting kind of laugh that only makes you laugh harder. Faisal's lip quivered, but he could lock it down. Sook's eyes got enormous and Munch shook his head in disapproval. But Maduro? His face grew so red, the pock marks accentuated on his mean, ugly face, and I laughed harder.

And then Dusty snapped out of it, awareness trickling into his eyes, and he grinned at me, a sweet and silly gap-toothed smile. "What I miss?"

I gasped for breath and struggled to get myself under control.

Faisal said, "Your weird little friend messed with the wrong guy."

Dusty's eyes quickly evaluated the situation: He'd spent some time locked up with these cons, after all. I don't know why he was acting loyal to me, someone he'd just met, but I knew I'd live to regret it. He puffed himself up and announced, "No, Maduro. You messed with the wrong dude. Lazlo can get you where you sleep."

Maduro silently appraised me. I gathered every ounce of my Hill attitude and scowled at him, feigning the toughness I did not possess. He nodded at me, adversary met, game on. I held his gaze until he turned his back.

Oh Dusty, what did you do?

Chapter Twelve

A couple of hours into the drive, Maduro, Munch, and Sook were snoring. Dusty, Faisal, and I sat awake, staring out the windows. We'd been climbing steadily for the last fifteen minutes. Expectation was building inside me; something was about to happen. My adventure was about to begin. The dust billowing around our vehicle clouded the vista. But yes, there was definitely something there. In the near distance, a hint of something dark, like a vast ground to sky wall, was becoming visible. I leaned forward intently.

"Dusty, you awake?"

"Yup."

"You see that?"

"What?"

"Out there, ahead of us. What is that?" The dark something touched the horizon. It came from eternity and spread into eternity, like the shallows blending into the sky, neither water nor air indistinguishable from the other.

Dusty squinted out his window. "Dude, that's—what is that?"

"The Line," said Faisal.

"That's—that's where we're going?"

"Sure is."

"It looks like, like—"

"Trees." I completed Dusty's thought.

"Of course those are trees," said Faisal. "That's the sweeper forest."

Dusty grinned at me, his eyes lighting up. His face expressed my excitement. "We're finally going to see it!"

"Where'd you think we were going?" asked Faisal. "Don't you know what the Line is?"

Dusty and I looked at each other, and he giggled. "Honestly? No clue. Just wanted to get out of that stinking prison."

"Same," I agreed.

Faisal glanced at us and shook his head.

The closer we drove to the trees, the less of them we could see. The startling desert sunlight of eastern Cascadia dimmed as we approached the vast shadows cast by the forest. This long drive from Coulee had taken us back to the sweeper forest, the geographical border between east and west Coulee. My home, the shallows I longed to return to, lay on the other side. They'd driven me halfway to home, if I could escape the work crew. But that was a big if.

The heliovan driver sped us off the road, such as it was, and we jutted along a path scratched out of the dust and scrub. All the cons awoke by the time the camp came into view. The driver downshifted and brought the heliovan to a stop.

The doors clicked open and boots thundered up the steps into the van. Three inmates clad in the Coulee yellow clambered aboard and spread out, snapping open our shackles. I didn't see any guards. No black uniforms or anti-PAP helmets. No respirators. Nothing but a small group of yellow coveralls and pitched tents.

The inmates unlocked me last. The driver gave me a meaningful look as I passed his pod. His unspoken kindness struck me, threatened to weaken me, and I steeled myself again. Standing in a huddle with the cons, my nose itched and something tingled in my head, and BAM! A full PAP alarm slugged me in the brain. It hit with such surprising force, and I was on my knees in the dirt, rocking in agony.

A flurry of dirt and pebbles struck my back, the van backing out, the driver abandoning us to our fate. Blinking through my neural haze, I saw a slender yet powerfully built convict holding a PAP tracker. As soon as the van was out of reach, he stepped back and released the button. The alarm subsided, leaving behind a throbbing trail inside my skull.

The surrounding prisoners were moaning, and Maduro cursed, *"Hundan!"*

"I'm Nelson," said the man holding the tracker, his deep bass calm and resonant. "I'm a prisoner, like all of you. For those of you who haven't noticed, there are no guards here. We patrol ourselves. That doesn't mean you can walk off the Line and go back to your pathetic, insignificant lives." He paced back and forth, a wolf guarding his territory. "In that direction," he pointed east from where we'd just driven, "is uninhabitable terrain. No shelter, no humans, nothing but sagebrush and rocks. The occasional grass fire and no water unless you have a drill that can break through the crust and penetrate deeper than fifty feet." He pointed west at the massive sweeper forest. "If you don't yet know what lies beyond the Line, I guarantee you will within twenty-four hours. And once you do, any dreams you have of escape will POOF," he snapped his fingers, "disappear."

"I control the tracker, so I know where you are at all times. And that is a good thing. You will want to have your location known when something comes for you. You will want to be found. The alarm is your warning that something bad is coming."

"At times, you will hate me." Nelson fastened the PAP tracker to his waistband, his black eyes glittering. "But only I stand between you and what lives out there. Disobey at your peril."

"You guys buy this? This freaking *hundan*—YEEOW!" Maduro grabbed his head between his hands.

Nelson released the button on the PAP tracker. "If there aren't questions—"

He swiped the digiscreen of the tracker and I tensed, waiting for the piercing of yet another PAP alarm, but it didn't come. He read the screen, squinted at us, pointed at each of the prisoners. "You, Clint Maduro. Armed robbery, you're with me. Also Mo Faisal, embezzlement? Who'd you piss off to wind up here? You look strong enough, though. You're with me. Armand Sook, the hell kind of name is that? What do you bench? Sixty, seventy kilos?"

Sook snorted and spit. "Shoot, eighty on a bad day."

"I'll bet. You're on my crew. And you, big guy. Maharasha Little." He scoffed. "You really go by that?"

"No sir. Friends call me Munch."

"Munch. You're with me." His eyes fell on me, slid off, and landed on Dusty. "Okay, what's the deal with you two?" He peered at Dusty. "You high, *hundan*?"

"I wish," said Dusty.

"Yeah, I'll bet you do." Nelson grabbed my hair and pulled hard. I kicked at him, but he pushed me away before my foot could connect. "Watch yourself, kid. What's Coulee doing sending me some scrawny teen? What am I supposed to do with you?"

"I'll take him, Boss." A tall, shirtless, sunburned man stepped forward. He was growing a massive, thick beard, compensating for his shiny dome up top. But the brown-and-gray streaked bird nest growing off his chin wasn't the most striking thing about him. On his left side, where his arm should be, a skin nob wiggled below his shoulder. My mouth went dry, and a little acid built in my stomach, but I couldn't look away. The fleshy bump mesmerized me, and I wondered where the rest of his arm was. "Give me that other one too."

"They're all yours, Kominsky. Make sure you keep them in line." He pointed at me. "Especially that one. Something about him." And with that, Nelson walked off, our fellow passengers following him like dogs. Dusty and I stood around with the one-armed man.

"Well then, what you waiting for? Come with me." He turned and strode through the campground toward a large military style canvas structure.

I stood, wiped the dirt off my pants, and followed.

Dusty jogged up behind me. "Dude, what did we get ourselves into?"

Chapter Thirteen

✦

Lending a strangely cozy sense to the darkening landscape, the canvas structure glowed from within. Kominsky swept aside the tent flap and walked inside. A small group of convicts lounged around a long table, eating and talking. The conversation quieted and stopped, all eyes on us.

"Get yourselves something to eat," said Kominsky.

Now that he mentioned it, I realized how hungry I was. Dusty hadn't waited for an invitation; he was pouring broth into a bowl and sprinkling protein flakes over the top. I followed his lead, grabbing some protein bars as well.

Kominsky had taken a seat at one of the long tables beside a small, wiry man who quietly hummed to himself. Dusty and I climbed on to the bench across from them.

"I'm Kominsky, this is Jan Oh." The man didn't seem to notice we'd invaded his space and continued eating and humming. "Your names are?"

"I'm Dusty, and he's Lazlo." Dusty slurped eagerly at his soup.

"Can't you talk for yourself, kid?"

"When I feel like it, old man."

My head hit the table with a brain jarring thump. Jan Oh stood over me, pinning me down.

"Your friend's wicked fast," said Dusty.

"Yes, he is. Everyone on the Line knows that about Jan Oh. Also, he's got a hard on for disrespect. I think it's cultural." He smiled at the man immobilizing me on the tabletop. "Thanks, Jan. Our new friend Lazlo is about to apologize."

I blinked up at Jan Oh's stoic face. He had me locked down with one muscular hand, my cheek pressed to a table that smelled of reconstituted food product and bleach. He'd restrained me without injuring me, and he didn't seem to be angry. To be honest, I knew I'd been acting like a punk since being sent to Coulee. My sentence was unfair; I was innocent. I was angry, but I was punching above my weight if an older man like Jan Oh could take me down so quickly.

"Sorry," I mumbled into the table.

Jan Oh released me, settled back into his seat, and continued humming.

"Let's begin again. Lazlo, I'm Kominsky."

"Hi, Mr. Kominsky." My eyes flicked to his shoulder nub, flicked back to his face.

"Yes, I'm missing an arm," he said. "Quite a few of us are. And it's just Kominsky. No mister."

I scanned the room and counted at least five older men with loose sleeves on one side or—if their chests were naked, like Kominsky's—shoulder nubs.

"Far out," said Dusty. "Was it that *hundan* Nelson? He's one evil dude."

Kominsky chuckled. "No. You kids really are young, aren't you? Born well after the arm implants. How old are you, Dusty?"

"Nineteen."

"The arm implants were fourth gen, or was it fifth?" His

full lips widened in a smile, and he stroked his mustache and beard thoughtfully. "Patriots like me, Cooper over there," he winked at a dark-skinned man with a loose sleeve who winked back, "even Jan here, we protested the implants. They haven't been about virus suppression for decades. When was the last time you heard of someone dying of the Bleed?"

"Population control," said Jan Oh. He began humming again.

"Right. And those of us who saw it, we cut those implants right out of our arms. Now patriots like me and Cooper, well, we were wise to the conspiracy, but not too knowledgeable about how to get the things out. In my case, wound got infected, by the time I got to a doc, had to amputate the entire arm. Hard to hide your crime when you're in surgery. And removing an arm implant, well, that was a federal crime."

"That's why you're here? Because you did a hatchet job on your own arm?" said Dusty.

"That's right. That's why we're here." Kominsky waved his arm to include the collection of older men.

"But—a federal crime?" How had I never heard about this? Not surprising, considering the first time I'd learned about neural mesh was after they had abducted me from the shallows and implanted it in my head—without my consent, I might add. Apparently, I wasn't the only one who'd had hardware stuck in their body against their will. "If I could rip this thing out of my head, I'd do the same thing!"

"Yeah, you and me both, Lazlo." Kominsky frowned. "That's why they developed the mesh. Can't cut it out of your own brain, not without a brain surgeon. No more arm implants, not for thirty years or more."

"They calling us traitors. Enemies of the state." Cooper carried a soup bowl to our table and pushed in beside Dusty.

"Said we was going to infect all of Cascadia with the Bleed. Ain't been no Bleed since, shoot—"

"Not in my lifetime," said Jan Oh.

Kominsky said, "They started throwing us in prison. Threat of jail time was supposed to deter folks from cutting out the implants."

"Didn't take long until they ran out of space," said Cooper. "All us implant dodgers crammed in there."

"And Mister Oh?" I asked.

The humming stopped, and Jan Oh's brown eyes met mine. "Arm implant."

"You've got two arms though," said Dusty.

Jan Oh rolled the sleeve of his coverall up over his bicep to his shoulder, revealing a small circular scar the size of a thumbnail.

"He was a doctor." Kominsky smiled at his friend. "He did it right."

Dusty said, "How'd they find out?"

Jan Oh shrugged. "Ratted out."

"But you dudes have mesh now, right?" said Dusty.

Kominsky nodded. "Prisons wouldn't work without the PAP alarm. And the Line? Sheer chaos without it. The threat of a PAP gets the laziest *hundan* working."

"Nelson wouldn't have a chance without it," added Cooper.

I ripped open a protein bar with my teeth, spat the wrapper to the ground. "He's a con."

"And never forget it," said Kominsky. "Makes him doubly dangerous."

"Nelson is Coulee's flunky, their muscle to keep us all in line. They pay him handsomely for it," said Kominsky.

Jan Oh took a break from his humming and added, "He likes it. Probably do it for free."

Kominsky chuckled mirthlessly.

"He must sleep with one eye open," I said.

Jan Oh held his soup bowl to his lips. "We all do."

Cooper shoved his empty soup bowl to the side and leaned across Dusty. "Nelson and those buddies of yours who arrived today. They ain't no implant patriots. Steer clear of them; you want to make it out of here."

"Keep your heads down, mind your business," said Kominsky. "Yes sir, no sir, nothing more. The Line's got more than one type of monster, and the human kind, they'd as soon stab you as talk to you."

Dusty threw me a meaningful look: Too late for that advice, it seemed to say. I rolled my eyes back at him: These prisoners haven't got a clue.

Kominsky saw what passed between me and Dusty and took offense. From out of nowhere, he dove across the table and yanked my hair, pulling me painfully away from the table.

"You're mine," he said. "And first thing I'm doing is shaving off this damn mop."

He dragged me across the dirt floor as I kicked and cursed. Coarse male laughter and a stupidly grinning Dusty followed us out of the tent.

Chapter Fourteen

❦

Outside the tent, Kominsky released me. I fell backwards on to the hard dirt.

I rubbed my head and scowled at him. "What was that?"

He pulled a multi-tool from his pocket and held it between his teeth. With the speed of practice, he whipped open a knife and waved it at me. I scrambled backward in the dust like a crab from scuttled stones.

"Whoa, dude!" Dusty jumped between me and Kominsky, his arms thrown outward.

"Relax, Dusty. Just giving the kid a haircut."

Dusty nodded and stepped back. "He could sure use one."

"*Hundan*, I got style."

Kominsky scoffed. "Not going to last a day with that hair. You'll get stuck before breakfast."

The way Maduro had made such a big deal of it, I knew he was right. I didn't like the look myself; it had been an impulsive move on my first day in juvvie that I'd lived with for three months. Couldn't back down then, and I would not back down now, not easily anyhow. I'd make Kominsky work for it.

"Oh yeah? What you going to do about it?"

"Cut it. Grab him, Dusty."

The dustrat chortled like the half-baked child he was and dove on top of me in the dirt. We wrestled for a few minutes until he'd pinned me, my arms to either side and him sitting on my chest. It was like that time with Big Danson all over again, and I wondered why this seemed always to be the move. I reached for Dusty's mesh, when, just like that, he climbed off me.

"It needs to be done, Lazlo. Let it happen."

He stood and reached his hand out, a tentative smile quirking his lips. I turned my head and spat dirt, then grabbed his hand and let him haul me to my feet.

I stood before Kominsky and offered my scalp. "Didn't need to tear half the hair from my head."

"Better I show you your weakness before one of these *hundans* uses it to kill you," he said. "Dusty, you do it. I'm at a disadvantage."

"For real?" Dusty grabbed at the multi-tool greedily. "Can't believe you gave me this."

"Why? You'll get your own soon enough. Standard gear on the Line."

He waved the knife. "But—"

"Guess they wouldn't care if we kill each other," I said. "Put us out here. Let us take out the garbage."

Dusty wasn't listening. He opened other tools on the gadget. "—scissors, a can opener—what are these for?"

"Screwdrivers," I said.

"What do we need screwdrivers for? Out here?"

"Gives us options. Keeps the stab wounds interesting."

Kominsky snorted. "Dusty, cut the kid's hair already."

With gentle fingers, Dusty held a section of my hair and sawed at it with the knife. Guided by Kominsky—"Shorter there; how'd you miss that hank?"—the ground was soon littered with long pieces of bleached and black hair. When he'd finished, I ran my hand over my scalp. Half my head throbbed, whether from the hair pulling or the memory of lost locks, I didn't know.

Dusty folded the multi-tool and grudgingly handed it back to Kominsky. He pocketed it and waved at us to follow him through the camp, strutting like he owned the place, greeting prisoners, shaking hands, cracking jokes, and trading insults. Suspicious glances fell on me and Dusty until Kominsky introduced us in a faintly proprietorial manner.

He pointed out the medical tent, a canvas structure about half the size of the canteen, and we met the nurse, a big, bearded man named Sid. Next, we stepped under a long stretch of vinyl tarps that housed shovels and many other tools I couldn't name or imagine a use for.

"See that stack of tarps in the corner?" he said. "Grab a couple of 'em, Dusty. Lazlo, you grab two of those long poles and about six of the smaller ones. One sleeping roll and a pack each. I'll show you kids how to pitch your tent."

We found a flat bit of ground at the edge of the camp, and Kominsky talked us through building a tent by draping the tarps over the long poles and fastening them on the edges with the stakes. He told us to lay another tarp on the ground as a barrier between the dirt and our sleeping rolls. And with that, he said goodnight and turned to go.

"Wait—where you going?" I asked.

"My tent and roll. Alarm goes off before daybreak."

"Hold on... umm..." said Dusty.

Kominsky pointed toward the south. "Past camp, follow your nose. You won't miss it. Don't wander at night. Stay away from the Line." And with those cryptic warnings, he left us.

I'd slept rough before—hadn't liked it then, and I didn't like it now. I dropped cross-legged to the ground. The hard stones and bumps jutted out against the ground tarp. Unfastening my pack, I took a quick inventory: three pairs of clean socks, three prison-issue, one-size-fits-most drawstring underwear, two bright yellow rags, work gloves, hat, and water bottle. The promised multi-tool shimmered in the fading light. I gripped it hungrily in my fist.

"I gotta drain the dragon. You coming?" Dusty pocketed his own multi-tool.

"Sure."

"Good. Lead the way."

"Why me?"

"Your enormous nose. You can sniff it out." I swung around with the knife in my hand, not sure I'd actually stab anyone but ready for a fight. But he was grinning, any sting from his words neutralized by the goofy space between his front teeth. "Dude, learn to take a joke."

"Learn to tell one." The anger had leaked out of me, though, and I slugged him in the arm.

You'd need to have been born without a nose to miss the toileting area. Kominsky hadn't lied: The eye-watering, bile-raising stench struck us before we'd walked far beyond the south end of the camp. Burying my nose in the collar of my coveralls, I breathed through my mouth.

"Dude, I'm out," said Dusty, unzipping right there where we stood. "If it smells that bad from this far out, I'm walking no closer."

I unzipped and joined him, and there we stood, peeing in the wide open, when the alarm began pounding. I clenched my teeth and zipped my fly. Dusty held his head and cursed. Someone kicked me in the back and I fell to the ground, scrambled back, and looked up. It was dark, but I knew it was Maduro glowering over me. A green glow behind him lit Nelson's face where he stood, tracker in hand.

"No pissing outside the sewer area," he said. "Ever. Get out of my sight."

Dusty and I stumbled back to our tent.

Chapter Fifteen

❦

An insistent brain buzzing woke me the following morning. Beside me in the dark shelter, Dusty groaned and softly cursed. "Did we even sleep?"

Awake and immediately hungry, I grabbed my coveralls off the tarp floor and dressed quickly. Dusty watched me, bleary-eyed.

"Nice bedhead," he said, his own light brown hair clumped to one side. He'd slept fully clothed, and the impression of a coverall seam stamped his cheek.

I threw one of his boots at his head. He caught it easily, groaned again, pulled on his shoes, and dragged himself from the tent.

The camp was awake, prisoners in various stages of undress, filling their water bottles and stuffing their pockets with protein bars. I ladled some nondescript food product, thick, steaming, and white, into a bowl, and slumped down on the bench I'd sat on the night before. Jan Oh sat there already, humming to himself.

"Morning," I said.

With downcast eyes, he grunted a hello.

Dusty dropped beside me. "Oh, hey Jan Oh. Lazlo, look at this." He tipped his bowl upside down. The food product stuck to the bottom of the bowl as if gravity didn't exist. "What is this stuff?"

I tapped my spoon against the glop in my bowl. The spoon stuck to the food product, squelching and popping, when I pulled it away. Definitely not an appetizing prospect, but my stomach was growling loudly now. I dug my spoon into the bowl and carved out a chunk of the white stuff. There was no discernible odor. I tapped my tongue to the glop and found it simultaneously salty and sweet.

"Jeesh, kid. Are you eating your oats or fellating them?" Kominsky took his usual spot beside Jan Oh. "Ain't you never tasted oatmeal before?" He settled into his own breakfast, shoveling food into his mouth with gusto.

Jan Oh explained, "Oats are a grain. Plants grow here in the east."

Kominsky stopped chewing and stared at me and Dusty. "You kids don't know what oats are?"

"Uh, sure—" I began, but Dusty spoke over me. "Nope. But I wasn't exactly a breakfast eater before. Not really a morning person." He looked at the bowl dubiously before scooping the smallest taste on to his spoon.

"What about you, Lazlo?"

I looked at the goop in silence and Jan Oh said, "You're a kelp kid."

"What the hell is that supposed to mean?"

Jan Oh regarded me placidly. "You're from the shallows, right? Raised on kelp and seaweed?"

"Yeah. You wanna make something of it?"

"No oats in the shallows." He nodded at the bowl. "Good energy for the day ahead. You'll get used to them."

The oatmeal coated my tongue blandly. I chewed, swallowed. A gooey texture, not much flavor, not much different from most food I'd eaten in my life. But there was plenty of it, so I dished myself seconds.

"Damn," said Kominsky. "Kids don't know what oatmeal is. Now I've heard everything."

"I doubt that," said Jan Oh.

By the time we finished breakfast, the sky was glowing with dawn. Jan Oh set off on his own, walking west with a group of older men. Dusty and I followed Kominsky to the tool tent. He pointed out several tools and named them for us: shovel, chain saw, weed torch. There were wires and circuit boards and canisters upon canisters of aluminum caulking, but he told us we wouldn't need those. Not today, not for a while. Dusty and I grabbed a shovel each and one weed torch.

"What you kids know about the Line?"

"We get half off our sentences and some crypto when we're through," said Dusty.

I bit my lip hard, remembering how the warden had conned me, then immediately regretted it as the scab reopened.

"That it?" said Kominsky.

"Pretty much," said Dusty.

Kominsky looked at me. I wiped the blood from my lip, nodded my head, said nothing.

"Damn," he said, shaking his head in disbelief. "And you signed up, not knowing—well, you kids know about the sweeper forest, right?"

You couldn't be a kid in Cascadia without learning about the sweepers and how they'd saved humanity from the brink of extinction. They were Cascadia's one contribution to the world. The geezer clearly thought we were naïve rubes. I said, "Uh, duh old man."

Kominsky only had the one hand, but it was fast. He

caught me across the face before I had time to duck.

"It cleans the air of excess carbon," said Dusty as though I'd never spoken.

"Damn, I don't have the patience. The amount you two don't know."

"You're right, we have a lot to learn," said Dusty, throwing me a look to keep my mouth shut. "So teach us."

We stepped out of the tent and met the morning sun. Standing beneath them on the transway in the dark, driving in at twilight when they were hazily visible, and seeing their shadows hadn't prepared me. My heart pounded out of my chest when I first saw the sweeper forest in the light of day. Massive tree trunks stretched from north to south as far as I could see. I tipped my head back and stared into the brightening sky, searching for their tops. The green boughs darted in and out of clouds. Now you see them, now you don't.

Beside me, Dusty gaped and blathered on and on about how beautiful and majestic the trees were. I was embarrassed for him. Kominsky laughed and said, "You kids really know nothing, don't you?" And then I was embarrassed for myself.

We walked out of the camp and into the field along with the other yellow-suited cons. A massive, shimmering, metallic wall of blocks ran along the edge of the forest, maybe ten feet high. The bright yellow uniforms swarmed the blocks nearest our camp. Others were working the field nearby.

"What is that?" asked Dusty.

"That's the Line." I said it, knowing it the moment I laid eyes on it. That metal wall attracted me, pulled me in, that line separating us from the forest. But it repelled me too. It was horrible and bleak; it severed us from the humanity-saving trees that sucked planet-heating carbon from our world. The Line caged us here in the eastern desert, far from the teeming cities and the peaceful Shallows. The Line was one more obstacle I'd have to cross before I reached home and Ami and the rest of my life.

"It's metallic foam. Lightweight, fire resistant, strong, and most importantly for you two, it conducts electricity. Never touch it, not unless I personally tell you to."

"There are men crawling all over it," said Dusty.

"Yeah, Nelson turns off sections of it during the day so we can replace bricks. Fill cracks. Repair circuits. Turns it back on when we're done for the day. Two cons got themselves electrocuted right before you all arrived, and we were short-handed even before that."

"Electrocuted?" said Dusty.

"That's why I say, and don't you ever forget, never touch the Line, not unless I give you the all clear."

Dusty hadn't asked the obvious question, so I did. "What's it for?"

"Ha, so this, well, this—" Kominsky scoffed, shook his head, looked from Dusty to me. "This is why you're such stupid kids. Not knowing what you got yourselves into. The Line—it keeps us safe. Keeps eastern Cascadia safe. The sweepers clean the air, but they also pump oxygen, make our air heavy. There are things that love that oxygen, that thrive on that oxygen, that live longer than any outsider in the heavy air. And those things live in that forest."

Dusty's eyes were starry. He was loving this, a dumb insider kid tripping on a made-up bedtime story. "Keep Cascadia safe from what?"

Kominsky growled low. He'd hooked a gutter rat, and he was hauling him in. "*Chongs, zhus*, biggest damn critters you've ever seen."

"Wait," I said, laughing. "Cascadia built a three-meter-high fence against *chong*s?" I'd learned the standard, non-Chinglish way to say "chong" was insect. "Zhu" was arachnid. No one I knew used those words.

Living in the shallows with Ami and Appei, I'd not had much experience with *chong*s. Sometimes in deep summer we'd have a burst of blood-stickers, but a passing windstorm would carry them away. My first encounter with brown backs had been at Miz Hazel's, a late night skittering the size of my foot. Miz Hazel had squashed it quickly with a broom, and the next day we had played outdoors while a team of masks gassed the house. By the time I'd made it to First City, masks and gas were commonplace. I hated *chong*s, sure, but building and fixing a vast fence to keep out some brown backs seemed a ridiculous waste of time and money, especially when a little gas could kill them easily.

Kominsky spun around and fixed me with a look. It was harder than if he'd punched me in the head again. I swallowed my laugh. He was serious.

"These ain't little city *chong*s. A little blast of spray ain't gonna take these out. Those city *chong*s are the babies. Leave them grow, they don't stop."

It was Dusty's turn to scoff. "Sounds like you had the worst dust trip ever."

"You'd know about that, I guess," said Kominsky.

But I believed Kominsky right off. Why else would Cascadia pour so much money and so many bodies into preserving this structure? It was easy enough to jail us beneath the ground in places like Coulee. Why drive a bus load of cons to the desert and load us up with tools, sharp knives, all of it? Did they hope we'd kill each other and rid them of the burden of housing us? If that was the goal, why feed us? Why bother creating a nightmare story like this to keep a few of us occupied? It made little sense.

"Dusty," I said. "Look at him. He's serious."

"You don't need to believe me, Dusty." Kominsky stopped in the middle of the field. "You'll see them soon enough."

Ami and the shallows were on the other side. I'd been so happy, thinking I was halfway to home. But I kept learning how difficult my escape would be.

Chapter Sixteen

Over five-hundred miles.

The Line stretched from southern Cascadia up to the Canadian border. Maybe they had a Line up there to keep the *chong*s inside. Kominsky didn't say, and I didn't ask. I was still getting my head around what was in front of my eyes here on the edge of the eastern desert. The eastern correctional facilities, Coulee among them, had prison crews working up and down the Line on the eastern side. Our crew was stationed farther north than any of them.

Cascadia intended each crew to have a minimum of thirty workers, but Kominsky told us between stabbings and work casualties, the Line lost workers faster than volunteers signed up. He said Nelson's crew had fewer con-to-con injuries than you might expect—a large part of our crew was patriots, old timers who'd maimed themselves, not hardened criminals—but because our crew was older, workers were going silent.

Our group of six propped up the crew's numbers. If not for the two who'd been shocked and sizzled before we'd arrived, Kominsky said, we'd be at a nice round twenty. And though we were far short of our minimum, and it was a fair guess that the crews south of us had the same problem, Cascadia couldn't force anyone to work the Line; there were civil rights laws and all. You had to volunteer, and you had to be paid.

Unless you were me, apparently.

And before you think, good for Cascadia with their civil rights laws protecting convicted prisoners, never forget, most of us hadn't chosen the mesh in our heads. The one-armed patriots certainly hadn't. Neither had I. Maybe some insiders had been lulled into it with promises of streaming stories and games and whatnot. That's what the Axon pills were for, after all: To soothe those insider minds, keep them happy and spending their insider crypto. But the rest of us?

Those so-called civil rights laws meant there were never enough warm bodies working to maintain the Line. They chewed up and spit out the few stupid *hundans* like us who signed up, replaced us with other idiots by promising a future they wouldn't live to see. I hadn't known what the Line was when I volunteered. How many cons did? I only knew what the warden had told me. He'd conned me worse than any slinger on the Hill ever had.

We hiked farther north along the Line as Kominsky schooled us. Sagebrush and grass and waist-high trees poked through the hard soil.

"You'll work the field today. Lazlo, you start here, scrape a shallow trench in that hard pan. Come on, put your back into it. Yes, that's the way. Dusty, you spark the grass and brush, real quick, like this—"

Pressing a button on the thin stick, Kominsky triggered a bright current of light. The heavy air grabbed the spark and breathed life into it. I jumped back as the dry grass at my feet burst into flame. The burning seam spread wide and ran away toward the shining bricks on the Line, leaving behind a smoking black trail. The flame reached my dirt trench and petered out.

"Both of you, keep those shovels handy in case the fire gets out of control. Don't let it jump the trench. If it does, shovel dirt on it like your lives depend on it. Because they do. If you don't burn your own hides, Nelson will do it for you."

"And that way?" I pointed west, toward the shimmering wall.

"The Line will stop the flames. Long as no one's working there, you're fine. Never use the torch unless you're north of the Line climbers."

I looked south to the Line. Maduro and Faisal had climbed halfway up the metallic wall. Munch and Sook were filling cracks. Nelson marched back and forth, eyes everywhere, barking orders up and down the Line. Yellow coveralls everywhere. We all wore yellow, the bright uniform of Coulee Correctional, instantly visible against the dead brown hardpan or the shiny metallic blocks or the dark shadows of the sweeper forest. We were going nowhere, no escape, not until our sentences were up or we were dead.

Whichever came first.

Kominsky handed Dusty the weed torch and strode across the field to a small tree standing alone. "These here are the hard work. This is a sweeper, one start. These things are fire resistant. Bred into their DNA. Part of the reason this work is so important. We need the forest, but we can't let it spread outside the Line. So when you see these escapees, you gotta dig them out. And in this hard pan, it ain't easy. But nothing you two healthy kids can't handle."

"What about that?" I pointed at the chainsaw we'd carried from camp.

"Saws can cut them if you get them young enough. But this far north, two decades of free growth—" He tapped the trunk with his knuckles. "The bark is damn tough. Couple years back, con here for robbery, one of the nicer ones, really. Tried to take one down, about this size. Got the damn chain stuck in the sweeper. Saw jumped in his hand. Poor *hundan* sliced into his own face. He survived. It got him off the Line, but damn. Not the way you want to go."

Looking at the chainsaw, I imagined how that chain would feel embedded in my head, and I shivered.

"Once the sweepers get like this, only way to kill them is to dig down to the roots. Dig them out entirely or saw through the roots. Weaken them so they wither. Let the wind take them down."

He turned around and began walking south toward the other crew members. Trees and brush stretched north into infinity.

"You're cracked if you think me and Dusty are doing this alone."

Kominsky's eyes narrowed. "You're new to the Line. Start small."

Dusty backed me up. "The other new dudes are working the Line."

"You think we're stupid?" I said.

"You think you got any rights?" Kominsky said. "Nelson decides for his crew. I decide for mine. Now shut up and get to work."

When he'd walked out of hearing range, Dusty cursed. "Kominsky is some *hundan*, right? Leaving us out here, digging like a couple of idiots. Thinks we're not good enough."

"So what's he gonna do if we don't work?" I said. "Not like he's sitting there, making us."

Dusty grinned. "Yeah, true. He doesn't have a PAP tracker. You told him off, and he did nothing."

"What's he gonna do if I throw my shovel down, like this?

And sit on the ground, like this. And close my eyes to take a nap, like this—"

Dusty laughed, dropped his tools, and sat beside me.

I wasn't afraid of working hard. A kid born in the kelp fields couldn't be: it was a point of pride. I was only flexing with Dusty. The false arrest, false conviction, being lied to by the warden, finding myself the lowest man on this work crew. But I was tired and when I pulled my pack under my head for a pillow, closed my eyes against the sun, I must have dozed off. The next thing I knew, a PAP alarm was piercing my brain.

Stumbling painfully, groggily to my feet, a grim-faced Nelson brought me instantly awake. Dusty rolled on the ground, screaming nonsense, completely dusted out. "Faisal, take the crazy one to medical. Tell Sid to trank him or something. Can't have the drama on my crew. Maduro, you stay here. Make sure this *hundan* works."

I watched as they dragged away the con I'd allied myself with, my only friend on the crew, a raving loon. Maduro stuffed something quickly in the pockets of his coveralls and kicked my pack away across the field. Sneering then, his beady black eyes narrowed, he cracked his knuckles and crossed his arms. "Give me a reason, *shashu*."

Grabbing my shovel, I scratched the first of the day's many trenches in the hardpan.

Chapter Seventeen

❧

By late morning, I longed for the marine layer of the shallows or even the moist clouds of First City. Again and again I pinged the dull shovel against the hard pan and pressed my prison boot against it. Inches of dirt crumbled bit by bit. Unused to the work, my hands grew red and sore and threatened blisters. Together, the sun and wind were two brutal prison friends standing shoulder to shoulder, beating me about the head and shoulders. I stripped to the waist, the top of my coveralls peeled back. The desert wind whipped me, cooling my skin and stealing every bit of sweat the sun dragged out of me.

Watching me work must have been even worse than the work itself, and Maduro had quickly grown bored. Half an hour after the cons had taken Dusty away, Maduro abandoned me to the field, and I labored alone. I almost welcomed the piercing burst of an alert to break up the tedium. Looking southward, I watched the cons climb down the wall and reach for their packs. Standing and sitting in discrete groups, they began eating and drinking. I figured it must be lunchtime, so I dropped the shovel where I stood and scarfed down the protein bar I'd brought from camp. My water bottle was nearly empty: I'd used it to cool my face and neck. Foolish! I would surely run out before the end of the day.

Barely had I swallowed down the last of the bar when the alert buzzed again. Yellow went up the wall again. Reprieve over. The heat played with the floating desert dirt and my dehydrated vision. Yellow shimmered in the haze, coming closer, resolving into a human. It was Dusty. He grabbed a shovel off the ground and strode over.

"This all you've done so far?"

"Shut up," I grinned. Was I ever happy to see him, but they must have used some crazy meds on him. Dilated black pupils nearly obliterated the blue of his eyes. "Feeling better?"

His singular smile, and then: "Not felt so good since the Hill."

And except for his eyes, he looked good. Calm and focused. The metallic clink of our shovels against stone was our conversation. I no longer felt the palms of my hands: the skin had numbed along with my brain, sensation disappearing into the monotony of digging. Was this how I'd spend every day for the next five years of my sentence? Was working on the Line with the threat of accidental electrocution better? It certainly couldn't be worse.

I bounced my shovel off the hardpan for the millionth time that day and felt a cool wetness on the handle. One of my blisters had burst. Blood mixed with the blister fluid and oozed from my hand. Dropping my shovel, I examined the other hand. My skin was torn open and bleeding. Once I saw the ragged mess I'd made of my hands, I felt fully the pain I'd blocked.

"Dude, where are your gloves?"

Dusty wore protective work gloves. Of course, why hadn't

I thought to wear mine? Walking back across the field, I retrieved my pack from where Maduro had kicked it that morning and rifled painfully through it. No gloves. But they'd been there, hadn't they? I'd had them; I was sure of it. Between last night and today, where had they disappeared to?

It was a sucker punch to the gut. I was an idiot.

"Maduro stole them."

"No kidding? Why?"

Fury joined the sharp stabbing in my hands, and my eyes searched the Line for him. Shielding my eyes from the sun and squinting through the haze, I could not see him. The yellow-suited bodies were indistinguishable from each other. I was a fair distance away and I couldn't see my quarry, but then, I didn't care about any of the cons on the Line. I didn't know them yet. If I accidentally hit someone else, tough luck. Not like anyone on the Line was innocent. Honestly, I never expected I'd land a thought pulse to anyone's mesh. But I was angry enough to try.

I closed my eyes and gathered the rage inside of me. I thought of Kominsky's warning about deadly *chongs*, imagined Miz Hazel's brown backs grown impossibly large. And then I thought of Maduro's smug expression. How I wanted to wipe the floor with him. I became the brown back, all waving antennae and dull hard shell and sticking legs. I tickled Maduro's ugly face with one antenna, then two. Stretched out one of my six legs, gripped his with my sticky *chong* foot and crawled up, the weight of my immense shell taking him down. I sat on him, my flat abdomen weighing on his back, then opened my jaws and took a bite from his shoulder—

The desert wind picked up the screams like leaves and blew them across the open field.

"What the—you hear that, Lazlo?" Dusty's shovel clattered against the hard pan and he ran over to me. "Someone get zapped on the Line? I mean, electrocuted?"

I pulled a pair of socks over my bleeding hands and picked up the weed torch.

"Let's burn some scrub before dinner."

Later in the canteen, I took my usual spot on the bench with Kominsky and Jan Oh. Bandaged and wrapped by Dusty's new friend, the nurse Sid, my hands struggled to hold a spoon. I gave up and cradled my bowl, slurping noisily at the warm broth. Sid had offered painkillers, which I'd found surprising. I hadn't imagined Coulee would care much about the discomfort of its indentured servants. But then, if it was so difficult to get volunteers, I supposed they needed to keep us happy, or at least, drugged into submission. I didn't trust pills, not since my time in care, so I'd turned them down. Sid had seemed surprised—clearly, he knew I'd been a slinger—and like most insiders whose knowledge of outsiders was based on the entertainment pulsing through their neural mesh, he'd assumed all slingers were also dusters.

No thanks. I'll keep both my pain and my reality, if it's all the same to you.

Dusty crowded in beside me, soup spilling from the sides of his overfull bowl. "What happened on the Line today? We heard screaming all the way from the field."

Kominsky said, "One of the new guys, muscular, dark crew cut, you know the one—"

"Maduro," I said.

"That his name? Tough guy. One of Nelson's new favorites. *Hundan* starts freaking out, screaming, tries to run—"

"Papped," said Jan Oh.

Dusty whistled. "Whoa... Dude! Where was he going? Was he trying to escape?"

"In broad daylight? Screaming like he was being gutted? I wouldn't think so."

I turned my face into my shoulder to hide my smile. Dusty saw it and his eyes grew large. At least, I think they did—his pupils were still pretty huge from the drugs Sid had given him. He knew I'd had something to do with it. I'd crossed his mesh that one time in the van, accidentally pulsed him. In his drug-addled state, it wouldn't take much for him to imagine I could do something to Maduro from across the field. He'd be right, but I didn't need him announcing it loudly to the entire tent. Not that anyone would believe a duster, but still. I quickly changed the subject.

"Kominsky, tell us more about the Line."

Ask Kominsky for information and, ooh boy. Better strap yourself in, because you'll be sitting there a while. He started right in, going on and on about how Cascadia built the whole thing a couple hundred years ago, before the east-west transway had become overgrown.

Jan Oh interrupted him, told him to go back even farther, and Kominsky did. Started school five hundred, maybe six hundred years ago when some egghead scientist planted some trees. Around the time of that scientist, I guess we'd heated the atmosphere and melted the poles. A century of wildfires and floods, hurricanes and diseases. Places like Coulee and east burned to the ground again and again, and people moved underground, letting the fires pass over them. Places like the shallows and farther west flooded, disappeared. Cascadia itself used to belong to a larger country from the shallows across Coulee to some place far east. Water on both sides.

But I guess the egghead overshot the mark a bit with his trees, because they took over. The places that didn't flood or burn were the places the sweepers loved. They spread, and at some point, some other egghead scientists figured out that the sweepers were going to keep spreading and pumping out oxygen. The *chongs* and *zhus* loved that oxygen. Their lungs grabbed it and those creatures grew and grew.

Kominsky told us the national guard designed and constructed the vast fence with financing secured by the Cascadian parliament. They hadn't thought to build in maintenance costs, though. They knew they wouldn't be able to secure the funding needed for that, not long term.

"A secret branch of the national guard maintains the western fence. Bet you didn't know about that, did you? Cascadia don't advertise that bit." Kominsky was beaming, loving this. He was a conspiracy theorist excited to be educating the next generation.

"Not a secret branch." Jan Oh mostly let Kominsky run the show. A word or two clarified or corrected his instruction. "Recruits. Basic training."

"And in the east?" I asked, though I'd lost interest in the lecture. I would keep Kominsky talking as long as I could. Give Dusty a chance to calm down.

"Cascadia neglected the eastern side for a long time—"

Jan Oh: "Decades."

"—until some eastern politician convinced the western politicians to make convicts do the work. The labor was cheap, and prisons were huge money-making enterprises."

Jan Oh: "Privatized."

"But by then, the Line was falling down. Sizeable areas unsecured. *Chongs* just walking across the desert. Didn't have time to focus on each section, like we do today. They had to do something fast."

Jan Oh: "Bombs."

That caught Dusty's attention. "They dropped bombs?"

Kominsky chuckled. "No kid. Cyanide land mines.

Explode when someone—or something—like a huge *chong* walks across them. Fast. Cheap. Easy."

"Why don't we just do that, then?" I looked at my bandaged hands. "Save time and money. Cascadia ought to like that."

"Once only," said Jan Oh.

"They explode one time," Kominsky explained, "and then what you got? Same problem—the Line still needs to be repaired. Our crew, the other cons on the crews south of here, we're all that stands between the eastern folks and an onslaught of *chong*s. This is our war. And we soldiers don't abandon our posts."

I scoffed. "Soldiers. Yeah, right. That's what Cascadia considers us. Real heroes."

"Don't matter what anyone else thinks. Certainly not those insiders down in Coulee." He lay his hand on my head, his sudden touch as gentle as it was startling. "What you are, that's up to you. Can't nobody tell you different. And don't let them try." Kominsky pushed himself up, groaning, from our table. "And now, I need to spend some private time on my bedroll." He nodded at my hands. "Get yourself a pair of gloves before you head to your tent tonight." Waving good-night, he left the canteen.

Dusty turned to me, "Dude! You do that to Mad—"

I kicked his shin, hard. "Not here," I said and fled the tent. Dusty wasn't far behind.

Chapter Eighteen

Dusty kept his mouth shut as we walked to the tool tent. He waited in silence when I grabbed a fresh pair of gloves. He didn't say a word until we were back in our shelter. But then, the floodgates opened.

"You did something, didn't you?"

I kicked off my boots. "Keep your voice down."

And quieter: "What did you do?"

"I was with you in the field. You saw me."

"No, no, no. You did that freaky thing—you got into his head."

"Shhhh!"

"You got into his head. Like you did with me. In the van."

Unzipping my coveralls with the tips of my fingers was difficult. I struggled to pull them off. My bandaged hands were thick and clumsy. I cursed and tugged, then stepped on the pants and pulled my legs free. Dusty lay on his side, head propped on a hand, watching me.

"Tell me."

"How can you sleep fully clothed?" I sat down on my bedroll, wincing as a stone pressed into my back.

"Don't change the subject."

"You good for a secret?"

"Lazlo, dude. Who am I going to tell? Munch? Faisal? Freaking Nelson? I got you, you got me, right?"

His face was earnest, and I thought trustworthy. Well, as trustworthy as a duster could be. I knew he'd give me up the second he needed some Axon. But who would give him that here? And even if he broke my trust, dusted out and spouted off, who'd believe him? Really believe him? Anyone would believe it to be the raving of a lunatic, an addict, a convict who'd fried his brain so badly he could no longer tell fact from fantasy.

Besides, I told myself, he technically already knew what I was capable of. I'd pulsed him once. He'd felt it. And I needed someone to confide in, someone friendship-adjacent, even if that person was of questionable sanity.

"You're right."

"I knew it! How?"

"Not sure. Been able to do it since I was... maybe twelve? Thirteen?"

"Someone teach you? Can you teach me?"

"No, nothing like that. I don't really know how it happens. It just did, one day, when I was in care. Slipped out, sort of."

"Like with me? In the van?"

"Yeah, an accident."

"But today—that wasn't an accident."

"No."

"Did you ever do that before? On purpose?"

I thought of Rajani, how I'd soothed her when she needed it. Stroked her neural mesh with images of gently rocking waves and the gulls crying over the kelp fields, and how I'd pulsed her pictures of Ami's flowers for her tattoo art. I said, "No."

"Lazlo, you know how big this is? Like—" He rolled to his back, put his hands under his head, and stared at the roof of the tent. "It's a weapon. And no one except us knows you have it."

"A concealed weapon."

"Yeah."

"But not really. It won't protect me. Like, if Maduro pulls a knife—"

"Why not? You can get into his head. Make him stab himself."

"It doesn't work like that, Dusty."

"Well, how did you do it today?"

"It's difficult to explain."

"Try."

My hands were hot and throbbing. Not like I was going to get much sleep tonight, anyway. "I make a picture in my head. And then I think of the person I want to send the picture to... and then... I don't know. It just, like, sends."

"So, you're like a transmission station?"

The Cascadian government kept sole control over the transmission stations. But Axon Corp owned the technology, so Cascadia licensed them to transmit consumption, encouragement, and entertainment over the networks. They engineered neural mesh to receive transmissions. I'd never believed it possible that an individual could use their mesh to transmit. At least, I'd never heard of it. And I didn't expect I ever would—Cascadia and Axon would work together to shut that down quick. That person would cease to exist. If they knew about me, I'd cease to exist. I knew that for a fact. Easy enough to disappear an outsider. And a throwaway—who'd notice?

I shook my head. "Nope. Nothing like that. Just a fluke."

"What do you mean?"

"Like, some weird side effect. Axon pills, you know. They test them on kids."

"Shut up. How could I get into that trial?" Dusty laughed. I didn't join in. "They tested on you?"

"In care. Yeah."

"And you think that's why—I don't know. The dust makes some crazy dreams."

He was quiet for a while and I thought he'd fallen asleep. I hoped he had. But I was not so lucky.

"More like a PAP tracker then, but you send pictures, not alarms."

I sighed. "Kind of, but not totally. I can't see where people are."

"How far can you send?"

"I've only done it when I'm right next to someone—"

"But today you sent to Maduro, and he wasn't close."

"No. I couldn't even see him."

"What picture did you send? Show me."

"No." Last thing I needed was Dusty flipping out here in the tent. It would probably trigger a full dust out.

"Pretty bad, huh? At least tell me."

"Giant *chong*. A brown back."

"You're right. I don't want to see that. But how'd you transmit so far? What do you think?"

"Got no clue."

Silence again and I waited.

"You sent me a mind picture and now you can send one a little farther. Maybe it's like a muscle. The more you exercise, the stronger it gets." I heard the crinkle of the floor tarp as he rolled to his side again. "Lazlo, you need to work out. I'll be your trainer."

I scoffed. "Yeah, right."

"That brain muscle needs to be stronger. It's your only

protection. I don't know if you've noticed, but Maduro's got it out for you."

"Kind of hard to miss. Even though I got this great new hairstyle." I moved to pat my head ironically before I remembered I wouldn't feel it through the bandages.

"Dude, I'm serious. No offense, but you're not exactly the biggest dude out here."

"My multi-tool doesn't care how big a guy is."

"I don't care what Cascadia says, Lazlo. You're no *shashu*."

And just like that, the crazy duster from the Hill became my friend. Until I could get back home to Ami, Dusty would be my safe place.

Chapter Nineteen

❧

The spun-out, lightheaded tipple in my brain was the first clue a major alarm was about to go off. A moment later, my mesh pulsed, my skull burned hot. The headache gripping my cranium would be a beast.

Beside me, Dusty's shovel clattered to the rocky soil. He held his head and rocked. "You feeling this?"

"Nope. You're the only one."

We'd been on the Line a month, working this section. Should move on soon, the old timers kept saying. An entire month, yet Dusty and I were still burning weeds and digging up trees. Kominsky hadn't even trained us for fence labor, and every time we asked, he came up with a new excuse: we didn't listen, Dusty's freak outs were too unpredictable, I was too young. Dusty spent several days a week in the medical tent, coming down off a neural break, and I spent several days a week being papped by Nelson or bullied by Maduro.

With each passing day, I quietly exercised my skills and kept a tally of how much time I had left to serve. Dusty would be out in four or five months. I still had four years and eleven months until my sentence was up. But I promised myself I wouldn't be here to see that day. I would have escaped long before that.

"*Chong!*" yelled Jan Oh at the other end of the fence line. "Big *chong!*" A redhead, a *chong* with a gleaming black back offset by red legs and head, had somehow found its way through the fence. It ambled shyly forward, antennae waggling. One of its back legs dragged in the dirt, a cloud of dust floating behind.

"Three feet long and half lame," said Dusty. He snorted and whacked dirt from his pants. "Not worth a PAP."

The other cons grunted in agreement. I shuddered, looked over my shoulder beyond the Line. An injured three-foot redhead might not seem much to my fellow prisoners; there were far deadlier *chong*s where that one had come from. With six working legs, that redhead would be on a man in seconds, boiling out its acrid spray with a pop. Cons who'd worked the Line longer than me spoke of the painful burn blisters as though they were a rite of passage. I didn't plan to spend time in the med tent with Sid, not because of a redhead. Lame or not, a redhead half the length of a grown man was plenty big to me.

Nelson had turned off the electricity for the section of Line for repairs. Kominsky worked that section today, and it surprised me that a slow-moving redhead had gotten through without him noticing. We had to watch our own backs. Coulee wouldn't care if some giant *chong* took us out. It would be inconvenient, sure, but they'd swap in another work crew.

The high frequency shriek of the zapper cut through my brain fog. The powerful thunk of current blasted through the hard shell of the redhead, sending cartilage and yellow pus outward in a 270-degree arc. Goo and guts splattered every poor loser standing near the former *chong*. Nelson grinned like a lunatic as he tossed the zapper from one hand to the other. He'd rigged a weed sparker to emit one focused ray of electrical energy. Like the PAP tracker, he kept it close by at all times. The only thing he seemed to enjoy more than threatening me was exploding *chong*s with it.

A fist slammed into the back of my head. I stumbled forward but didn't fall. Maduro leered at me, all acne-pocked skin and shaved head, daring me to try something, anything. He'd have me on the ground with an arm pulled behind my back before I could get a punch off. I reached into my mind, but my mesh blazed, the headache pounding. No way I could throw a thought pulse.

"Clean it up, *shashu*," he said, clenching his tattooed fist.

I grabbed my water bottle and shovel and walked toward the Line. Nelson's eyes were on me. He pointed the zapper at me, following my path across the rocky landscape.

"Bang."

"Give the kid a break, Nelson," said Kominsky. "He's serving his time, like the rest of us."

"Mind your business, old man. Shame if you lost the other arm," said Nelson, but he lowered the zapper.

I took a long draw on my water bottle before getting to work. Mixed into the liquid was the day's supply of electrolytes, protein, and carbs. I craved caffeine, aspirin, anything to dull the throbbing between my temples. Nelson had turned off the alarm right before zapping the *chong*, but this headache would be with me for hours. The PAPs hit me extra hard these days; I was increasingly sensitive to them, becoming more so as I exercised my ability.

If I could do it and survive, I often thought I'd gouge the mesh from my brain like Kominsky and Jan Oh and the other patriots did, drilling the implants from their arms. But not before I escaped the Line. The implant kept me captive, a puppet to whoever held the PAP tracker. But it was also my only defense against men like Maduro who outweighed me two to one. I needed to learn how to block reception so I could prevent the debilitating headaches and preserve my strength and ability to transmit.

Halfway up the fence, Jan Oh rewired the metal blocks. He was a small man; shorter than me. Work on the Line was muscling out my torso and arms, but Jan's frame had gone wiry. The power in him simmered, taut and on edge, just beneath the surface. No one messed with the old timers, only a few lame insults—they were slightly crazy—they'd sliced into their own flesh to remove hardware, after all. And Jan was a special breed among them: smart, silent, unknowable, slightly off.

On the ground, Kominsky had been patching the break with aluminum foam. He mopped *chong* juice from his face. He shook out his sweat rag, inspected it, wrinkled his nose, then jammed the rag into the back pocket of his nuclear yellow coveralls.

"Don't know how it got through," he said. "I was patching the fence, turned to grab a new can of foam. Next thing I know, there it is."

"Could have happened to anyone." I lied. My skin would have crawled long before I'd seen the thing.

I wondered how Kominsky had missed it, lumbering in his direction. Maybe his eyesight was going. He was probably in his forties, the age Appei had been when he went silent. Only Jan was older, and he'd been an insider once. Gave him more time than the other old timers, the ones who'd lived their entire lives without air processors. Jan even looked younger than the others, with his sleek, black hair tied at the nape of his neck. His skin was light brown, still smooth. Not like Kominsky and the other light-skinned cons. Their skin dried out and cracked, grew brown spots that multiplied across their arms and faces. Jan even seemed younger than the dark prisoners, men like Cooper, who seemed out of breath after walking across the field. I'd seen Cooper in the med tent several times, though I didn't remember him ever burning or cutting himself and needing first aid.

But I often forgot how old Kominsky was. He seemed younger somehow when I talked to him.

I scooped a pile of *chong* guts and flung them toward the metal blocks. They dropped wetly; yellow goo coated the surface of the shovel. Kicking at the ground, I scraped rocks from the surface of the soil before stabbing the shovel into the hard packed earth. I dug into the soil again and again, scraping the shovel clean.

I worked silently, shoveling and tossing, clearing the field beneath the blazing sun, feeling my skin roast.

This wasn't a punishment; it was a slow torture to the death. You wouldn't work the Line if you had anyone to fight for you. Anyone to live for. Anyone left who cared.

Kominsky and Jan finished the repairs on the fence before dark. I'd finished cleaning up the *chong* an hour before and had moved on to torching the ground cover that would hide any others. I was supposed to be uprooting saplings with Dusty, but Nelson was elsewhere, tormenting other members of the crew, so I took my chances. My headache had gotten worse, and all I wanted was my bedroll and sleep.

"That should do it," said Kominsky. "How's it looking up there?"

"Nothing getting through." Jan climbed gently down, running a finger along each section he'd caulked, feeling for weak spots. He stepped to the ground and stood beside his friend. The patriots, they were like that. They'd been together so long; you couldn't imagine one without the other.

The younger cons hung together, sure, but that was more of an unspoken agreement. You watch my back and I'll watch yours. Not like what Jan and Kominsky had. You messed with one, you'd get it from the other. But it wasn't an earned and owed protection, not like what Maduro enforced with his gang, not a beat down and fearful gang. I enjoyed being around those two. I hoped me and Dusty would be like that one day. It was the closest thing I'd felt to home since I'd been here. Well, since long before I'd arrived, honestly. Life with Ami and Appei on the float had been the only home I'd known.

Kominsky wiped his bald head with a sweat rag, looked over his shoulder at me. Grinned. "You're torching the ground pretty good. Dirt don't burn, Lazlo."

I felt my cheeks reddening. "Taking pride in my work."

"That's the way, kid." He chuckled, scratched his beard, winked at Jan. "It's getting dark. Rest of the crew is knocking off for the day."

I glanced at blocks, the only thing standing between us and the *chong*s. Looked to be solid, but it wouldn't be secure until Nelson turned the current back on. Grabbing my tools, I followed them back to camp, Dusty joining us as we walked. To most of the cons, I was the lowest of the low, a constant punching bag for Maduro and his gang, but walking through camp with Kominsky, Jan, and Dusty, it was almost like I belonged. Like I had a family again.

Chapter Twenty

The next day, my head was still pounding.

"How you feeling, Lazlo?" Dusty's bloodshot eyes searched mine.

"Death would be an improvement." I cleared my throat, spit dust and phlegm at the ground. The clot left a dark stain as it disappeared into the parched earth.

Dusty tilted his face back and squinted into the blue sky. "So no different from most days."

I barked a laugh and grabbed my shovel. Dusty grinned through chapped lips and wrapped a sweat rag around his forehead. His name suited him better with each passing day. Though he had light skin, he hadn't sunburned red like Kominsky or tanned browner like me. Filth protected him from the harsh glare of the sun, from the silt coating his skin and hair to the dirt caked into his once yellow uniform. The grit emphasized the startling blue of his eyes. They blinked clear in the light, but I'd learned they could cloud over with no warning and he'd be off, surfing the gray zone. Most of the time, he sang or talked to himself placidly when a flashback hit. But sometimes he ranted and raved, bringing down the wrath of Nelson and a trip to the med tent.

Dusty was like Jan Oh and Kominsky and the other patriots. Basically innocent. Or innocent of anything that really mattered. I knew he was incapable of hurting anyone other than himself. What he was guilty of: bad choices, being in the wrong place at the wrong time. Easy enough to do for a person hooked on a hallucinogen. That's what happened to people like him, people who were susceptible to people like me. Insiders who took a walk on the wild side and couldn't find their way back home.

Dusty would have been the ideal customer for me back in the day, back when I was slinging Axon dust. The only dust I was slinging these days was *chong*-soaked, sun-baked Coulee dust. Digging up sweeper saplings along the Cascadia border. Keeping the *chongs* inside the sweeper forest, away from the law-abiding citizens east of Coulee. Those obedient little families in their sub-earth homes breathing their processed air, following the rules of the Cascadian government. As addicted to the opiate transmissions on their Axon Corp networks as any rat on the Hill. They surfed the mesh between their two ears and remained oblivious to the reality out here on the Line.

But I hadn't been Dusty's slinger. He wasn't on my conscience.

Not like Rajani.

I'd been thinking of her more often as I worked the field. Not much else to do out here but work on my tan. That and dig, torch, dig some more, and think.

A dust slinger and a collector, I had focused on the crypto I was earning, not thinking of the consequences. I had hung with Rajani, worked with her, but I had never used with her. I certainly hadn't killed her. At least, I didn't think so. But what if I hadn't traded her the Axon pills when I first landed in First City? What if I'd never met her? Would she still have died?

"What's the plan?" Dusty leaned on his shovel.

"Got no energy to dig saplings this morning. You?"

"Nope. Trench and burn?"

"Think so."

We stood side by side and scraped outward from the center. Kominsky liked us to stay well north of the Line crew. Those hours spent cleaning up Nelson's *chong* mess the day before had put us behind. Not our fault we'd lost some of our advance. I didn't much care about random guidelines, anyway. If we worked ahead or behind or beside the crew, did it really matter? And besides, if field work was so awfully important, why not assign more cons to it?

The glaring light was making my head hurt worse: the pain was so bad I thought I might vomit. I poured lukewarm electrolyte water from my bottle to my sweat rag and wrapped the moist fabric around my scalp. The sun and my head heated the rag nearly as soon as I slapped it on, and I regretted wasting the liquid. I knew Sid could give me something for the pain if I asked, but he played fast and loose with the tranks. Who knew what else he was using to dose the cons? I couldn't chance it. I'd gotten through bad days before, and I'd beat this one too.

Tomorrow, when this headache was history, I'd exercise again. First thing, I'd get even with Maduro, throw him a thought pulse like he'd never had. Think up something really great, then sit back and watch. Because during those weeks in the field, when I'd grown tired of feeling guilty about Rajani, I'd found other ways to pass the time. When my head was killing me, like today, there was nothing else to do but wallow in regret. But when my brain was calm, while I burned scrub and dug out saplings, I'd been practicing.

Once the lab rat, I was becoming the researcher. I was

getting better at seeding thoughts and projecting them, but I couldn't control the outcome. I had moved on from images to sounds, smells, even flavors. And some results were, well, interesting. Tears sometimes—that wasn't the reaction I wanted, ever. Not fun to watch, some grown man sobbing. Last week, Nelson had sent Faisal back to camp to "dry up" after I'd sent him a memory of Ami's lightly spiced fish and kelp stew. Made me feel bad: I liked the man and thought he'd enjoy it.

Recently, I'd begun pulsing two cons at once. It took a lot out of me and often triggered a headache, not as bad as the one I had today or any PAP alarm really, but it would put me out of commission for a day. Hopefully, the continued practice would strengthen my brain. Dusty was certain it would.

The multi-pulsing went like this: I'd pick out two prisoners, send them the same picture, and compare their reactions. For example, I sent an interesting question to Sook and Munch: would a desert rock taste salty or acrid? Munch reached out a finger, touched the rock, rolled it around in the palm of his hand, and put it back on the ground. Sook, and I hadn't expected it, actually put a rock into his mouth and sucked on it. Same thought. Entirely different responses, and not the way I thought it would go. Some people were more sensitive to the suggestions than others. Unfortunately, because that *hundan* deserved several ugly images, I had no luck with Nelson. But Maduro?

The best reaction I'd ever gotten remained that thought pulse I'd thrown at Maduro. He was a stupid, vicious man. Didn't think for himself. He followed Nelson blindly, obeying his every order, looking for scraps from the master's table like a dumb, ragged mutt. It had been a weak pulse; I knew that now. I'd gotten much stronger since that my furious attempt at revenge. But that pulse—how it had landed?

Maduro screamed, screamed like he was being murdered by an actual *chong*, and then took off—until his hero Nelson papped him. I hadn't been able to see it from the field, but my imagination had painted the picture for me and it was probably better than the actual event. Honestly, he'd had it coming.

I never pulsed Jan or Kominsky. It felt disrespectful, like lying to your father, if you'd had a good one, like I'd had. And the old Lazlo of the shallows would never have dishonored Appei. I guess there was a piece of the old Lazlo in me still. Dusty asked for it sometimes, said it was to check how my abilities were coming along. But I often sent him unrequested thoughts, soothing ones just because, like I'd done for Rajani. Tried to keep him from dusting out. Sometimes I was successful.

The air prickled, lifting the tiny hairs on the back of my neck. When I sparked the weed torch, my neck hairs would stand up, but I hadn't sparked it. But I wasn't even holding it, which could only mean Dusty had turned it on—and hadn't bothered to warn me. My trenches weren't remotely ready for a controlled burn.

"Dusty, what the—"

I spun around in time to see him running across the field toward the Line; he held the sparking torch over his head, streaks of electricity shooting from the tool like lightning. Ground fire raced toward the trench I'd only begun digging, speeding ever faster as it devoured dry brush. I tripped over the lip of the trench and stumbled backwards, grabbing up my shovel at the last possible moment. The flames lapped against the trench and bounced backward, spreading outward in three directions.

Yelling for Dusty, I swung into action, digging and tossing dirt and rocks on the fire, my headache forgotten. I jumped on the smoldering brush, smoke drifting up under my boots. My heart pounded in my ears and my vision narrowed, focusing in on one section I needed to extinguish, then the next. Acrid fumes pricked my eyes, tears and sweat mixing and running down my cheeks. I caught a flash of yellow as nearby crew members joined me.

Voices filled the air, curses and shouts mixing with the smoke, and when it cleared, Kominsky and Jan, Cooper and Faisal, even Sook and Maduro pounded down the dying embers, faces and clothes coated with grimy, black soot.

Faisal touched my shoulder. "How did that happen?"

"Lucky it didn't burn anyone on the Line, *Hundan*." Maduro whacked the back of my head.

Kominsky grimaced, flexing his hand. "Where the hell's Dusty?"

I scrubbed at my itching eyes and blinked through stinging tears. And there was my friend, scaling the blocks in the distance, weed torch forgotten beneath him.

My head was pounding, my thoughts jumbled. I raised my hand silently and pointed.

"Where he think he's going?" asked Cooper. We all knew the answer was nowhere. He was going nowhere.

Up and over the fence, and he'd land directly in the sweeper forest among the *chongs* and a world of nighttime dark. Besides, Nelson could track all of us. He knew where we were at all times, whether on the Line or in the field or back at camp or taking a crap. The mesh imprisoned us in our own heads. So what was Dusty doing?

"The ground is alive! Don't you see it? They're swarming! They're after us!"

I closed my eyes, seed a pulse, tried to transmit: "No *chongs*, Dusty. The ground is clear." The pain was intense, but I pushed through. Ami's flowers, bottomless glasses of cool water, moon and stars on a cloudless night. I aimed soothing images at Dusty's mesh, but if I was landing them, they weren't making any difference.

"They're crawling up my legs! Hundreds of them! Thousands!"

Dusty was in a full break. A PAP alarm rang through my brain and I bit my tongue, dropped the pulse. Nelson hadn't needed to set off a general alarm; he could have focused it directly on Dusty's mesh.

We stood in the field, bone-tired and burned, clutching our heads against the sadistic alarm. My friend clung tightly high up the wall, his mouth open as though he were yelling, but I couldn't hear his cries over the shrill piercing in my head.

Superhuman against the pulsing pain he must certainly have felt, Dusty continued climbing upward, mouth open, trying to escape the nightmare in his own mind. He clearly wasn't thinking. There was no way he would suddenly snap out of it and climb down on his own. I knew that. Everyone knew that. Nelson must have known that.

I stumbled forward toward the Line, walking, then running, not sure what I'd do when I got there. Did I think I was going to catch Dusty in outstretched arms or give him something soft to land on? Because he was going to fall, that was the only way he was coming down. And the farther up he climbed, the harder he was going to hit.

And then it happened. He lost his grip, grabbed at the aluminum blocks, skidded down their slick surface, stretching and tearing open a huge rift in the wall. His body whacked the hardpan soil, and he lay still. I ran to him, slapped his face, and his eyes shot open.

"They're on me! Get them off! Get them off!"

Maduro shoved me out of the way and hauled Dusty to

his feet. He'd drag my friend to Sid, where he'd be pumped full of something and tranked. These were the long-term effects of dusting, and you could never predict when they'd hit.

"Jan Oh, patch that fence," said Nelson. His eyes narrowed as he looked at me. He cleared his throat and spit.

Chapter Twenty-One

❧

The excitement over, the crew had cleared out back to the Line where they set to repairing the blocks Dusty had damaged. Jan Oh had stayed behind to help me with the field work.

"Kominsky, you know."

He waved his left arm. Meaning Kominsky would be here digging beside us if he had the use of two arms.

I grunted in reply, relieved to have something to do with my body. Watching Dusty hit the ground, the sound of it—how had he not broken every bone in his body? And Maduro had dragged him away in his usual rough way with no thought of what injuries Dusty might have suffered. I was seething with anger—at Nelson, at Maduro, and at my friend for losing it, again. Frankly, I was tired, exhausted of being angry and on guard. I was always watching my back and hating my life. Being angry took so much energy, but on the Line, anger was all I had. My ability to seed thoughts in another's neural mesh was my sword. Anger was my shield.

Kominsky dug quickly, efficiently. I watched his technique, how he moved his slight body with intent, adding its weight to the shovel, breaking the hard pan with the edge of the metal like it was nothing. I mimicked his movements but eventually gave up, resorting to the brute force I was used to.

He hummed while he worked. The monotonous tune relaxed me somehow, and I forgot for a while that I was nursing a headache. After a time, he broke the comfortable quiet between us.

"That one is *zhong shi*."

"Sorry?"

"The crazy one."

"Dusty?"

"*Zhong shi de peng you.*"

"I don't understand."

"It means faithful friend. That is rare in society. Even less common here, on the Line."

I scoffed, hiding behind my anger. "He's an addicted *hundan*."

Jan rarely spoke, at least not to me. He started humming again, and I figured we were done.

"Kominsky is also *zhong shi de peng you*. I take care of him. You take care of Dusty. You are each other's strength."

He said nothing more, which gave me plenty of time to think about his words. He wasn't wrong about Dusty: that *hezui* was a lot of things, but loyal was at the top of the list. The more I thought about it, the more guilty I felt. I shared most things with Dusty. He was my self-appointed coach, cheering me on as my mental strength grew. But I had kept one thing secret from him. One very important thing.

Since landing in corrections, I'd been trying to crack reception, mainly, how to block it. Nelson wasn't stingy with his PAP alarms. In fact, he was worse than the most button-happy prison guard. The alarms overloaded my dendrites and seemed to affect me more painfully than the others. I needed to figure out how to interfere with the reception, if not to block the alarms completely, at least to mute them. It was a matter of self-preservation.

Several times, Dusty had asked why I was holding my breath. I hadn't realized I was tensing up, trying to muscle my way through the problem. But thinking about it as an intellectual exercise had gotten me nowhere.

The pulses didn't require physical strength. Their power relied on the mental focus and on the accuracy of the images. Visualizations and suggestions. If there was a solution to the problem, I'd find it there.

I'd landed on this theory: I could block alarms in the same way I had learned to send images, smells, sounds—through suggestions. But rather than sending the visualizations to others, I would keep them to myself. Focus my mind on them, block my mesh with the images.

The trouble was, I hadn't yet figured out what visualization would work. It needed to be something that would surround and protect. Like the Line. A huge fence of blocks. I thought I'd build a wall around my mind made of something soundproof, but any image I visualized would have to come from memory. My knowledge of the world consisted of kelp farming in the shallows, dust slinging in First City, and now Line work. The Line was metal and blocks and electricity, none of which could keep out sound. Ami's and Appei's float was wood and plastic. Every sound had seeped through the walls. In First City, harder stuff, stones and rocks, sand and shards, were bound in a thick, hardened slurry of concrete. That concrete, used for city streets, was the best material I could think of for a wall. It was the closest thing to sound-proof I had seen.

So I had tested my theory. Right before the alarm announcing quitting time, I'd built a vast wall of thick, rough composite strengthened with rebar. Enclosing my mind with the structure, I expected to protect my sensitive mind from noise invasion. It had seemed so obvious.

But I had forgotten something vital in my quest for a soundproof material: Transmissions have no sound. They're not audible, but only felt when the mesh pulsed, sending electrical impulses into the synapses and dendrites, stretching and overlapping and growing like the roots of the sweeper saplings. Alarms hit the mind as though a thousand sirens were piercing the eardrums, but alarms didn't affect the ears.

When I wrapped myself in the hard surface, the sound-proof wall, my mind sensed the thought alarm, dragged it inside the wall, and set it loose. My brain, encased in visualized concrete, dispersed the alarm and it reverberated from one end of the image wall to the other, ricocheting around my mind like a cacophonous bullet, hitting my dendrites again and again, unceasing, unrelenting.

The pain had been unendurable. I awoke stretched on a cot in the med tent, Sid hovering over me. He had suspected heatstroke or malnutrition or dehydration. Anything physical could have laid me out in the desert along the Line. It never occurred to him I'd done it to myself within my head.

And Dusty had been there, holding him back from dosing me, knowing I would be against any drugs. The thought of my drug-happy friend fighting for my right to not have them administered to me made me feel even worse about keeping secrets.

By the time we finished for the day, I felt so guilty about Dusty that I didn't stop for dinner at the canteen. I kept right on walking until I reached the medical tent. Maduro stood there like a self-appointed guard. I wanted to punch his stupid face.

"Little *hundan* got an owie?" He sneered. Like he'd said

something funny. I pushed past him. He whacked me with his shoulder, so I stumbled through the doorway.

"Idiot," I muttered under my breath.

"What's that? What you say?" His voice through the canvas. "Come say that to my face." His arm, his thick torso, and a fist against the side of my head. I was lying on the ground, cheek shoved into the hardpan, spitting sand. "Didn't your mama teach you no respect?" He tried to crack my head against the ground and I silently thanked Kominsky for making me cut my hair.

His stomach growled loudly, and he lost interest and left the tent. Probably to shove his stupid face full of food. I got to my feet and spat to clear my mouth. The physical pain on the outside of my skull from bouncing off the dirt was a welcome distraction from the throbbing on the inside. As soon as I could transmit again, Maduro would get what was coming to him.

"Why did you piss him off?" Dusty's voice was weak. Sid had tranked him more than he normally did.

"Can't help myself." I walked to his cot. The metal springs creaked as I perched on the edge. "Don't worry. I'll get even tomorrow."

Dusty gave me his lazy, gap-toothed grin. It was endearing and a little goofy, making him seem younger than he was. I pushed down an unwelcome prick at the back of my eye.

"What are you thinking?" he asked.

"*Chong*? Think I should do it again?"

Dusty nodded. "An oldie, but a goodie."

"They springing you tonight?" I asked.

"Nope." Sid's voice boomed out before the tent flap fluttered open. He carried two steaming bowls, one in each of his meaty hands. Sid was a large, solid man with thick black hair and a beard to match. His furry unibrow shaded his eyes like a dead caterpillar. If not for the pale blue medical garb he wore, he could easily be mistaken for a convict. "That was a nasty fall he took. I'm keeping him here tonight." He handed Dusty one of the two bowls and slurped from the other. Looked at me silently. Kept looking.

"What?"

"Just thinking."

"Do you have to look at me while thinking?" I'd never trusted the nurse, the only non-prisoner among us. What kind of honest civilian signed up for Line work? Nobody who didn't have an ulterior motive, that's what I thought. He was probably a spy or a creep or a wannabe slinger, that's what I figured.

Dusty wiped the soup from his mouth, blinked at me sleepily. "Huh? What's that?"

"What did you give him?" I asked Sid.

Sid shook his head. "Don't worry about it. He'll be okay by tomorrow." He took another mouthful of soup and kept looking at me. "Dusty told me you got a headache."

"And?" His pale green eyes blinked from beneath the dead caterpillar. "Could you stop staring at me?"

"Want something for that?"

"Did I ask?"

He shrugged. "Up to you, you want to suffer."

"Yeah. I guess it is."

"Sid! Got one for you." Faisal and Sook carried an unconscious Cooper into the tent and lay him on an empty cot.

The nurse bent over Cooper, pushed and prodded at him, checked something on a tracker, then sighed. "Silent."

Faisal stumbled backward. "What do you mean? He was just eating dinner, flopped down."

"No pulse, no respiration." Sid waved at the tracker. "And no brain activity."

"Just like that?" said Sook. "He didn't cough or grab his chest or—"

"No warning." Faisal ran his hand over his face.

"What? First time you ever seen someone go silent?" I shoved myself off the cot. "Dusty, I'll catch you in the morning." I stalked from the tent.

Anger was with me again, my constant companion. Anger was my *zhong shi de peng you*, not Dusty. I'd been ten when I'd seen Appei go silent, watched as his funeral pyre burned, and comforted my wailing mother. After Appei's death, Ami and I had carried on, the two of us against the world. One time, I'd overheard the neighbors talking. What could Ami have expected, marrying someone so much older than her? That's when anger first introduced itself to me as a loyal friend.

I cut around the back of the camp, avoiding everyone. I was in a foul mood and I was bound to say or do something I'd pay for quickly and painfully. Reaching the tent Dusty and I shared, I grabbed my bedroll and sneaked off toward the Line.

My heavy leather boots kicked at the ground, knocking away loose stones. I dropped my bedroll to the ground. I found a boulder the right size to lay my head on and tossed my work gloves on top for cushioning. The field was entirely in deep shadow. The smaller trees just inside the fence, the offspring of the vast sweeper forest, were no longer visible.

The Line crackled and sizzled, electrified to life. Safe again, protecting this section of field and, farther, the sleepy towns east of Coulee; a wired sentry against *chongs*, but only those sections we'd repaired. Directly north of camp, where we'd work tomorrow, were countless unsecured openings. Farther north, toward the border with Canada, no one had repaired the Line for two decades or more, if the old timers were to be believed.

My stomach complained, reminding me I'd forgotten to eat. I had intended to visit the canteen after seeing Dusty, but somehow hunger pains seemed less uncomfortable than being around people. I knew from experience that I could sleep through it.

But I didn't want to sleep. I didn't want to have the dream again, and seeing Cooper's silenced body would bring it back, I knew. I'd had the dream almost nightly, right after Rajani died. And then I didn't have it anymore.

I rolled up the leg of my coveralls and brushed the dirt from my calf. There was the flower Rajani had given me, a tattoo traded for dust. A simple flower, the daisy, but how detailed she'd drawn it. Petals bent back, welcoming the heat of an invisible sun. Center puffy and suggesting softness. Leaves pointed, veins running through to the stem. Roots dangling hairy from the bottom, trapping bits of soil. Beauty in the natural reality of it. She'd asked me what I wanted and drawn the flower from my imagination. A stamp upon my memory of Ami's tall daisies in a pot fueled the thought pulse I sent her.

Her brow furrowed in concentration, holding the pen clenched in a fist like a little girl. She flicked her tongue back and forth across her lip piercings as she drew. She'd gotten it right the second time she sketched, and then she made it permanent. Thinking back, I could feel the stinging jabs on my skin. The pain of leaving Ami behind mixed with the pain of the tattoo. The tiny spatters of blood, Rajani dabbing at them as she worked, the rag pink as my canvas traded blood for ink. And then she sat back, her multicolored braids falling about her face, blowing loose strands of hair from her eyes, judging her work.

"What do you think, Harish? Does it look like a days-ee?"

Focusing on the tattoo now, I could half-close my eyes and imagine the daisy stretching its head toward the sun, sinking its feet deeper into the soil, planted by Ami in the rusted bucket on the deck of our float. Ami's favorite flower, the daisy. She said it was a happy flower, always smiling, growing anywhere. I thought it smelled of dirty feet, but how I missed that smell now that I no longer had it. I traced the tattoo on my leg. As long as I had this leg, this tattoo, the daisy was with me. And with the daisy, both Ami and Rajani sat beside me.

Resting my head on the boulder, I curled into the bedroll. My eyes were dry, tired of seeing. Rajani smiled at me, all rosy-damp lips around tiny white pearls. Her heavy-lidded black eyes were sleepy, lazy. Her hair was loose from the braids, all the colors billowing around her slender shoulders. She wore a red sari—why? I'd never seen her in anything like that before. She reached a thin arm toward me, motioning me to follow. We were in First City. She was running, and I chased her. Fog surrounded us, moist and cool on my skin. Flashes of red through the gray mist, floating now at my feet. I stepped on an empty sari, but where was Rajani?

My chest clenched, and I couldn't breathe. I was holding the sari; I draped it over my arm, and then it flickered, on and off, a light switch. First visible, and then vanished. Gone, like Rajani.

I opened my eyes to darkness. The Line crackled.

Chapter Twenty-Two

The warm red glow on my eyelids woke me before the neural blast of reveille. Gingerly, I reached into my mind and prodded around, searching for remnants of pain. My brain felt cool and alert. Today was the day I'd have some fun with Maduro, assuming there were no PAP alarms that set off another debilitating headache. But that was a big assumption.

My neck was stiff from my night spent on the boulder pillow. Jamming my fingers into the muscles and sinews, I loosened the kinks. I bunched up the bedroll and rotated my body into a seated position, my legs crossed and my ankles resting across my thighs. My eyes drifted shut, and I stretched out my arms and turned my palms upward, my hands resting on my knees.

On the float all those years ago, my morning practice had been much different. Standing beside Appei at the basin, I'd washed my hands and face, our ablution before prayer. Appei and Ami had taught me the ways of our people, a religious tradition my ancestors had brought with them centuries ago when they'd abandoned the desert for the rain. And here I was again in dirt and sand, far removed from the waters of my home, far from the faith I'd ceased to practice when they stole me from Ami. Would I pray again when I returned to Ami, kneeling in front of her on the carpet? Would I remember the order of prayer and the verses of the holy book?

Allowing my mind to float and relax, I turned those thoughts over in my mind and let them pass through me. My meditations continued, and I visualized the inside of my brain, all its twists and turns, my dendritic spines that burned so hot. Focusing on my inhalations and exhalations, I soothed myself and searched for pulsing, errant transmissions. Quiet, empty. No signals. The camp slept.

The perfect moment to work on my defense.

I needed to break the code—to learn how to block the alarms. Only then could I prevent the headaches. In my relaxed, meditative state, ideas ambled through my mind, none of them sticking. Memories of Miz Hazel's care home floated in, when I'd stumbled across the secrets of transmission—when my first crude stabbing at Big Danson's mesh with a kelp fork had evolved into Ami's pin thrown at a cushion.

A thought drifted in: I'd been going full warrior on the problem, meeting it head on, going toe to toe. Like trying to battle Maduro with my fists, meeting him on his turf. No way I could win—he was stronger, always would be. I had to be a guerilla, outsmart him, come at him from an angle he didn't see, that he didn't even know existed. Perhaps the answer to outsmarting the alarm was something softer, something indirect. Sneaking up on the issue, catching it by surprise. Maybe I didn't need to block the transmissions entirely. What if I simply muted them? Filed away their edges to lessen the stabbing pain?

I needed to visualize something soft, something that

would absorb the transmission and cushion my reverberating brain. My mind pulled up memories of soft things, a revolving door of images and smells from my past. They paraded through, grazing me lightly, and moving on as the next demanded to be let out.

What was soft? Water could be soft. But liquid distorted sound, and I wondered what ill effect that would have on the alarm transmissions. My work gloves weren't exactly soft, cushioned more like, and they hadn't been an adequate pillow. The crick in my neck from the rock proved that. Ami had been soft. She used to wrap warm arms around me when I woke from a nightmare. Her gentle lips were on my forehead, soothing me back to sleep. Her long, flowing black hair, covered by a silky headscarf when she ventured into public, had been soft. Work-roughened though they were, her hands had touched my wounds softly when they'd bandaged a skinned knee. Her voice, musical and lilting. Her laugh, light and kind. But none of these memories would absorb the harsh alarm pulse.

Crawling deeper into my memories, I lay on the floor of my childhood home, rocking gently as the shallow tide moved beneath our float. How many times had I lain there, my skinny brown arms outspread, the bare skin of my back itching from the wool carpet covering the wood slats? That carpet, jeweled reds and bright blues and golden speckles, had been in Ami's family for several generations, a treasure from the desert country, fringe fraying at the corners, worn and bald in spots from the touch of my ancestors. The carpet that we had shared during daily prayers. I wondered if Ami still thought of me and Appei when she kneeled upon that carpet.

I stroked Ami's carpet, feeling the bare spots, the rough wool. My fingers teased the fringe. Grown now, I stood and pulled the carpet from the floor. In my mind, I saw myself. I saw the carpet. Nothing else. I bundled myself into the carpet, wrapped it around my shoulders, pulled it over my head. It was heavy, weighing me down. My nose tickled from the dust woven into the warp, the slight tinge of moisture, the musty hint of mildew.

Warm and cozy in the carpet's darkness, I heard a faint buzzing, a thrumming. A motor boat passing, perhaps a kelp farmer on his way to town. A mail boat arriving with bills and an occasional letter. I huddled beneath Ami's carpet and waited for the boat to pass. When I peered through its folds, the boat was gone.

I opened my eyes and realized the sun was high overhead. I heard loud voices coming from camp. My fellow convicts were awake—had neural reveille sounded? It must have. How late was it? I hadn't been aware of the waking alarm, or had I?

Stretching and gathering my belongings, I thought of what had happened. I'd visualized Ami's carpet. Though I hadn't intended to select it, I had become lost in the memory. But I'd interacted with the memory. The visualization had included a grown Lazlo wrapped in the carpet. I hadn't done that as a child—the carpet was large and would have been too heavy for me, the scrawny kid that I had been.

And then I wondered about the buzzing, what I'd thought was a boat—had that been the neural alarm?

I followed my feet into camp, thinking through the possibilities, when I heard Nelson bellowing at me. "Lazlo! Where the hell you been?"

And then there was Dusty, throwing his body at me, knocking me to the ground in his enthusiasm. "We thought you'd gone silent—"

"Overslept—" I shoved Dusty off me and stood. It slowly dawned on me what I'd done. Not only had I successfully blocked an alarm, but I'd discovered another skill.

"Don't let it happen again." Nelson whacked the tracker with his palm. "Signal's back. Must be something wrong with the tracker." He glanced at the device again to make sure my green dot was still there, then walked off saying, "Breaking camp today. You got latrine duty."

Dusty grabbed my bedroll off the ground. "Dude, don't scare me like that again. Shoot. First Cooper, then you." His eyes were wet, and it embarrassed me.

I punched his shoulder but had to look away. "Be a long time before I go silent. Unless I don't get some food soon."

"Yeah." Dusty cleared his throat. "Me too. Starving."

Squaring my shoulders, I walked with my friend to the canteen. Maduro glared at me and I glared right back, daring him to mess with me.

Go ahead. Try it. Today I learned how to disappear.

Chapter Twenty-Three

❧

I regretted skipping dinner the night before. My stomach grumbled angrily. Protein drinks were the only food on offer this morning; two cons were breaking down the canteen.

"Figures it's gonna be a scorcher on a move day," said one of the old timers loading supplies into a crate.

"What you griping about?" said Maduro, sneering at the man's empty sleeve. "It's not like you cripples carry anything heavy."

The patriot towered over Maduro, his fist clenched. "I carry plenty. Ain't no lightweight."

Maduro's eyes narrowed. If he'd had something sharp in hand, I knew he'd have cut the man. He was that type. Out of curiosity and because I could, I thought-pulsed him a tent stake. He struck out at the big con, his rounded fist clasping air, and nudged his opponent's torso impotently. The patriot only had the one arm, but it was quick. He gripped Maduro's wrist and twisted it sharply. Maduro cried out, whimpering like a kicked puppy. I forced myself to cough and smother a snicker.

"*Hundan!*" Maduro cradled his limp hand to his chest. "I think you broke it!"

"Sprained, more like." Jan Oh's bored voice came from behind me. "Won't hurt so long as you carry nothing heavy." He slurped his protein drink and nodded at me and Dusty.

Maduro nearly collided with Kominsky as he stomped off, likely toward the medical tent and Sid's pills.

"What's with him?" Not caring about the answer, he grabbed a shake and stood beside me. "So what's this I heard? You dropped off track?"

I shrugged. "I guess Nelson needs to charge his gear."

Kominsky guzzled his breakfast and belched loudly. He filled his water bottle and turned to go. "Could be a problem for him if his gear stops working. This crew would love to get loose."

Two helpings of breakfast in me and a full water bottle in hand, I turned to leave. Dusty tugged at my sleeve, his eyes intent and sparkling. "No one else dropped off. Just you. You made that happen—with your mind, didn't you?"

"Shhh, keep your voice down." I grabbed his elbow and shoved him outside, away from the other cons. There was probably no need for it because Dusty and I were lower than nothing, not interesting to anyone. We may as well have been stones on the dirt floor. None of them would believe that the teen *shashu* could use his mind to outsmart tech. Still, I whispered, just in case. "Yeah, I guess I did."

He whooped, pumped his fist in the air, and stirred up a cloud of dust with an impromptu dance.

"Stop it! People are looking."

He grinned, dazed and happy. "I'm *hezui*, remember? I'm totally out of it."

We blinked at each other stupidly, awkwardly. I didn't know what else to say, and I suspected Dusty was still half tranked, half in reality. I elbowed him in the side. "Let's get the tent down. I have latrine duty too, remember?"

At our tent, I shoved my prison-issue briefs and socks into my backpack. Yellow, yellow, everything yellow. I wrapped a rag around my neck and grabbed my field hat. Didn't need a worse sunburn on my neck and head than I already had. Dusty and I dragged our backpacks outside, then pulled the poles and watched our tent flutter down. Dusty pulled the stakes from the edges while I rolled up the tarp and stuffed it into my pack.

"See you later. I'm off to shovel *goushi*."

"Laz," said Dusty. "You know I'm going to help."

Good old Dusty.

At the tool tent, I took a shovel off a pile in the corner. Sook grabbed it out of my hands. "Where you think you're going with that? We're packing up."

The con who was working with him, a street thief I think, said, "You two got the poop scoop?"

"Yeah."

He nodded, and Sook gave me back the shovel. "We been here a month. You poor *hundans*." He chuckled.

"Yeah. It's a total laugh riot."

Shovels on our shoulders, Dusty and I hiked to the toileting area, what Nelson called the latrine. Though it was upwind of camp, we smelled it way before we saw the privacy screen. I quickly realized this job was not for the queasy. The hardpan made it next to impossible to dig a deep enough hole for a real latrine. The cons who'd set up this latrine before we'd arrived on the Line had only bothered to scrape a shallow rut in the earth. Our crew had dug at the rut to widen it, relieving themselves in multiple scratched furrows. The resulting "latrine" was a stinking morass that spread out in all directions. For the first time, I was happy our crew was far smaller than it should have been. A month, tallied by excrement, was a long time.

When prison staff had still guarded Line convicts, there'd been rules about this sort of thing. Convicts covered their crap immediately. No open sewage. But the neural mesh and PAP trackers were so efficient that private prisons soon realized they didn't need so much staff, or any. Now convicts guarded each other. The smart, sadistic cons, like Nelson, could run a crew on the cheap. Convicts guarding themselves saved the prisons an unnecessary staffing expense, but some rules, well, cons weren't exactly a group that followed rules.

The problem was if you didn't cover your poop-crap-*goushi* —things found it. *Chong*s. Big *chong*s. Graypills, sure, they loved crap. Devoured it. But crap attracted more substantial *chong*s; that's what Kominsky said. No shortage of *chong* varieties. So although Nelson wasn't enforcing the immediate cover rule, he made us throw some dirt over the top of the sewer before we packed up.

Dusty and I pulled our rags over our noses and mouths, which did little to block the stench. I reached the edge of the sewer and forced back a gag. I visualized the salty, fresh sea air around the shallows, sent a thought pulse to Dusty, watched him inhale.

"Thanks, dude."

"Don't mention it." Too bad the visualization had no effect on me. I bent my shoulder to the shovel, dug into the hardpan, and tossed the dirt onto a pile that sank into the brown wetness. "This will take a lot of digging."

"Not afraid of a little digging. Saplings or *goushi*, makes no difference."

Dusty's chill vibe made the work, if not better, at least more tolerable. When he was calm, like he was today, there was no one I'd rather be around.

Smells brought memories to life like nothing else. This

mound of reeking sewage brought Miz Hazel's care home into the present. I was a kid again, crammed into a bedroom with four others. The bedroom across the hall housed another five. Ten of us kids for one bathroom. The flush toilet was always overflowing, the salt water running into the sewer and backing up the pipes. Several times a week, a kid hadn't waited for the salt water to retreat. One flush and the mess would spill over the toilet bowl, run along the floor, and escape under the doorsill. Miz Hazel always made me and Big Danson clean it up, the two oldest. Yes, I was good at shoveling *goushi*, even from a young age.

Together, Dusty and I got the mess covered in less than an hour. We were finishing up. A few shovels more, and we'd be done.

"Don't look now," said Dusty.

Maduro marched across the field, his wrist wrapped in a wide bandage. "Oh great, my toilet awaits." He dropped his pants and squatted, making no attempt at privacy. He proudly squeezed out a pile and pulled up his coveralls. Sneering, he said, "Clean it up."

Dusty caught my eye and winked.

A tiny pinprick, the laziest of images—poop on Maduro's hand, wet diarrhea oozing down his forehead, dripping down his nose, hovering over his lips. He screamed and stepped backward. Waving a hand and scrubbing his face, he yelled, "Get it off! Get it off!" And then he tripped. He sat down, hard, on his own deposit.

Dusty exploded into laughter, great gulps of joy erupting from him. Maduro sat frozen, his face burning. He scrambled to his feet, yelled, "Shut up! Shut up, or I'll, I'll—" Forgetting his bandaged wrist for the moment, he swung at Dusty, grimaced, and cursed. Dusty was gasping for air, tears rolling down his face, unable to control his amusement.

I leaned on my shovel and watched Maduro, straight faced and silent.

Maduro glared at me. "Watch your back, *shashu*." He marched back toward camp, swatting at the brown mark on the back of his coveralls.

Chapter Twenty-Four

❧

Shoving each other playfully, we slowly made our way back to camp.

"Poo? *Goushi*? That's what you sent him?" Dusty was giggling, stuck in a loop, and it infected me.

"Dripping... down... his... face..." I gasped for breath in between words.

"Dude! That is twisted!"

"Twisted like genius."

"Evil genius, yeah. Remind me not to get on your crap side, Lazlo." He wiped tears from his eyes. "*Goushi*! That was a crappy thing to do."

"Aw, don't give me that crap. You know he deserved it."

"Yeah, he's always pulling all kinds of crap on you."

"I know. He and Nelson always give me the crappy jobs."

Kominsky's voice cut through our hilarity. "Pyre before we go. You didn't forget, did you? Coop went silent last night."

It's not that I had forgotten about the patriot taking his last breath, but my life was, well, complicated. I hadn't known the man, not really, not more than his name. It was sad that he went silent, sure, like it was sad when anyone went silent, but it didn't weigh on me much. I mean, I hadn't caused it. But the look on Kominsky's face—he was choked up, I could tell—he and Cooper had been on the Line together for a long, long time. Of course, they'd been friends. Kominsky was grieving.

Suddenly, it occurred to me that Kominsky and Jan and Cooper were all about the same age. A few years separated them, like me and Dusty, but all in their 40s, at least. It must be on their minds constantly that they were nearing the end, close to taking their last few breaths of heavy outside air. Hard labor and exertion shortened their life spans for sure. So when one of their vintage fell silent, they felt more than sadness for the poor man. They felt afraid for themselves.

Wrapped in a scratchy gray blanket, Cooper's body looked like a huge hunk of broken roadway. Gone with his signal were his bravado and swagger. Nelson passed Sid the rigged weed sparker, the zapper. Without so much as a goodbye, no prayer or ceremony, Sid fired up the zapper. Sizzling and popping, the electrical current slammed into the unmoving package. The wrapped corpse shuddered and jumped with the impact and glowed blue before bursting into a devastating orange flame. The heavy air around it ignited with an oxygen sucking boom, and within minutes reduced Cooper to ash.

I'd witnessed a pyre once before when we'd said goodbye to Appei with words of prayer and benediction to Allah. Ami's arms had locked around me and I'd felt the wet of her tears in my hair, the shivering of her body as she wept for her beloved. Our community of kelp farmers had stood with us, each on their own float, as the pyre erupted across the water. The sea breeze had carried Appei's ashes into the sky, to heaven, Ami had said. Appei had gone home.

That pyre had been sad yet strangely uplifting. This one

was matter-of-fact. The former prisoner Cooper, a patriot or traitor depending on who you asked, the gentle giant who'd been brave or crazy to cut a tracker from his own flesh and lose an arm, had ceased to exist.

Such was the way with throwaways. I refused to be one of them.

While Dusty and I had dealt with the latrine, the crew had packed most of the food and supplies into boxes and loaded them into the heliotractor. We divided among us what didn't fit on the tractor, jamming tools and foodstuffs into our packs, then set off for our new camp. Our long, yellow blemish walked behind the slow-moving tractor, moving north along the Line. The group thinned out rapidly, the bigger prisoners hefting their load easier than the rest, speeding forward.

Dusty and I kicked along in the back, still chuckling amongst ourselves about my revenge on Maduro.

"Lazlo, Dusty, get a move on!"

A faint tingling in my head indicated a signal was about to go. Grabbing Ami's carpet, I wrapped my mind. We were together in musty emptiness, me and the carpet, and I was content and happy. Dull thrumming, distant buzzing, and then silence. I opened my mind, peered through the carpet fringe. The alarm had ended and I hadn't felt a thing. Kominsky rubbed his ears. Jan Oh was tipping his head side to side, pulling his ear lobes as though water were stuck inside. A few of the cons groaned. I looked at Dusty, holding his head and rocking like he usually did after an alarm, but his eyes were wide and staring at me.

"You did it again, didn't you? Dropped off?"

I nodded. "What was the transmission?"

He closed his eyes, grimaced, and guzzled water from his bottle. Taking a deep breath, he said, "Orders from Coulee.

Electrical short detected twelve miles north. We're hiking straight through."

"We're not fixing the next section of Line first? Walking through an unsecured area? Must be a big short."

"Don't know. That's all the message said."

"Terrific."

A twelve-mile hike wasn't all that bad. At our current pace, we'd cover a mile every half hour, and we'd already been hiking an hour, so only five more before we'd arrive. We had gotten a late start; it had taken a while to break camp— we'd have time to pitch tents, set up the canteen, scratch out a latrine site.

But I knew from Kominsky and Jan that it had been at least a decade since a crew had tested the section of fence we'd be passing and ignoring. We'd have to double back to the area we were now hiking past. We had nothing better to do, but none of us wanted to backtrack. Moving forward was the same as looking forward to a Line con. Going backwards seemed like having more time added to your sentence. We never wanted to add more time on the Line. Moving forward was all we had, that, or becoming like Nelson, the leader of a crew. And Coulee would never consider former dust slingers and rats like me and Dusty for that role.

We lagged even farther behind, our heads bowed in submission to the beating sun. Dusty found a big rock and toed it forward, alternating between his feet, left, then right. He kicked it in my direction, and I nudged it with my boot, getting the feel, the weight. I blasted it too hard, and it tumbled out of reach. My pack bouncing against my back, I jogged forward and kicked it back to Dusty. Then he too was jogging, running to the side, juggling the rock between his feet, passing it to me.

Kominsky glanced back. "Con football," he said, and then he was part of the game. He was pretty good with his feet, which shouldn't have surprised me; Kominsky was agile. When I ran at him and tried to steal, he turned his body to his good arm, elbowed me, and sped off.

The three of us were at the end of the line, running forward, stopping, going sideways. We were keeping up with the group in our way. Just ahead of us, Jan Oh hiked alongside Nelson. Neither man spoke. Nelson held the tracker, counted signals, yelled over his shoulder without looking, "What are you three doing? Keep up."

"We're right behind you, Boss," called Kominsky. You had to hand it to him: He knew how to stroke Nelson's ego. It wouldn't be the worst thing to get along with people like Kominsky did. He'd worked the Line a long time. I had five years of bullying from the likes of Maduro to look forward to —I didn't want that. But I wasn't desperate enough yet to kiss up to Nelson. Nowhere near ready to grovel in front of Maduro. Not when I could make him believe he was covered in poo.

I grew tired of the game and called over to Dusty. "Foot check."

"Good idea," said Kominsky, and the three of us sat on the ground, removed our boots and socks, and checked for blisters. I poked at a tender spot before pulling on a dry pair of socks.

"How long we been hiking?" I asked.

"Dunno. Two hours maybe. Certainly no more," said Kominsky. He removed his hat and tipped his water bottle over his shiny head. "*Goushi!* That feels fantastic!" he said as the water cascaded down his face.

Dusty threw me a look, but I was the first to sputter.

"*Gou... shi,*" chortled Dusty, rolling in the dust.

Kominsky regarded us with serious eyes, but his lips quirked. "I'll never understand you two." He got to his feet, flicking drops of water from his hand as he walked.

I dribbled some water on my handkerchief and wrapped it around my neck to cool down. Kicking a rock around probably hadn't been the best idea, not in this heat, but it had broken up the hike. Dusty reached out a hand. I grabbed it and he hoisted me up. I pulled my hat brim over my eyes, shading them from the sun. We marched along in silence.

I'm not sure when the terrain changed. I suspect it was gradual, a pale green fuzz on the hardpan, a clump of grass here, a clump of grass there. Soon, there were more clumps than hardpan, and then there was low scrub and bushes. The scrub was growing along the fence, and then some taller green stuff, and before you knew it, short trees. Some had leaves, mostly green but turning yellow and red. And other trees, trees with needles, miniature sweepers. At least a decade without maintenance, and it showed. The sweeper forest was breaking through the Line here, spreading rapidly.

What else was breaking through the Line, hiding in the brush? I shivered.

Chapter Twenty-Five

❦

It was now maybe three hours into our hike. I figured we were halfway there. The ground sloped steadily downward. Grass whipped about my legs, leaving wet green stains on my coveralls. I didn't like this. I threw a worried glance in Dusty's direction, but he didn't seem to notice, or if he did, he didn't care. Up ahead, Kominsky was walking in a group with Nelson and Jan Oh. I could see over their heads, beyond them. Maduro marched with Sook. Close by was Sid, turned toward Munch, talking. They were heading down, way below me and Dusty, on the steep slope. That's why I could see them all.

The forest was casting a shadow over us, a deeper darkness than usual this early in the afternoon. The farther we traveled into the valley, the darker it became. Light flickering from the west caught the corner of my eye, and I peered into the sky. Flashes beyond the Line lit the sweepers from behind. During the canteen lectures, the old timers had told us the forest was so tall, stretching so far into the sky, that it could create its own weather.

I didn't realize I'd stopped until I heard Dusty's voice. "What are you looking at, Lazlo?"

"Up there, those flashes," I said. "The color of the clouds."

"Dude, that looks gnarly."

Another flash, and then a rumble from the forest. "Thunder."

"You mean, we're going to get rained on?"

"Yeah." I took in our surroundings. Bright green grass. Thickly growing bushes. The trees. So many small trees. "This area gets rain."

"Dude! That's awesome! Rain!" He had little long-term memory left and couldn't tell me where he'd been born, but his excitement was a clue that he was from coastal Cascadia. I still suspected he'd been an insider, but maybe an insider from an outlier community. No long-term First City dweller I ever knew welcomed rain. Water liquefied the street chemicals, mixing them with refuse, and the place stank until it finally dried out again. Second City was even worse—overflowing toilets like at Miz Hazel's care home were common. Thinking he might be from the rain coast, if not the shallows, made me like him more.

I clapped him on the shoulder. "Yeah. Rain! It's raining in the sweeper forest."

"Think it's headed this way?" he asked.

Crashing thunder and an explosion of light answered his question. A torrent of water gushed from the sky as though it had cracked open directly over our heads and soaked us instantly. The cold, piercing needles of water shocked my senses, and then my skin adjusted and the glorious rain washed the dust from my face and arms. I observed the crew in the valley below. The rain delighted the hardened criminals and cynical patriots alike. Heads tipped to the sky, mouths open, yellow-clad convicts dancing and laughing—even Maduro was celebrating.

Apparently, you didn't have to grow up in the shallows to enjoy a good, hard rain. You only needed to work without end in a desert.

Another crack of thunder, and I felt the ground beneath my feet move. "Dusty," I said. "Something's not right—" The water poured down, unceasing, growing in strength, violently washing the soil away.

His frightened eyes met mine. "Grab a tree!" I yelled, and the two of us lurched, jumped, grabbed the branches of a small, solid sweeper. I wrapped my arms and legs around the trunk and Dusty scrambled as high as he could manage into the boughs. The ground where we'd been standing loosened and crashed downhill. A tsunami of mud, rocks, and small shrubs were heading toward the entire crew beneath us on the slope.

The heavy slurry swept down the valley, knocking Jan Oh's legs out from under him. Nelson went down, then Kominsky. Jan Oh lay on his back, pack heavy beneath him, his arms and legs waving in the air like a tipped *chong*. Nelson threw a muscular arm over the sludge, one after another, swimming in mud. He grabbed Jan Oh and hauled him away from the moving stream. Like us, the two men gripped trees, the only non-moving objects on the sliding earth.

Horrified, I watched Kominsky struggling with his one arm, impotent in the sludge. Kicking his long legs, he tried to shove himself up the slope, against the rush of mud. He lost traction and tumbled head over heels down the slope, the strap of his backpack catching the limb of a tree. He looped his arm around the trunk and held tight.

I blinked water from my eyes and looked for Dusty. He was still there, hanging in the tree beside me, hair glued to his face, his expression stricken as he watched the mudslide decimate our crew. Beyond Nelson, Jan Oh, and Kominsky, the moving earth had reached the center of the valley. Mud and debris had collected below and water was pooling in the valley. It was raining too hard for the earth to absorb it all. Maduro, Sid, and the rest were being pummeled by water, mud, and rocks. They were flailing desperately in the rising sludge. A wave of mud swept aside the heliotractor, and it sunk out of view.

Dusty called over the wind and rain, "Do something, Lazlo! Do something!"

I hated Maduro, but I couldn't stop thinking of his injured wrist. And Faisal, that sly hustler who reminded me of home, I kind of liked him, actually. Munch never missed a meal—he was an arsonist, I think. Another man, spiky sun-bleached hair and a scar on one side of his face. He kept to himself mostly; I didn't know what he was in for. And then Sid. I couldn't let Sid drown. Dusty needed Sid.

All the cons had higher prisoner status than me, the teen *shashu*. But I was higher on the slope than any of them, clinging even higher in a tree, and that was the only height that counted right now.

Dusty was right. I couldn't let them die.

I'd never pulsed to this many people at once. I didn't believe it would work, if I had the strength, if I could shoot so many pulses so far. How could I hit all the cons at once? But I had no choice. Kominsky, Nelson, Jan—none of them could help. It was all on me.

What thought would get them out of this trouble? Munch was flailing insanely, yet I could see a tree less than an arm's length from him. He could simply reach out and grab it to pull himself out of the mire. But he didn't see it. Why didn't he see it? He wasn't seeing or thinking. Munch was panicking, and surer than the mud or water, panic would kill him.

None of them were thinking clearly. Not even Sid. I mean,

in that situation, we'd all panic, wouldn't we? The crew needed a calm moment so they could think.

I closed my eyes and imagined each of their faces, stuck them like posters to the wall of my mind. Sid: bushy eyebrows, beard, and greenish eyes. Maduro: ugly pock-marked face and constant sneer. Munch: watchful eyes and round belly. Faisal: short dark hair, close-set brown eyes, stooping walk. The light con: I wasn't so clear on his face, but I focused on the face scar. And the next one: yellow bandana do-ragged around his balding head, huge honking nose. I went through the list of cons, their faces and something memorable about them. Lined them up on the wall of my mind.

And affixed to another wall in my mind, facing my wall of prisoners, I aimed Ami's old red pincushion. I chucked those pins in all directions, piercing the posters, the perp shots of the cons. And the thoughts I sent—I didn't know their past lives, so I pulsed what calmed me: lying on the deck of the float, the sun warming my bare chest, rocking gently on the tide, a light drizzle coating my shoulders, paddling lazily in the shallows. I kept the faces of the men on my mind wall, kept pulsing my memories, a light breeze and a gentle lapping of water against the side of the float and the swimming. I reminded them to swim.

Pulsing thoughts as I was, I didn't feel the rain or hear the thunder or see the mudslide. I was in my mind, my neural mesh a sandbox. Playing with my toys, my thoughts, my memories, I hoped it would be enough. Without warning, my energy was gone. I had no more left to give. My head was heavy, my thoughts blurred, my pins blunted, bouncing off the mesh of the others: Sid and Maduro, Faisal and Munch. Coming back to myself, I felt the cold clamminess of my soaked clothing and the rough bark of the tree I still gripped.

"You did it." Dusty clapped me on the back. "They're going to be okay, Lazlo."

And I wanted him to shut up, stop talking. His voice was too loud. Everything was too bright, too loud, too cold. Too much. But across the valley, a group of men rested, breathed, lived. And as rapidly as the storm had started, it ended. The rain dripped lightly from the sky, a leaky faucet, and then abruptly shut off.

Nelson's voice sliced through the dizzy feeling in my head. "Let's go." He dropped to the muddy ground and tumbled down the slope. Jan Oh sat down, pushed off, slid past him, and stopped by Kominsky's tree.

"You okay, Lazlo?" asked Dusty.

"Never want to do that again."

"Feeling like *goushi*?" he said, but it wasn't a joke this time.

I dropped out of the tree and squelched my way down the slope.

"I doubt they can survive under that desert hardpan," said Jan. "But here? Where the soil nourishes so much plant life? Yes. They're probably part of the reason the plants are growing here."

"I felt better not knowing all that." Dusty shuddered.

"You're sure they aren't dangerous?" I asked.

"I'm still alive, aren't I?" Jan Oh removed the earthworm from his neck and placed it gently on the ground. "Unlike that poor *hundan*."

A pair of hiking boots jutted out of the mud half a meter away from where I stood.

Chapter Twenty-Six

❧

In the valley below, a mud-slimed Nelson was checking the tracker, counting signals, I guessed. Nothing like a well-timed emergency for a convict to attempt a runner.

I descended into the valley sideways, planting one foot firmly on the sucking ground before moving the other. The sudden storm had left me drenched to the skin, but other than the mud covering my boots, I was comparatively clean. Across the valley, grime covered Maduro and the other inmates who'd nearly drowned, the yellow of their uniforms masked by the brown mud.

Behind me, Dusty cursed and struck a blow against my back, then we both went down, hitting the mud wetly. I rolled sideways, my flailing arms useless to stop my rapid downward slide. Dusty whooped and yelled, having the time of his life. Mud invaded all my openings: it was up my nose, in my ears. I even think I swallowed a little. When a mucky pile at the bottom of the slope finally halted us, sludge and grime coated us as heavily as the rest of the crew.

"That was awesome," said Dusty. "Let's climb back up and slide down again!"

Clearly, he had eaten less dirt on the downward run than I had. I coughed and spit out muck-tinged phlegm. "We have to climb the other side. Maybe you'll get lucky and slide down again. But try not to take me out next time, okay?"

He grinned. "Aw, you know you loved it!"

I dug mud from my ear with a grimy finger and scowled.

"We're missing three." Nelson wrinkled his brow in thought and pointed at the destroyed heliotractor. "Maduro! Take a crew, salvage what you can, carry it up. Pitch camp. I'll message Coulee, have them send fresh supplies. The rest of you, fan out. Those three *hundans* didn't just disappear. Let's find them."

Dusty whispered, "Think they figured it out? How to drop off the tracker?"

I'd only just discovered how to mute the alarms. Dropping off the grid for short periods of time had been a happy accident. If I hadn't been focused on saving our crew, it would have been a great time to make a break for it. If I had anywhere to go. So who knew? Maybe the three missing cons had muted their signals and gotten out. But I doubted it. If any of these cons knew how to do what I did, they'd have skipped out a long time ago. Wouldn't they?

I shook my head. "Nope."

After what had just happened—the sudden rainstorm and the mudslide—it was more likely that the three missing men were dead. That's why the tracker couldn't pick up signals. Cellular energy powered the neural mesh, and cells only had energy if they were alive, so if the inmates' meshes had gone silent, the obvious answer was that they had gone silent first.

The valley we stood in was less valley than a long wound gashed into the ground. The rut began beyond the fence on the west side and stretched far east into the desert. Dusty and I struggled through the thick, stinking mud toward the Line. The going was slow and arduous; we had to wrestle each step from the greedy soil and climb over uprooted bushes and bracken. The sun was disappearing behind the forest. We needed to find the bodies quickly and leave the valley; I didn't want to be stuck in this rut at nightfall, a climb up the slippery slope still ahead of me.

Kominsky's voice yelled from the east: "Here! Found someone!"

Dusty swiveled his body around, feet immobile in the muck. He pointed back east, where the rest of the cons searched. "Most of the dudes are over there."

"They don't need us then, do they?" I wrenched a foot from the mud and set it on a coiled cable.

"Pull," said Faisal.

"Got him—poor devil."

The cable gave way, squished into the mire. Except it wasn't a cable. There was nothing remotely metallic about it. Another coil lay to my right, and a loose, long cable lay to my left: maybe six or seven feet long, as wide as my arm. But these weren't cables. Maybe they were some ancient rope from a decade ago, the last time anyone worked on the Line this far north. That made little sense, though. We didn't use ropes on the Line; it didn't hold up well in the elements and the *chong*s chewed right through it. And more importantly, it couldn't conduct electricity.

"He's gone silent," said Kominsky.

And then Nelson said, "It's Shah. Dead. Two more to find. Jing and Manson, come here. The two of you carry Shah up."

"Dusty, look here," I said. I reached down and touched the rope-thing. Unlike rope, it was soft and smooth, cool and wet. Rings looped around it. Tiny holes covered the surface, like pores on skin almost. Driven by curiosity, I bent and picked it up; it was lighter than I'd imagined. I poked a finger into the soft surface and it moved in response to my touch.

It actually squirmed!

This was no discarded item from a long-gone Line crew. It was alive. Disgusted by the slimy creature, I tossed it as far from me as I could. Mud imprisoned my feet, and the force of my throw sent me flailing backwards. I sat down squarely on the watery earth. It sucked at the seat of my coveralls, the wet ooze seeping into my groin and running down my thighs.

"You okay Lazlo?" Dusty labored toward me. "What was that?"

"I don't know. But it was alive!"

"Did it bite you?"

I checked my arms and hands. "I don't think so." Why had I touched it? Why had I picked it up? Stupid.

"Earthworm." Jan Oh appeared silently beside us, his arms crossed. "Looks like we stumbled on a colony." He waved his arms wide, pointing out the entire valley that more than half of our crew stood in.

"*Chongs!*" I pushed myself from the earth and saw my horror reflected on Dusty's face.

"Am I dusting, Lazlo? This feels so real—"

"It's real. A real nightmare."

"Boys, boys. Calm down." A hint of a smile passed over Jan's solemn face and disappeared. "Earthworms are harmless." As if to prove his words, he picked up one of the creatures and wrapped it around his neck like a long, wet, squirming scarf.

"Ew!" said Dusty.

"Did they cause the mudslide?" I asked.

Jan shook his head. "No, they're victims of the storm as much as Shah was. They came to the surface for air when the water filled their tunnels."

"Wait," said Dusty. "They live underground?"

"You mean we've been walking over the top of them this whole time? Dusty and I dig every day. Why haven't we seen them before?"

"I doubt they can survive under that desert hardpan," said Jan. "But here? Where the soil nourishes so much plant life? Yes. They're probably part of the reason the plants are growing here."

"I felt better not knowing all that." Dusty shuddered.

"You're sure they aren't dangerous?" I asked.

"I'm still alive, aren't I?" Jan Oh removed the earthworm from his neck and placed it gently on the ground. "Unlike that poor *hundan*."

A pair of hiking boots jutted out of the mud half a meter away from where I stood.

Chapter Twenty-Seven

❧

After searching for the better part of two hours, we'd discovered only the two bodies. Nelson called off the search. The third inmate was presumed dead, buried beneath piles of mud. The valley was socked in shadow, and Nelson ordered us to get out of the rut and to safety. We all eagerly obeyed.

What this morning had started as an easy hike to the next camp had turned into an arduous slog through a wild, unmaintained area. Three members of our crew were now dead. Mud and debris had buried most of our supplies, and we hadn't yet arrived at the major breach we were supposed to repair.

The light of a smoking campfire beckoned to us from the plateau. Maduro, Sid, and a few others had rapidly pitched camp. The low light flickered on our tired faces, our relief at having made it out of the valley alive quickly disappearing as we took the measure of the campsite.

"Maduro." Nelson barked his name, barely masking the quaver in his voice. "You walk the Line before you set up camp here?"

"Ummm..."

"Great. You just arrive on the Line this morning? New to things?" He coughed, spit. "Idiot."

I couldn't see Maduro's expression in the dim light, but from experience I knew his face had darkened. He'd be looking to beat down someone later to feel better about himself. Would not be me, not if I could help it.

Scrub and brush covered the site, protected by a section of Line neither inspected nor maintained for over ten years. Without having performed that most basic of tasks, walking the Line to check for minor breaches and the field to check for roaming *chong*s or nests, we were at the mercy of fate. There could be *chong*s hiding behind plants, *chong*s burrowing beneath the Line, *chong*s surrounding us on all sides just beyond the firelight.

Nelson scanned our faces. He was about to volunteer someone to perform a suicide mission, walking the Line in the dark, and I had a sneaking suspicion the volunteer would be me. I ducked behind a big con hulking in front of me, yanked Dusty down beside me, and that's when the rumble of a heliovan interrupted Nelson's thought process and saved me.

We followed the headlights out, four of our crew carrying the two bodies to the heliovan for transport. No Line pyre for these corpses, not in the wild among flammable brush. Back in Coulee, they'd incinerate the bodies.

A new prisoner stumbled out of the van as we arrived. Nelson papped him to his knees, then ran through his speech, "You will come to hate me" and all that. I could tell his heart wasn't in it, though. The new prisoner took one look at our crew hovering there, monstrously mud-caked and exhausted, wondering what he'd signed up for, and I almost felt bad for him. Almost. At least he was getting paid.

We loaded up with the supplies we needed and carried

them to the campsite, a line of grimy *chong*-looking cons, marching back and forth. And finally, the pay off—the powers at Coulee had sent us several barrels of water and clean coveralls—we took turns hosing down our stinking, itching bodies. We formed an assembly line of cleansing: efficient, but far from comfortable. And, like the rest of my experience in prison, utterly dehumanizing.

When it was my turn, I peeled off my coveralls and dropped them on the pile of discarded uniforms, chunks falling from the stiffened fabric. Naked except for my thick-soled boots, I stood shivering. Dried mud caked my skull, and I silently thanked Kominsky again for forcing my haircut that first night. The tepid spray struck me, hard and stinging. My skin grew numb under the onslaught and I watched the mud slide away, the brown water turning clear. I rotated my body slowly in the steady stream, rubbed the water into my itching scalp and over my grimy face. The water pooled around my ankles and dripped into my boots.

"Next!" called Sid, who was controlling the hose, and I stepped aside, brushed the water from my body and grabbed a clean yellow coverall and underwear.

Dusty waited for me as I pulled on my new clothes and we squelched back to camp, water seeping from our wet boots with each step. Our clothes and bodies were clean, but our packs were trashed. Fastened correctly, they would repel rain, but how had they held up to mud? I scraped the dried soil from my pack before opening it. My gear was dry, mud-free.

Dusty upended his pack, and a rivulet of brown water dribbled out. "*Goushi!*" he complained. "Everything. It soaked through everything."

It didn't surprise me. Dusty never closed his pack when we worked the field. And this wasn't the first time he'd trashed his gear. I knew he'd hang his wet, gray socks and underwear up to dry overnight, then shove them back into his pack in the morning. I could remind him to close his pack tomorrow, but he wouldn't. Brain reset, no memory, or sheer insider laziness, I didn't know.

At least I'd been the one to carry our tarp. We assembled our tent quickly, shoving posts into the ground, tossing the clean and dry tarp over the top, and punching the stakes into the sides. Someone had thrown together a makeshift canteen, and we were each given a couple of protein bars to make it through the night. Never remembering such hunger, I inhaled mine. I was bone-tired, my legs stiff and sore from plodding through mud for hours. My arms and shoulders were aching, and the morning's latrine work felt like a week ago. I stretched my arms over my head and yawned loudly. All I wanted was to collapse on to my bedroll, also clean and dry, and close my eyes. And then I realized Nelson had seen me. I turned to leave quickly, but it was already too late.

"We need sentries tonight," said Nelson. "Lazlo, Kominsky. You're on."

It figured. Why not Maduro, I thought. He'd been the numbskull who hadn't bothered to walk the Line. And he'd been sitting on his backside the entire time we were all slogging through the mud, searching for bodies. But I didn't dare say it, not to Nelson.

"All night?" Kominsky looked drained, the dark circles under his eyes hollowing out his pale face in the firelight.

"You got something better to do?"

"Sleep."

"I don't mind staying up," said Dusty. "I'll take Kominsky's spot."

Nelson's response was instant. "Not a chance in hell."

"But I'm nocturnal. I can stay up all night—"

"Crew doesn't need you dusting out halfway through. Got enough drama."

"But—"

"Dustman. No." Faisal clamped his hand on Dusty's shoulder. A flicker of something—shame or maybe resentment—appeared on Dusty's face.

He shrugged Faisal's hand off his shoulder, scowled, and slunk off toward our tent.

Kominsky shoved a flashlight into my hand. "Let's go, kid. Don't know how we pissed off Nelson, but you and me are in for a fun night."

Swinging our flashlights from side to side, we headed westward toward the Line.

"*Chong*s could be anywhere," I said. "All these bushes." I shivered, thinking of those earthworms crawling along beneath our feet, digging their tunnels under our tents while we slept. Unseen by any of us, they were munching out caverns in the soil. What would prevent us falling through the earth into those holes, suffocating in the dirt as they crawled around us? Perfectly harmless, Jan Oh had called them. But if earthworms lived below, unknown to us, what nameless *chong*s were running around up here?

"We're going to the Line, kid. Anything comes out of those bushes, you and me, we're as good as silent. Unless Nelson gave you his *chong* zapper?"

I shook my head, no.

"Didn't think so. No zapper, no sentry. Not me. No way I'm sacrificing what I got left of this brief life for Nelson and Maduro, or any the rest of them."

"But Jan? You watch out for him."

"He can take care of himself. Or haven't you noticed?"

He might have confidence in Jan's ability to survive a surprise *chong* attack, but I was worried about Dusty. What if something had a taste for convicts and came looking for a midnight snack? Our tent was just there, right beside the bushes. Well, all the tents were beside bushes. Bushes and big saplings covered the entire field. Plenty of hiding and nesting places. If I didn't watch the area and warn the crew, something bad could happen to Dusty.

"Lazlo! Dude! Wait up!" And there he was. Grinning, hair sticking straight up in the beam of my flashlight, waving our two tent poles. "You didn't think I'd let you fight off *chong*s without me?" He lunged dramatically forward, slicing the night air with the poles, and then handed me one. "So you don't have to fight them barehanded."

I could have hugged him.

"Glad to have the extra eyes, Dusty," said Kominsky. "No dancing in the gray zone tonight, agreed?"

"Try my best."

Now that Dusty was beside me and not unprotected in camp, it was easy to agree with Kominsky. The safest place for us was, oddly enough, the Line. It was closer to the sweeper forest and the big *chong*s, sure. But the electrified blocks would offer some protection, more protection certainly than the wide-open spaces beside the valley and the unexplored areas around the camp.

The three of us walked single file. I was out in front, shining my flashlight forward, whacking a path through the brush with the pole. Kominsky went behind me, panning his light from side to side, watching for movement. Dusty brought up the rear, dramatically crouching and wielding his tent pole like a javelin, poised to throw it at any moment and in any direction. He was having fun.

We made it to the Line and spread out, tamping down low growth and tugging out low shrubs and higher grasses, clearing a space to rest.

"I'm gonna walk the Line once, just for us. Make sure there's nothing hiding close by," I said.

"I'll come with you," said Dusty.

"Leave me a pole, would you?" I gave Kominsky mine,

then Dusty and I set out, walking south back toward the valley. Dusty held the pole behind his neck, his arms resting across the top. I shone the light on the bottom of the fence and panned it slowly upward, checking for obvious breaks. We turned back when we reached the edge of the slope.

Kominsky sat calmly in the small clearing we'd made.

"Anything happen?" I asked.

"No movement beyond the Line. I saw nothing." He pointed with the flashlight.

"Now what?" asked Dusty.

"We can walk north, check the Line that way."

"Knock yourselves out," said Kominsky. "Think Nelson's going to give us a break on the hike tomorrow? He won't care that we haven't slept all night, that we've walked back and forth around the camp for hours protecting him from— as far as I can tell—nothing? You kids can do what you want, but I'm getting some shuteye." He made a big show of curling up on the cleared ground and closing his eyes. I noticed he clutched my tent pole tightly in his hand.

"Right here?" said Dusty.

"Where else?"

Dusty shrugged, dropped beside Kominsky.

"I'm not lying down on this ground," I said. I sat down, facing south. Dusty sat up, pushed his back against mine, faced north.

"Yeah, that's a better idea," said Kominsky, sitting up. He rested his long frame against us, facing away from the crackling Line. I left my flashlight on, facing forward, and stared into the darkness.

At some point, I guess I must have drifted off. When I first heard the scream, I called out for Rajani. Was she in danger? The second scream brought me fully awake, and the third jolted me off the ground.

Chapter Twenty-Eight

My flashlight was rolling on the ground, its beam bouncing along the ground until it stopped dead against a shrub ten feet in the distance. I dove forward and snatched it up as Kominsky said, "You hear that?"

A final shriek, wet and guttural, pierced the darkness. Dusty said, "What was that? Was it human?"

"If it was, the poor *hundan* is done for," said Kominsky. He cursed, and I turned my beam toward him. He was whacking his flashlight against his thigh. "Damn flashlight's dead."

"We need to check it out." Dusty thrusted and parried with his tent pole.

"Hard to do with no flashlight," said Kominsky.

"Lazlo's works. That's all we need."

Kominsky scoffed. "You must be dusting right now, kid, if you think I'm heading toward that sound, no zapper and now no light."

"What if it was you calling for help, and no one came? Or me or Laz? What about Jan?" Dusty's eyes gleamed in my wavering beam. "Lazlo, you know we need to investigate."

"It might have been *chongs*, one eating another, something

like that." I hedged, but in my heart, I knew. That had been a man's voice, a man's scream. It was one of our crew; I was sure of it.

"I'll go on my own to check it out, if that's what it takes."

Kominsky shook his head. "No, Dusty. Nelson ain't right about much, but he was right not to make you a sentry. Sorry, kid, but the threat of you dusting out when we need you is too real." He sighed. "Much as I hate to say it, me and Laz gotta check this one out."

"But—"

"Hey Dusty," I said, "I got a bad feeling. We're going to find something we don't want to see. And me and Kominsky, we need that zapper. Can you get back to camp without a light? Take the pole, be careful, get Nelson."

"He'll think I'm dusting."

"Convince him. Because whoever that was—he'll go silent if we don't help. And we'll go silent if you can't convince Nelson we need help."

"You can count on me, Laz." He pushed his tent pole into my free hand. "But you need this more than me." He whooped and took off, running blindly through the scrub toward camp.

"Either he's the bravest *hundan* on this sorry con Line, or he's half dusted right now," said Kominsky. "Well, what you waiting for? You've got the light, not me."

Flashlight clenched in one hand, tent pole in the other, I led the way north. Cold sweat dampened my armpits and my heart echoed loudly in my ears. Though Kominsky had only one arm, knowing he was but a footstep behind me strengthened my courage. He was tough, strong, and fierce. And despite his unwillingness to defend the Nelsons and Maduros of the crew, I'd always thought he held warmer feelings toward me, maybe even miss me if I was gone.

"You think someone got up to take a leak?" I asked.

"Zapped himself on the Line?" More than one crew member had learned the hard way not to piss on the electrified blocks.

"I hope that's all it is," said Kominsky.

We were silent, eyes and ears alert, watching for movement and listening for the faintest of murmurs in the dark night. The tent pole was slippery in my right hand. I stopped a moment and rested it on the ground, then dried my sweaty palms on my pant leg. I took up the pole again, ready to strike whatever attempted to cross my path.

I panned the light across the ground as we walked. The beam stretched out, strong and narrow at my feet, spreading wide and faint at its furthest reaches. Clumps of grass and small brush became instantly visible close by. In the distance, vegetation cast ominous shadows outward. The flashlight and my methodically stepping feet moved in an unplanned rhythm: step right, swing left, step left and swing right. And with one left swing, the beam of light caught and held. I stopped walking, wondering what I was seeing. Circles of iridescent blue reflected at me from the fence. Two larger circles in the middle, four small ones beneath, two medium circles on top.

Behind me, Kominsky gasped. "Don't move. Whatever you do. Don't make a sound."

"What are those?"

"Eyes. Eight of them. *Zhu.* A damned big one."

My skin prickled, and it became difficult to breathe. Everything in me screamed, run away, as fast as you can. It took all I had to remain still.

"It's a night hunter," whispered Kominsky. "Lies in wait, hidden in its burrow. Feels vibration and strikes. Faster than you can imagine. If it realizes we're here, we won't stand a chance."

I shuddered, sweat beading on my face, on my scalp, running down my neck. The eyes were right there, eight of them, staring forward, glowing. I wanted to switch off the flashlight, not see the awful eyes anymore, but I couldn't. With the flashlight on, I knew where they were, where the *zhu* was. I hated knowing it, but it would be worse not knowing, imagining. The sheer terror of it, the *zhu* staring at me yet not seeing me.

The hint of an itch teased my nose. A sneeze was building, growing bigger and more inevitable by the moment. Nothing I could do to stop it. The sneeze was coming, and then what? Would the *zhu* strike immediately? The grotesque eyes in the distance and then, springing forward suddenly, on top of me? Or would the attack be more stealthy, the hideous reflecting circles moving closer, closer, slowly closer, until the fangs pierced my skin? And the sneeze was growing bigger, tickling deep inside my nose, up in my sinuses. The more I tried to hold it back, prevent it from happening, the louder it would be when it finally exploded out of me.

Closing my eyes, I climbed under Ami's carpet. But it did no good. The sneeze followed me there, tickling on the inside, between my eyebrows. I threw off the carpet and was back again, the freakish eyes unblinking, Kominsky breathing heavily behind me. I could smell his fear sweat and that made my terror so much worse.

I threw out some thought pulses then. No images, no odors, no sounds. Feelings only.

To Sid: dread, terror.

To Faisal: fear, hatred.

To Maduro: kill it.

I was pulsing so hard I missed the twinge that preceded the alarm. The full neural siren went by then, agony lacing through my mind. They know! They're coming! The sneeze slipped away, defused by the piercing lance of an alarm. My hands flew up in a protective gesture and the flashlight went tumbling from my sweat-dampened fist. It hit the ground and rolled.

Kominsky gasped, and I held still. A rush of air against my fear-heightened nerves, an enormous shadow hovering over the flashlight beam, a furry leg, the light racing backward toward the fence, and then stillness. The beam glimmered faintly and expired.

Kominsky's fear was palpable, and it blanketed me like fog. The two of us stood immobile, sweating together, waiting, hoping, our lives passing before our eyes.

We heard the prisoners coming, voices hushed and excited. Light streams cutting through the air. The crew had to be stealthy or the *zhu* would be on them before they knew it. Hot pain lanced through my mind. I'd never been able to send a thought pulse after an alarm. A sharpened branding iron impaled my head from one ear to the other, but I had to try. I squeezed my eyes shut and plunged my mind into the water of the shallows, outside the float of my childhood. And as I cooled the red-hot throbbing in my mind, I sent one pulse, everything I had, to the one person who'd been immune to my suggestions.

To Nelson: *Zhu.* Eight eyes. Death on the Line.

Searing light. The sizzle of a zapper shooting its killing beam. The wet thunk of newly dead animal flesh.

Flashlights sending beams in celebratory circles. Whoops of fear-laced tribulation. My eyes followed the lights to a burrow beneath the fence, a mere six feet from where I stood. Half-clothed men struggled to pull the heavy remains of the *zhu* from the tunnel. Though collapsed in on itself, the eight legs held in tight to the round hairy body, the dead creature was nearly six feet wide.

"There's someone in here!"

"Who is it?"

"Get his arm. Get him out of there!"

I saw Sid bend over the body that belonged to the scream. "He's still breathing! Quick, help me get him back to camp!"

Two men hauled the body past me. I heard the excited voices, the waning adrenaline. Light beams shifted and turned, receding back to camp.

And still I stood, silent and unmoving. A hand closed on my arm and I leaped, barked out a cry, and swung around with my tent pole.

"Whoa! Dude! Watch it. You almost hit me!" Dusty pried the pole from my frozen fingers and guided me back to camp.

Chapter Twenty-Nine

The next hours were a blur; Dusty and I switched places for a while. He became my voice of reason and sanity, and I behaved like the *hezui* with a neural short who needed to be tranked regularly. Those eight glowing eyes were seared on my brain. I saw them everywhere, like the phantom traces that remain after staring into a bright light. I couldn't stop shaking.

Dusty sat with me in our shelter as I'd so often sat beside him in the med tent. His voice was calm and reasonable. "The dude's gonna live. Sid will make sure. We're safe. Nothing coming for us here."

And I knew he was right; I needed to get hold of myself. Both Dusty and Kominsky had heard the death screams. Kominsky had seen the same monster I had. Why was I the only one traumatized? Or was I the only one who couldn't control his emotions?

"Let's get some food," said Dusty. "Not much of a canteen, but we can find something."

I hugged my knees to my chest and rocked back and forth. "Not going out there."

"Fine. I'll go alone and grab us protein bars."

"No!" I grabbed his arm.

He shook himself free. "Dude, when'd you get so clingy? Look, if you're not ready to go out there, sure. I get it. But I'm starving. If you don't want to stay here alone, I don't know what to tell you. I'm going."

Drawing a deep, cleansing breath, I relaxed into my mind and pulled up a memory. A log of bull kelp rocked back and forth on a gentle tide. When I opened my eyes, Dusty had left. Forcing myself, I ventured out into the pale early morning light.

Sook fed the smoldering campfire twigs while Munch looked on. Jan was distributing protein bars to a line of hungry cons. Dusty smiled as I approached and wrestled me into a playful headlock. "Good to see you, Laz."

I slugged him gently in the gut and he released me. Unwrapping the bar Jan handed me, I bit off a mouthful. Chewy and sweet, the food triggered a flow of saliva, and I realized I was actually hungry. With every swallow, I could feel calm returning to my body and mind, the fear not exactly disappearing, but shrinking enough to be manageable.

Around the campfire, several prisoners discussed the night's excitement.

"How big was the thing, Lazlo?" said Munch. "We got a bet going."

"What are you asking that little *shashu* for? I was there. You don't believe me?" said Sook.

Munch snorted. "If you were there, I'm eating nothing but cold oatmeal from now on—morning, noon, and night."

"Anyone hear how the guy's doing?" Kominsky blew on a steaming cup, nodded an unspoken good morning to me.

"Is that coffee?" said Munch. "Where'd you get your hands on that?"

Sook said, "Hand! Just one," and laughed.

"*Hundan*," I thought, not realizing the word had slipped out of my mouth.

"What'd you call me?"

Sook was a big man, stronger than me, but he wasn't deadly. Not a *zhu*, that was for sure. He wasn't the bully Maduro was, but I had no use for him most days. He certainly wasn't worth even half of Kominsky. I raised my chin and faced him, man to man. "You heard me. I can say it louder, though, for everyone else to hear. *HUNDAN!*"

He lunged at me, but his size slowed him down. I ducked out of his reach and he punched empty air. I bounced around the other side of the campfire, energized by protein bar and *zhu* fear and adrenaline, singing, "*Hundan, hundan,* Sook is a *hundan!*" Yeah, it was childish and stupid, but it really pissed him off, and it was funny. Faisal was grinning, Munch was laughing, and of course Dusty couldn't hold it together.

The madder Sook got and the more appreciative my audience became, the more stupid I acted. I don't know how long my antics would have lasted if Kominsky hadn't tripped me. I hit the dirt hard, scratching my palm open as I landed.

"Enough." Kominsky sipped his coffee calmly.

My hand stung as the abrasion pinked up with blood. He ignored me as I glared at him from the ground. I stood stiffly and brushed the dirt off my knees, trading brown marks for red blotches when my injured palm grazed my coveralls.

"Anyone know how the injured man is?" Kominsky repeated his question.

"Not great." Sid stepped up to the campfire. "Anyone seen Nelson?"

"Walked to the Line this morning with Maduro," said Jan Oh as he organized the food supplies. "Took the zapper to clear out any *zhus*."

"Here they come now," Faisal said.

The zapper slung over his shoulder, Nelson neared the

camp, Maduro trotting along beside him like a lucky dog. Halting by the fire, Nelson laid the zapper on the ground and pulled the PAP tracker from his coverall pocket. Once he was content that all live bodies were visible on the digiscreen, he spoke.

"Maduro and I walked the Line this morning, zapped anything that moved. A few small *chongs*, nothing poisonous. No other *zhus*—that one last night probably hunted the area clean." He accepted a steaming cup from Jan Oh, nodded his thanks, and took a sip. "Our plans don't change. We got several more clicks before we can repair that short up the Line. No telling what we'll find once we get there."

"Not me," said Sid. "I'm staying put until a heliovan comes for Noonan."

So that was the new prisoner's name: Noonan. Sid didn't have to go anywhere with Nelson. He wasn't a con, just some sicko nurse who enjoyed camping in the wilderness and dosing prisoners.

"No heliovan coming," said Nelson.

"What? Why not? Noonan's in terrible shape. I can't help him here. He needs proper medical care back in Coulee. What reason did they give?"

"No reason. I didn't message them," said Nelson. "Bad enough I called for help yesterday."

Why wouldn't Nelson message for medical transport? The new prisoner, that could have been me or Dusty, any of us on our first day. Noonan hadn't known what he was getting himself into when he signed on to work the Line. He hadn't lasted a night, not even a few hours.

Sid wrinkled his forehead. "What are you saying, Nelson? You're going to sentence him to death?"

Nelson regarded Sid over the lip of his mug, finished his coffee, then dumped the dregs on the ground. "We both know you won't let him die. You're too good a nurse for that to happen."

"I don't have the equipment—"

"You'll figure it out. And while you argue about it, Noonan's alone and probably dying. Go on, do your job."

If looks could kill, Sid's blazing eyes would have severed Nelson's head from his shoulders with laser heat. "He can't make the hike. We don't even have a heliotractor to move him. Not that I'd recommend that, not in his condition." He stalked back to the hastily erected medical tent. "And I'm staying with him until he's healed. If you continue on, you'll be without a nurse."

I didn't understand Nelson. Surely Coulee would send a heliovan to bring Noonan back to prison for medical attention? Why wouldn't Nelson message for one? I glanced at Dusty, and he seemed as confused as I was. If Nelson wouldn't get help for a prisoner who'd been half eaten by a *zhu*, a man who hadn't annoyed him, would he behave differently if Dusty or I were gravely injured? Considering how little he thought of us, probably not.

Nelson sighed, rubbed his chin, and said, "Sid's staying here with Noonan. And the Line repairs begin today. We're already a day behind."

"What happens if we wait a day or two, however long it takes for him—" Faisal started speaking. He didn't finish. We all knew the end of that sentence: however long it takes for him to die. Because those of us who'd seen the *zhu* couldn't imagine anyone could survive that attack.

"Repairs start today." Menace laced Nelson's soft voice. He raised the PAP tracker high so we could all see it. Let no one forget who's in charge here. The Line wasn't a democracy; the one who controlled the tracker controlled the Line. And that was Nelson.

"We can't abandon Sid and Noonan."

I don't know why I said it. Perhaps it was the giddiness from nearly dying the night before. The words snuck past my lips, a voice that didn't sound like mine. It was high-pitched and reedy, embarrassing really. The thing was, I didn't care about Noonan. I felt bad for the man and didn't want him to die. None of us did: We didn't know him enough to hate him yet. But we all needed Sid. He was our nurse; he kept my friend semi-sane. And unlike Nelson, who wouldn't bother to message Coulee, Sid actually wanted to keep us alive.

"No one is abandoning Sid," said Nelson. "Some will hike north to repair the short, and the others will stay here and work this section."

"You're splitting the crew in half?" Kominsky frowned. "Are you sure that's a good idea? Our crew is too small. That mudslide that took out three experienced men. And Cooper —and now the new guy—"

Nelson's eyes sparked. "I know how big our crew is, old man." He was in control of himself, but his rage simmered dangerously beneath the surface of calm. "Most of the crew stays here, strengthening and repairing the fence as we move north, like we should have done in the first place. Those *hundans* in Coulee! I lost good men because of them. No way are we making the same mistake twice. Not sending good men unprotected through the bush. But this is no prisoner revolt. No one wants time added to his sentence, right, old man?"

"They can do that?" Dusty asked.

Maduro said, "Yeah, the *hundans* at Central erase your time served, then add on another two years for good measure."

My dreams of escape faded away as I imagined my sentence increasing to twelve years.

"So what's the plan?" asked Kominsky.

My mouth went dry when Nelson turned his glittering

black eyes on me. "Lazlo will lead the way north. He's young and quick. It won't take him more than a couple of hours to get there. He can wire up a fix while the rest of us repair the Line here."

Bile rose into my throat, and the camp began spinning around me. Dusty's hand gripped my shoulder. "He's not going alone."

"Suit yourself," said Nelson.

"Like hell those kids are going! They don't know what they're doing." Kominsky's bald head glowed pink. "They're field workers. You know they've never laid blocks or fixed wiring. And they're my crew, not yours. Why not send Maduro and Faisal?"

Nelson chuckled, a sound completely devoid of humor. "Old man, you never had a crew. Coulee sent me a joke. What was I supposed to do with a crazy duster and a *shashu* kid? I would have left them in the desert to fend for themselves, if I could have. But that would have been wrong; you might say criminal, even." He sneered. "So I gave them to the old one-armed con, the con so desperate to have a crew before his mesh shorted. I mean, what you got? A month, maybe two, before you drop like Cooper did? You know you're not getting off the Line alive."

Kominsky's hand squeezed into a white-knuckled fist. Nelson's eyes glanced at the fist and back up, met Kominsky's glare. "Thing is, old man, if your pathetic little crew isn't ready for the job, you got no one to blame but yourself. A month on the Line, and they've never worked the fence. You spoiled them." He turned his back to Kominsky, the ultimate insult. He wasn't afraid of Kominsky's anger, his one clenched fist. Nelson controlled the PAP tracker, and between that and his cruel pragmatism, he controlled every member of the crew.

Nelson called back over his shoulder as he walked away,

"Grab your packs, your food supplies, and tools, and get lost. We'll follow in a week, maybe two."

"We got this, *Shashu*," whispered Dusty.

"Hell yeah, *Hezui*."

"Hey Nelson!" yelled Dusty. "Any chance we can get our hands on that *chong* zapper?"

Maduro snorted. "You always were a funny *hundan*. I might even miss you."

In that moment, Kominsky's knuckle connected with a target: Maduro's face. Maduro went down fast, unconscious, before he hit the ground. Kominsky wiggled his fingers, relaxing his fist. "Damn, that felt good. C'mon boys, let's pack our bags and get out of here."

Chapter Thirty

❧

Laden with a chain saw, shovels, a weed torch, and backpacks weighted down by whatever food supplies we could carry, the three of us set off. Once we arrived at the breach site and got the lay of the land, Kominsky said one of us could hike back to camp for additional supplies. He never mentioned we had nothing we could use to repair the Line once we arrived, blocks or foam or wires or whatever. Even if we'd had construction supplies, our crew's heliotractor lay broken and useless under drying mud at the bottom of the valley. I hoped the *hundans* in Coulee had thought to transport whatever supplies we would need to the job-site.

I realized Nelson had only selected Dusty and me for the job to get to Kominsky. He'd known Kominsky would step forward to protect us. Of course he would. And unlike any other con Nelson could have chosen for the suicidal job, Kominsky wouldn't try to run. Saddling the old timer with two clueless field workers, two workers he had taken responsibility for, two workers he actually liked, was Nelson's way to ensure that Kominsky actually did the work to repair the short.

North we went, Kominsky leading the way, blazing our trail with the weed torch. Dusty jogged along behind him, digging and tossing dirt on the low fire to keep it under control. I brought up the rear with the chainsaw, zipping through whatever saplings I could, always mindful of their girth and the unreliable chain. I'd shoved two soft noise-canceling plugs deep into my ears, and I heard nothing but the faint, monotonous hum of the saw ripping into young bark.

We cleared our path as we hiked, leaving the detail work for the crew. I felt morbidly gratified that someone else would have to clear the field. Shouldn't have killed off your field workers, Nelson.

Our goal was to arrive at the breach and set up shelters before we lost light. Kominsky hoped to rig up a temporary current to secure us for the night. He'd have no choice but to educate us, and fast.

It had been thirty-six hours since Coulee alerted us to the fence short. We didn't know why a section of the Line had blinked out. How long before the monstrous creatures inside the forest discovered there was no electrified barrier confining them?

The *chongs* were huge and ugly and terrifying, but did they understand we were at war with them, that we built the Line that shocked and ignited them if they tried to cross? Would they realize it was no longer electrified, or merely stumble over it unthinkingly?

A straight hike would have taken two hours, but clearing the path as we went slowed us down. Would we stop for lunch? Probably not. Kominsky was still going strong, work-horse that he was. I was thinking of the protein bar at the top of my pack, my mouth watering as I tried to will myself through a few more sapling cuts, ten more, nine more, eight more, before I allowed myself to stop, open my pack, and tear into the chewy, sweet snack. Between fantasizing about food and trying not to amputate my hand, I didn't notice Dusty was twitching and pacing. If I'd paid attention to what was happening right in front of me, his impending neural break would have been obvious.

Kominsky was well ahead of us by then—the oxygen-rich air feeding the trail of fire, speeding it along. Only four saplings to go before I allowed myself to take a bite of protein bar. I don't know why I glanced up, but it was good I did. A giddy streak of flames ripped away to the east while Dusty gazed emptily into the sky, transfixed by whatever was happening in his mind.

I closed my eyes and broke my vow to never intrude on Kominsky's mesh. Fire! Heat! Danger! I pulsed rapidly at Kominsky, who was unaware of the wildfire half a mile behind him. I pulsed a fire thought at Dusty, then thought better of it, saving my strength. Nothing short of a PAP alarm would make it through his grayed-out mind haze. Dropping my heavy pack to the ground and gripping the chainsaw tightly, I stumbled frantically over the uneven terrain toward the leading edge of the fire.

Sweeper trees were always escaping their fenced boundaries, their seeds spread by wind and birds. Remembering that sweepers didn't catch fire like other trees, part of the reason that the field work, the digging up and sawing of the saplings was so important, I used them to create a noncombustible barrier against the fire. I ran past the fire, outflanking it on the eastern side, and revved the chain saw's engine. Walking back toward the lapping flames, I swatted down small saplings. The blade sliced swiftly through the trees; their bark and cores were soft and unresisting.

"No! No!" Kominsky raced toward me, Dusty's shovel gripped in his hand. "Those aren't sweepers!"

I stopped mid-slice; the chainsaw wedged in the middle of

the trunk I'd been cutting. Kominsky was jamming the shovel into the hard dirt, throwing his body against the handle, struggling to hurl load after load on top of the raging fire with one arm.

The chainsaw was stuck fast, and I tugged the handle to release it from the tree. The saw jumped free of its bark prison, but the chain slipped off the saw, useless to me now until I repaired it. And the middle of a raging inferno was no place to fix a dislodged chain.

The fire leaped suddenly forward, and I tripped backwards in my rush to get away. The flames devoured the saplings I had just cut down, sap and needles blazing into orange life with a savage hissing. Kominsky was right: I'd not constructed my fire barrier from fireproof sweeper trees but with one of their non-genetically modified cousins. I'd never bothered to learn the difference, and now it was too late.

I tossed the useless chainsaw to the ground and yanked the shovel from Kominsky's hand before running beyond the fire, farther east. Working quickly, I gouged a trench into the soil, lassoing the fringe of fire and digging my way westward. All conscious thought ceased as I worked, my body becoming one with the shovel. My backs and thighs and arms bent and dug and threw. I was a machine, moving ever forward, reining in the fire. My engine hummed, sweat pouring from my soot-caked skin.

Kominsky raced along behind me and farther to the north. Through drifts of smoke and haze, I glimpsed him moving his way ever closer to me. The fire wasn't spreading north, but I couldn't imagine what a one-armed man without a shovel could do to stop the blaze.

Strength and energy were coursing through me like blood as I raced to contain the inferno. Mindlessly shoveling my way forward, I was a mere wind kiss away from immolation. Scared for my life but unable to stop, something bigger than me forced me onward, stopping the uncontrolled wildfire before it reached a town many miles away, populated by complete strangers. A fire started in the quest to protect that anonymous town and countless others from an onslaught of giant *chongs* and *zhus*. Why was I doing this? Why did I care? Those strangers didn't know me, nor I them. And even if they had, they wouldn't care about me. A nameless 17-year-old con, an accused *shashu*, a throwaway. But I kept working, shoveling, containing the fire.

When I noticed my body again, the adrenaline dried up and leaving me exhausted, Kominsky and I stood side by side. Our chests heaved, drawing oxygen, and we watched the fire peter out in the west against the blocks of the Line. His body stood erect and proud, taller than mine, his grizzled, smoky face turned toward the dwindling flames.

"You didn't have a shovel," I said, leaning on the one I'd stolen from him. He held a canister. Metallic foam. He shook it and squeezed the trigger, sending nothing but air from the nozzle. He tossed it on top of the smoldering ground.

"I packed five cans. That was the last one." The Line workers used the foam to fill the spaces between metal blocks. Five cans wouldn't have been enough, not by a long shot. But now we had none.

"Do we have to hike back? Get more?"

Kominsky kept his eyes on the dying fire. He didn't answer. My thoughts returned to the morning, how Nelson had looked at me, sent me and Dusty on a deadly errand knowing full well neither of us had the skills for it. How he'd insulted Kominsky, how Kominsky had walked out on the crew and joined up with me and Dusty. If I realized Nelson had played him, he did too. No way he'd go back now.

We headed back along the burn, stopping to retrieve the broken chainsaw. Dusty was mumbling to himself when we arrived. He didn't notice he'd burned down the eastern slope.

"Lazlo, dude," he said, pupils wide and glassy, "you see that butterfly too? Purple it was, man. Huge."

I slugged him. Punched him in the face with all I had, knocked him to the ground, and kicked him. Kominsky hauled me off him. Scary how strong he was. He grabbed me around the chest and tossed me to the side like I weighed nothing. Spitting ash, I scowled at Dusty. He lay on the ground, his nose bleeding from where my fist had connected, still going on about some stupid butterfly.

Kominsky stood there silently, probably wondering why he'd signed on for this.

Then his face wrinkled. He scratched his sooty beard and barked out a laugh. Just one. "You damn kids." He shook his head. "That's it. No more clearing. The next time we stop, we camp." He broke down the weed torch and stashed it in his pack, and then he swung a shovel over his shoulder and walked away.

            # Chapter Thirty-One

❦

The trail wound west and inclined upward. I hiked
behind Kominsky now, not caring where Dusty was,
not really. He could wander around hallucinating purple
butterflies or green clouds or flying transports or dancing pill
bottles for all I cared. Wander around spouting nonsense
until a *chong* ate him. That would serve him right, the waste
of space that he was.

But every time I turned around to check, there he was
right behind me, the blood from his nose congealing and
drying on his face like he didn't even know I'd punched him.
And I'd turn around again and imagine sitting on his chest,
hitting him again and again in his stupid face, but what if a
chong chased him? He wouldn't notice, wouldn't warn me
and Kominsky that we were in danger. So I turned around
again, just to be sure he was there, and not some eight-eyed
zhu, and he grinned at me. Stupid space between his stupid
front teeth. And I said, "Shut up *hundan.*" Even though he
had said nothing.

The broken chainsaw was hanging from my hand, and
yeah, I knew I could fix it, wrap that link back around where

it belonged, but it was a complete pain to do that, and the light was fading fast. It was after lunch. Midday had come and gone while Kominsky and I had chased that stupid wildfire that would never have happened if Dusty hadn't been such a dumb *hundan*. And now that I was thinking about it, I'd been just about to start sapling four and I hadn't taken a bite of that protein bar and as far as I knew, Kominsky had eaten nothing either, and Dusty was so out of it he probably didn't even feel hunger anymore and is he still behind me or did he wander off? And there he walked, still right behind me, but he wasn't smiling anymore and his eyes looked normal.

"Did I do it again?"

"Yeah."

"Oh no. What happened? You and Kominsky—you two look scorched, dude. But me—" He held out his coverall covered arm, yellow except for the green and brown smudges where I'd wrestled him to the ground.

"Wildfire."

He gulped and a worry line creased his brow. "It was me, wasn't it?"

I said nothing.

"Dude, I'm... I'm so sorry."

"Shut up," I said. "I want to be mad a while longer."

He jogged up beside me, pulled me into a headlock, and scrubbed his knuckles against my scalp. I swung at him sideways and he released me, ran ahead of me and raced past Kominsky.

I chased after him, the broken chainsaw slowing me down, but I didn't get far. The slope had grown steep quickly, and I had little energy left after battling a wildfire for half the day. Holding my knees and sucking wind, I remembered the protein bar. I was chewing it contentedly when Kominsky caught up.

"You hear it?" he said as he approached.

I cocked my head, listened. A bit of wind rustled the saplings growing around us. The sizzle of the Line. "Hear what?"

"Electricity. The Line is live."

"Yeah? So?"

"So, we should be close to the job-site. Nelson should have turned off the section if he wants me to fix it. I can't repair the short and reconnect the circuit if the Line is still conducting."

The sweeper forest was already throwing shadows. They weren't deep shadows yet; we would have had an hour of daylight to work on the Line.

"Maybe we aren't there yet."

"Kominsky, Lazlo!" We couldn't see Dusty through the brush and trees, but his voice didn't sound too far ahead. "The Line didn't short. It's gone!"

Kominsky threw me a look and strode away. I swallowed my last bite of the protein bar, strapped on my backpack, and grabbed the chainsaw. Kominsky cursed, and I hurried to catch up.

Dusty hadn't exaggerated.

We'd all assumed some circuits were fried. A big problem, leaving a section of Line without electricity, but nothing that Kominsky couldn't fix. The transmission, or what I'd learned about it, had communicated as much. Maybe a cracked metal block or three. Something a bit more extreme than what we were used to, a bit more spray foam needed, some knowledge of electrical circuitry to rewire a faulty connection.

But what the message from Coulee hadn't said was that the Line had an actual breach, a physical breach, as in a vast gap in the wall stretching from the sloping ground up to the sky. We hadn't counted on a breach large enough for ten giant *chong*s to walk through side by side. Foam blocks lay on both sides of the Line, some seemingly in perfect shape, others shattered. Something had gnawed on several of them. We didn't need to replace a few blocks and wire circuits. We had to rebuild the Line.

"We can do this!" Dusty was full of energy fueled by an insider's naivete. I didn't share his optimism. He bent to pick up one of the intact metal blocks.

"Stop!" Kominsky pointed at the intact section of the Line, crackling with *chong*-repelling current. "The second that block in your hand touches the live section, you'll fry."

"What does Nelson expect us to do?"

I clenched the saw. "I think he expects us to die."

"No need to be dramatic," said Kominsky. "Lots happening. Probably just forgot." He scratched his beard, thinking. "Still, I don't want to waste the daylight we still have. Here's what we'll do. We'll gather the blocks we can reuse... carefully." He looked pointedly at Dusty. "Find a flat spot outside the Line and stack them there. That's where we'll set up camp."

"The blocks will protect us from *chong*s at night," said Dusty. "Our personal wall."

Of course, those blocks wouldn't be conducting electricity. They wouldn't keep away anything that really wanted to eat us. I didn't say that out loud. We all knew it.

"Dusty and me, we'll clear the job-site as best we can in the light we have today," said Kominsky. "No way Coulee could drive a heliovan up here. Lazlo, you hike down to the flats beyond the scrub and trees. See what supplies they left us down there. No way to fix this without more blocks, foam, wire. And we got no heliotractor, so we'll have to carry everything back by hand. But that's work for tomorrow."

Happy to be excused from site clearing, even if it meant hiking up and down another steep hill, I shrugged off my pack.

"Hey kid." An object hurtled at my head and I reacted without thinking, reaching up to block my face and plucking a flashlight from the air. Kominsky grinned. "So you can find your way back in the dark."

I shoved the flashlight into the long leg pocket of my coverall and jogged down the slope toward the east. In the declining light, I didn't see the end of a rotting log and caught the tip of my boot on it. I sprawled over it and continued tumbling down the hill. Coming to a stop, I stood and brushed leaves and dirt off my soot-caked coverall, then raced against the dark.

My strides down the hill were long and sliding. I grabbed new saplings and old snags as I walked, propelling myself quickly along. The shadows had caught me by the time the ground leveled out, and I flicked the flashlight on, the beam spreading through the gloaming. To my left, the northeast, the light twinkled, catching something, and reflected to me. Casting the light on the ground to place my footsteps carefully before flicking it up to find the reflection again, I made my way to a large stack of metallic blocks and cartons of foam canisters resting along a dusty track, the road to Coulee and eastern Cascadia.

Kominsky was right. Coulee had provided. The pile was huge, and the only way to transport the two-person pallets of aluminum blocks would be to haul them manually up the slope, through the rocks and trees, to the Line about two miles away. The individual blocks were lightweight, but pallets of them weren't, and as I clambered back up the slope toward the Line, I realized how much stamina we would need to climb up and down the slope while simultaneously maneuvering pallets in and out of uncleared sub-forest.

Only Kominsky knew how to repair the circuits. He was too valuable to waste hauling construction materials, even if he'd been able to do it. Obviously, he'd stay on the Line while

Dusty and I labored. And if Dusty slipped off into his neural oblivion... there would be no way I could carry the pallets on my own.

I climbed the slope, the light of my flashlight picking out rocks and stumps. In the dark, I expected to lose my way and wind up on another section of trail, but the looming shapes of the sweeper trees kept me heading in the general direction of the Line. An uncleared area such as the one I was walking through, especially with evening coming on and nocturnal creatures waking up, was not a place to hang around. Adrenaline and fear surged through me and I quickened my pace, feeling the burn in my lungs and thighs.

The closer to the sweeper forest I hiked, the darker it grew. My flashlight barely pricked a hole in the thick, dank air. I crested a hill and leaned against a sweeper sapling to catch a quick breath.

A colossal boom shook the ground and tossed me to the ground. The night sky burst into view, the vast trunks of the sweeper forest spotlit from below.

A swooshing sound clouded my hearing. It took me a moment to realize I was hearing my blood pumping. With the strange sensation that I was swimming deep down in the water of the shallows, I crawled forward, running my hand along the ground to find my flashlight. A low ridge of fire blazed nearby, and I stumbled toward it.

Now I was on the trail where I'd eaten my protein bar and talked with Kominsky a few hours ago. The fire was ahead of me, along the Line. Had Dusty spaced out again? Bumped into the live section of Line with a metal block and electrocuted himself? Was he on fire? I sprinted toward the blaze and spotted a smear of yellow, a body facedown on the trail.

My hand was on his head. Warm fluid covered my fingers. So sticky. Blood. My arms were rolling the body over.

Dusty.

Blood dripped from his right ear. His eyes were closed. I called his name. My lips moved, and I felt the vibration in my throat, but I couldn't hear my voice, only the sloshing of the heartbeat water in my ears.

There was warm air on my hand, my hand that touched his face. His chest rose and fell. He was breathing.

He was alive.

The flames lapped up the pine resin, the blood of the trees that weren't sweepers, the flammable ones. Fire and smoke and chaos.

Where was Kominsky?

Dusty was suddenly conscious, sitting up. His eyes were wide. He was coherent. I asked him, or at least, I think I did, but I still couldn't hear myself. My throat burned, the smoke scratching as I soundlessly screamed, "Where's Kominsky?"

Dusty pointed to his injured ear, wiped the blood away, and shook his head. He swiped a finger across his throat, but I wasn't sure what he meant. He couldn't hear me? His ears were dead? Or... Kominsky?

Was Kominsky dead?

So I said it again, but this time I didn't use my ragged voice. I moved my lips slowly, mouthing the question. I pulsed it to his mesh. No way he could misunderstand me. "Where. Is. Kominsky?"

Dusty shook his head, and I followed his eyes. All the way to the breach in the Line. The enormous gap between the two sections. The area that ten *chongs* could walk across side by side.

A large black circle scorched the ground. Off to one side stood a smoldering sweeper; several others lay uprooted and on their sides, as if tossed about by a ferocious wind.

Just beyond the circle. What was that? A log... a stick... no. No.

An arm.

I vomited, the half-digested protein bar ejected in a stream of hot stomach acid.

Then I was crying, wailing like a little baby. In an instant, Rajani was lying dead on the floor, dust powdering her lips. Appei's pyre was burning. Flames reflected on shimmering water. My arms were being gripped by strangers' hands. I was being hauled away. Where was Ami? Leave me with my mother—

But Dusty was standing, nudging me with his boot. He was pulling at my arm, hauling me to my feet. I saw him grab his pack, then Kominsky's, then mine. He strapped things on me, strapped things on him. Anything we could carry. Everything we could carry.

He walked through the breach, stepped over Kominsky's severed arm, skirted around the black circle.

Before I realized, before my hearing came back to me, before I'd even stopped crying, we were in the sweeper forest, flashlight beams stretching ahead of us, running.

Chapter Thirty-Two

I followed Dusty's lanky form, the light of the flames behind us receding into darkness. A light clicked on ahead of Dusty; he'd turned on his flashlight. In those first moments, it didn't occur to me to switch on my own. I didn't realize I was still gripping mine in a bloodless fist. I wasn't thinking; my feet were moving, self-propelled, as if by some base survival instinct. Back there, what I'd left behind, that was death. Where I was going, running behind Dusty into the unknown, that was life.

My physical body allowed me to be guided by Dusty while my brain struggled to wake up, catch on, become lucid. Somewhere deep in the folds of my cranium, I was closer to Dusty than I'd ever been. I wasn't dusting out, not like he did, but my mind had ceased to function.

Within the forest, the sweepers hid. They were sinister, silent creatures that revealed clues only as we stumbled into them. Dusty would nearly collide into the massive girth of a tree trunk, and my body would follow, stepping blindly into his footsteps, tripping over the same things he did.

The firelight vanished behind a wall of giant sweepers and it slowly dawned on me we were on the wrong side of the Line. As my thinking brain returned to me, I became slowly aware that we were racing heedlessly into the depths of the sweeper forest, the lair of the monstrous *chongs* and *zhus* we'd been trying to keep out. The breathy roar in my muffled ears was deafening, my eyes shrouded in nighttime, and my only connection to another human was the weak light at the end of Dusty's arm.

I called to him, yelled his name until my throat burned. Either he still couldn't hear me—I couldn't hear me—or he didn't care. We were moving as quickly as the flashlight would allow deeper and deeper into a situation we wouldn't escape. A slow pressure built in my left ear and ended with a painful pop. Suddenly I could suddenly hear my boots rustling on the ground. My right ear popped, and I yelled Dusty's name again. This time I could hear myself, and so did he. The light stopped moving forward and swung around.

"Ow! Stop shining the light into my eyes!"

"Sorry, dude."

Only then did I remember the flashlight in my hand. I clicked it on and aimed it at Dusty. Sweat poured down his face, leaving trails through the smoke black coating his face. His expression was grim, his eyes serious. Dried blood smeared his right cheek.

"Are you dusting?" I asked.

"Do I look like I'm dusting?"

"No. You hurt?"

"I don't think so. But I can only hear on one side."

I panned my beam slowly around the forest. The light stretched away from me, then came up short against a tree trunk until it located another gap between the rounded walls of wood. "We shouldn't be here. This is a bad idea."

"This is the only way."

"No, no no. We can't be here." I shone my flashlight straight up the tree trunk. The dark split the light into weak dust motes, expanded them to a hazy glow. Not enough force to see any creature hazards, but just enough suggestion to ignite my deeper phobias.

"Lazlo. It will be fine."

"No! No, it won't be. You didn't see the *zhu*, the one that me and... Kominsky... found. Those things live in here, and worse. We're heading straight for them—and blind."

"Lazlo. Think about it."

"That's all I'm doing! I'm telling you, this is a bad, bad, bad idea."

"You got a better one?"

"Um. Yeah. Not be here. Let's go back. Right now."

"To do what? Kominsky's dead."

That arm. I felt the acid in my throat again, gulped it down. "Dusty—" I wiped cold sweat from my face and bent over, struggling to keep myself together. "What... what happened?"

"Dude, I don't even know. We were piling blocks, you know, for the camp. Old dude goes through the breach, I heard him curse, next thing—blam!"

"He didn't touch the electrified part?"

"No way. You saw him, I mean, what was left of him." He gulped and cleared his throat. "An electrical short... would have fried him, sure. But he, um... exploded."

"It was almost like—"

"A bomb. Yeah."

I remembered those lectures in the canteen, in the early days, when me and Dusty had first arrived on the Line. The old timers had told us about the first cons who worked the Line.

"You think it was one of those cyanide bombs? Those were from, what, forty or fifty years ago? Longer?"

Dusty was probing his injured ear with a finger, clearing out dried blood. "Guess they missed one."

"Or they never made it this far north."

"Maybe."

"You think Nelson knew? That there were bombs here still?"

"Dude, this is what I'm saying."

"No. Wouldn't happen. We're his crew. You, me, Kominsky. If Nelson had known, he would have warned us."

"Lazlo. Am I the only one thinking right now? Nelson sends you and me up here, a death sentence. He hates us that much—and we can't fix the fence. I don't know how. Do you?"

"Not without... Kominsky."

Dusty rested a gentle hand on my shoulder and I straightened up. "So, we hike back... tomorrow. Tell Nelson what happened."

"Really? That the best you can do?" He scoffed and shook his head. "You surprise me, Laz. You want back in to that snake pit? I've only got five more months. But you? How long have you got?"

"You know how long I got."

"When are you going to have a better chance of getting out? Nelson's got no love for you. Only a matter of time until he gets you killed, especially now. No Kominsky to have your back."

He was making sense, but was this what I wanted? I'd fantasized about escaping, but I never thought I'd have the chance. Not really. "But what about Jan Oh?"

"That old timer doesn't care about us," said Dusty. "He's Kominsky's friend, not ours. And how you think he'll react when he finds out his *zhong shi de peng you* died? Blew up after trying to protect the two sorriest cons on the whole crew? Won't be a huge fan."

"But—"

"And Nelson? How long's it going to take him to fit you and me up for Kominsky's murder? Or more likely, silence us both and tell Coulee the bomb killed us all? You heard what he said. He never wanted either of us on the crew."

"If Kominsky hadn't claimed us that first day—"

"We'd be dead. Even with your... um... mind skills. And if we go back without Kominsky, we'll be dead."

Dusty had a point. And apparently, a very dark mind. He'd obviously learned more on the Hill and in prison than I'd given him credit for. Maybe he wasn't such a naïve insider after all.

"Okay, so we can't go back, not to the Line. I'm with you on that. But, Dusty, come on!" I panned the flashlight around the forest. "This? Here? This place? I mean, what was wrong with heading north or, I don't know, east to where the *chong*s are smaller and we can, you know, see?"

"Dude! This is where you need to follow the mind of the duster!" He held the light under his chin and illuminated the tip of his nose and its nostrils. "Where do you think Nelson is going to look for us? Where would a normal con run to? Think anyone in their right mind would set a foot in this forest—mwaaa haaa haaa—where the giant *chong*s dare to roam."

He'd only ever seen redheads and slow-moving and stupid graypills. We'd sent him back to camp to get Nelson and the zapper; he'd never laid eyes on the *zhu*. And neither of us had any idea how big the things could grow, here in the forest, away from human eyes.

There had to be another way to escape. Not through the forest.

"You're wrong, Dusty. Once Nelson gets in range and

checks his PAP tracker, he'll see us. We can't move fast enough in here. I mean, we can't even see! We'll be stumbling around in here for days, moving in circles, going nowhere. He'll pap us soon as he can and bring us back. That's if we're still alive."

"Lazlo, Lazlo, Lazlo." He shook his head with mock sadness. "My young friend. How little you know of criminal life." He laughed. "I knew you weren't *shashu*, but I'm doubting you're even a dustslinger. Such a naïve, trusting young man."

"So educate me. You think you're so smart."

"Why do you think Nelson didn't send for help after the *zhu* attacked the new dude?"

That had bothered me. Still did. But I shrugged and said, "The guy didn't need help. Sid took care of him."

"That dude had no chance without special care. You knew it, I knew it, Nelson knew it. But two emergency calls within twenty-four hours? They would have reassigned Nelson. That's what they do to lead cons who mess up." His teeth sparkled in the flashlight's glow, a gleaming schadenfreude grin. "Coulee would send him to someone else's crew, a newbie, but worse off than us. Because the minute another crew hears he was a lead con, he'd be lower than a *shashu* or a *hezui*. They'd be volunteering to silence him, and I don't mean just the crew. The lead con of his new gig would be after him. Can't have two hard cases in one crew. Nelson wouldn't last a week."

"So, what you're saying is—"

"There won't be a search crew. Not in here anyhow. And not for a while. Depends on when they hike north."

Dusty was making sense, and that scared me. If he was right, there would be no choice but to keep moving deeper into the forest. And I wasn't sure I could do that. "Nelson will check the tracker every day. He'll see that Kominsky is silent and that we're off the Line. He'll know."

"Neither of us knows the range of that tracker, but if Nelson could pick up our signals, why hasn't he papped us yet?"

I had no answer.

Dusty kept talking as though he hadn't expected a response. "We're out of range. And Nelson doesn't care. He knows Kominsky would never run. None of those old timers would. They're proud of being so-called patriots. They'll serve their time and go home or go silent and be martyrs in each other's addled brains. And Nelson figures you and me, if Kominsky hadn't—hmm—" He cleared his throat, began again. "We would have stuck with him, PAP tracker or no."

"Because he's family."

"Family. Right. So, the way I figure it, if we keep moving away from the Line, by the time Nelson gets close enough to check, we'll be out of range. And by the time the crew gets up here and finds Kominsky's... his um... remains... um... they'll search the likely places first. And that's north on the Line or east back towards Coulee."

"They won't imagine we'd be stupid or crazy enough to wander into the sweeper forest."

"You got it! We move fast now, elude capture, make it out to the west side. And then, we stay clear of dust patrols and, you know, anyone who has access to Cascadian criminal files."

"So long as we steer clear of trackers scanning our mesh —" I said.

"We'll be as good as dead to Cascadia. But not actually dead." Dusty laughed. "Free. We'll be free."

"Yeah. Freedom. Sounds great." I scanned the area with my flashlight to be sure nothing had crept up on us while we'd been talking. "But right now, I'm more worried about evading hungry *chong*s than outsmarting Nelson."

"Well, I can't help you with your anxiety. You got your demons, I got mine." He tapped his head, and I wondered if he meant his mental state or his deaf ear. "One question, though. What makes you think we'd be any safer out there, next to a busted section of Line, than in here? The blocks have been gone for how long? Couple of days? Weeks maybe? All we know is the message, the one Coulee transmitted. You trust that?"

I shook my head. No.

I'd never seen Dusty this coherent; I'd never had such a long and logical conversation with him. He was my best friend on the Line, yet this was the first I'd ever seen this side of him. I didn't know who was more pathetic: him for frying what must have once been an incredible brain, or me for only just realizing who he was.

"Way I see it, we've got just as much chance of getting attacked by *chong*s out there as in here."

His arguments were breaking through, convincing me. My thinking brain was taking control again, pushing down my fear. "In the forest, we won't have a false sense of security," I said, encouraging myself. "We know how dangerous it is. We'll be more alert than we were on the Line."

"In here, the *chong*s eat each other," said Dusty. "We're not the only ones on the menu."

"Out there, we'd have to worry about both *chong*s and Nelson."

"That's right!"

Aiming my flashlight at the ground, I took a step forward. "How far can the trackers reach?"

Dusty began walking again. "No clue. That's why we have to keep moving. West and away. We'll know if Nelson can reach us. We'll feel it."

"Northwest," I said. "Northwest will take us out of range sooner."

What I didn't say was what I was imagining. My dreamed future was now a possibility. The shallows lay to the northwest.

With each step, I'd be closer to my childhood home and to Ami.

Chapter Thirty-Three

❦

Dusty was jogging, weaving around the vast tree trunks. I sped up and ran beside him, lending my flashlight beam to his, creating a wider swath of visibility. A dark thing scuttled just beyond our combined light field.

"What was that thing?" My voice cracked, embarrassingly. There was no hiding how scared I felt.

"A *chong*. Guess we'll get used to it."

"I won't ever get used to it."

"Watch out—there—your right," called Dusty, pointing his light into the near distance, about a meter from my head.

A long string stretched from one trunk to another, straight across the gap where I'd been aiming to run. I stopped, raised my beam, and eight points of light glittered back at me. A *zhu*, much smaller than the one that had attacked Noonan, hanging lightly in the air and not hunting on the ground, but still. A *zhu*.

Then I remembered the chainsaw.

"Dusty, when we ran, did you take any tools?"

"Why?" Dusty stood several feet away from me. "What are you looking for?"

"Chainsaw. You take it?"

"It was broken—but, yeah, I think I shoved it into Kominsky's pack."

His light wavered in the distance, came closer. He stopped in front of me and dropped the pack off his right shoulder. The handle of the broken chainsaw poked out at the top.

"Spot me."

I sat on the ground, my back against a tree, and held my flashlight in my mouth to direct its beam to the chainsaw. My fingers were shaky at first until I blocked out the thought of the *zhu* hanging mere feet from us. I bit down hard on the flashlight, harder each time the chain stuck to itself or fell off the saw, but as my nerves calmed, more and more of the chain wound around the saw until I'd repaired it.

We set off again, Dusty carrying two packs, me carrying one. But I had weapons now: a flashlight in one hand, a chainsaw in the other. I was ready for whatever beast crossed our path.

Dusty and I traveled all night, flashlight beams crisscrossing, skittering movements slightly beyond the reach of our artificial light. I was bone-tired, but sheer terror propelled me through the black expanse. I didn't want to be left behind, alone in the dark, so I raced along, barely keeping pace with Dusty's manic energy. The chainsaw gripped in my fist gave me courage. Our chances of survival might be slightly better with a weapon.

When the air lightened to a misty gray, we turned off our flashlights to conserve their remaining helioenergy. The diffuse light breaking through the ceiling of sweeper trees wouldn't be strong enough to recharge their solar cells. Soon, we'd only be able to travel by day. When the flashlights no longer worked, we'd have to take our chances with the *chongs* in the dark. I tried not to think about it.

I shoved the flashlight in my pocket and called to Dusty. "Let's stop here. Have a bite to eat."

"Bad idea. We should keep moving, stay out of range."

Rapidly scanning the area for *chongs*, I rested my chainsaw on the ground and slipped off my backpack. "We've been walking and running all night." I dropped to the ground, soft and fragrant with brown needles, and dug into my backpack. "Aren't you hungry?"

He stuck his hand into his pocket, pulled out an empty wrapper, and dropped it on the ground. "I eat while I move, don't you?"

I was having no luck feeling out a protein bar or a packet of dehydrated food-product, so I tipped my backpack upside down and sorted through the debris. Three bars, ten food packets, and a quarter bottle of water. No way was I going to waste the water rehydrating the food packet. I tore it open with my teeth, sprinkled the powder on my tongue, and swallowed. Chalky and salty, not much to it, but it had calories. After I'd licked the packet clean so I didn't waste a single calorie, I drizzled water on my tongue to wash it down. Not much of a meal, so I chewed my way through a bar.

"You done?" Dusty walked away from me.

"Hold up! I've only got two protein bars left. How many you got?"

"Does it matter right now?"

"Yeah, it does. You've got two backpacks—yours and Kominsky's—which means you've got his rations."

"You wanna carry his pack, be my guest."

"Don't get mad. All I'm saying—let's pool our resources. See what we've got."

"Dude, really? Right now?" He rocked from one foot to the other and looked anxiously back the way we'd come.

"Yeah. Right now. Or you got something to hide?"

"What's your problem? Here, take it, you want it so bad."
He tossed Kominsky's backpack at me.

The contents of the unzipped pack were disordered. I
upended the bag and sorted through what I found. Kominsky
had packed an assortment of wires, little tools I didn't know
the name of or purpose for, an extra coverall, and some clean
socks. No food. That didn't seem right. "Give me your bag," I
said.

"No way. You wanted Kominsky's pack. You got Kominsky's pack."

"There's no food in here. You know as well as me the old
timer would never travel without rations. No way he ate
them all before—"

"Fine." He dropped his backpack to the ground.

I searched Dusty's backpack and found four protein bars.
No other food. "Is this all you have? No food packets?"

"Didn't occur to me."

"You're kidding. Where are Kominsky's rations?"

Dusty avoided my eyes.

"We have six protein bars and nine food packets between
us."

"That's all?"

"Yeah, *hundan*. That's all we've got, and most of that's
mine."

Dusty flew at me, all fists, and pounded my head into the
soft ground before I got a punch off. He took me completely
by surprise—granted I'd only known him a month, not
counting crossing paths with him on the Hill—but in all that
time, he'd never been aggressive. Never violent toward me or
anyone else. I didn't remember him ever losing his temper or
even saying anything slightly angry about anyone. He was a
harmless, goofy joker, only slightly dangerous when he had a
dust flashback.

"Dusty—get off! What's with you?"

He rolled off me and away, shaking, holding his head in his hands. "Sorry, sorry, dude. Sorry, I'm um... not feeling so good..."

Pushing away from him, I brushed dirt and leaves off my clothes and stood. He was bent over and hugging his knees, tears streaming down his face. What was going on?

"Dusty, dude. It's okay." Awkwardly, I patted his head. "Everything we've got, we share. I didn't mean... I'm hungry, that's all... you didn't think I'd take all the food, did you?"

He drew a shuddering breath, then ran his fingers through his hair and leaned against a tree trunk. "No, no Lazlo. Wasn't thinking of food. Just, um." His right hand shook. He glanced at it, grabbed it with his left hand, forced it to be still. "Not feeling myself right now. That's all." I don't know if it was the gray light surrounding us or the vestiges of smoke on his skin, but his face seemed even whiter than usual. Honestly, he didn't look great.

"Look, I'll repack our bags," I said. "Kominsky had a bunch of stuff we don't need. We'll break it down to two packs, ration our food, figure out something as we go. And we need to rest. I know I do. You'll feel better after. Okay?"

Dusty glanced at me, subdued now, and nodded. He leaned into the tree and closed his eyes. I packed Kominsky's coveralls in Dusty's pack; they were much too long for me. Split the socks between both our packs. Packed the food in my bag. Dusty had made it obvious I couldn't trust him with our precious rations. He seemed to be dozing, but I couldn't be sure. I tucked my pack tightly beneath my head, draped a hand over the chainsaw, and curled up beside Dusty against the tree. A quick nap, that's all I needed.

The minute I closed my eyes, I felt the thunder of the explosion again, the heat of the flames, and I saw the severed arm. My stomach was roiling with the memory; the dry food-product was choking me. Rajani floated five inches off the ground, her naked toes pointing downward, her colorful braids floating around her head in all directions. That white dust under her nose. I reached for her and she vanished. I turned around, searching for her, and behind me rose a mountain of gray skulls, empty eye sockets gaping. Rajani stood in their midst, a faint smile on her lips. Again, I tried to touch her, and she dove into an eyehole. I dug for her, reaching into the socket. It expanded to encompass my arm, my torso, and it drew me in, then closed around me—strangling me—and I couldn't breathe—

I flung open my eyes and gagged, but it was only dry heaves. I reached for my water bottle and drank greedily, emptying it. Dusty still slept. I didn't know how much time had passed. The air was still gray, no lighter or darker than before, so I thought it might have only been a few minutes, half an hour, no more. But then, how much light could penetrate the sweeper forest? Perhaps this was all the light that we could hope for and I'd actually slept for hours, so I nudged Dusty awake.

He groaned, rubbed his face, and opened his eyes. He blinked at me, and I watched his memory of where we'd been and what we'd experienced alter his sleepy expression. "How long have I been out?"

"Not sure." I stood and slung my pack over my shoulder. "I fell asleep too. Packed the bags. We should go."

"Yeah." He stretched, laid his hands on the other packed bag, and looked at me. "Only two?"

"All we need."

"Which way we walking?" Dusty looked around, confused. "Everything looks the same. You remember which way?"

I reached into my pocket, pulled out an old analog compass. "Look what Kominsky had." I pointed northwest. "That's the way. Uphill, looks like."

And we climbed. The flat, soft ground between the trees rose gradually at first and then all at once. We scrambled over boulders between groves of sweepers, happy for the bright blue sky and its illuminating sunlight. But as pleasant as the daylight felt, we knew the time spent crossing the uneven terrain was slowing us down. We cut back into the forest and the gloom.

Dusty was silent as we walked, which was unusual. I expected he was tired and hungry, as I was, and simply saving his energy. My mind was an anxious place, my thoughts racing with worst-case scenarios. How long would our food rations last? Would we pass out without more food? How many miles lay between us and Nelson's tracker? When would Nelson catch up and hit us with an alarm? Were we far enough away yet to be untraceable? How many miles long was the passage through the forest? What would we do when we reached the other side? Would we reach the other side or would we be *chong* food?

And most perplexing, why had Dusty attacked me?

Deeper and deeper into the forest we hiked, the sweepers becoming larger with each passing hour, as though they had spread outward from some central location we hadn't yet reached. I wondered whether they really were getting bigger or if my lack of sleep and physical exhaustion were playing tricks on my mind.

Dusty broke our hours-long silence with a curse and rubbed his head.

"What?"

"Headache. Little one suddenly."

Had Nelson found us? Besides a tired, woozy feeling, I felt nothing. "Maybe you're dehydrated. Have a drink."

"Tracker found us."

"I don't feel it."

"It's still faint. But I could take an aspirin." He sighed. "I'd love an aspirin."

Aspirin was code for something else, something much stronger, I knew. Someday soon, he'd short out. I wasn't sure what I'd do when that happened. One more thing to worry about. I pushed away the nagging thought.

"It's not the tracker, or I'd feel it too. You know I'm more sensitive than you. I bet we're off grid."

Dusty was quiet; the excitement he'd shown the day before was gone. "An aspirin would feel good."

"You don't need an aspirin." Grabbing him by the shoulder strap of his pack, I tugged him along. "If we keep moving through the night, we'll be far out of range. Make it impossible for Nelson to track us."

"But he knows where we are, where we're going. The crew will have plenty of rations to chase us. No way we can get away."

I stopped in my tracks. Spinning around to face him, I said, "Don't."

"It's just..." He kicked a hole in the ground with the tip of his boot. "I'm not sure this was such a good idea."

"Don't!" I shook my head, not believing what I was hearing. He kept staring at his feet. "This was your idea, remember? You said we should run. You said!"

"I know. I did." He wouldn't look at me. "But... it's like... really far. And... we're almost out of food... and... Nelson will catch us."

"No, he won't. He won't set foot in the sweeper forest." I was talking fast, pacing in circles, repeating back to Dusty all the things he'd said to convince me mere hours ago. "Even if he knew where we were. He'd never be able to convince the crew to go into the forest, no way. Not even by papping them. And he'd never come alone. He doesn't care about us.

Nelson wants us dead; he even said so. He'll tell Coulee we're dead, just like Kominsky is—"

When Dusty looked up, his eyes were sad. "Lazlo. Dude. I can't."

"No, you don't. I won't let you." I stepped away from him. "You can't take it back now. It was your idea."

He brushed tears from his face. "My head isn't good. I need... I need..." His voice dropped. "Sid's pills."

"You no-good *hundan*! You stupid *hezui* dustrat idiot!" I rounded on him and shoved him, hard. He stumbled backward, and I hit him in the jaw once, twice. His body dropped, limp and uncaring. He didn't raise a hand to fend me off, didn't even try to fight back. He lay there silently, his eyes glassy and leaking, letting me beat him. My lack of energy stopped me before I did much damage, but my rage was still red hot. I imagined my body smoldering until it burst into flame, scorching everything in my path.

Lying immobile on the ground, Dusty whispered, "I'm sorry."

"Sorry? Sorry! You know what happens if we go back? We get time added, remember? Might not matter to you—how long you got? They'll give you another year. Coulee will keep you numb and happy with their drugs. But what about me? Huh? Think about that!"

My knuckles were raw and swollen. They matched the fist-shaped mark reddening Dusty's cheek. His face and my fist were swelling, threatening bruises. Cause and effect, the proof that I was a criminal, a danger to those around me. A throwaway kid, not safe to be around.

Ten more years. That's what I'd get. Another decade in a cage. Might as well feed myself to a *zhu* right now. Twenty years would mean I'd never have a life. No wife or family. No home of my own. I'd grow old and go silent in prison.

Alone forever.

Pacing back and forth, I pounded circles into the dried sweeper needles as my mind reeled. I could do this by myself, right? Walk through the forest alone, protect myself against *chongs*, find my way out the other side? There was no alternative.

Dusty drew a loud, shaky breath. "Okay."

"Okay what?"

He pushed himself off the ground and adjusted the pack across his shoulders. "Well? What are you waiting for? If we're going to outrun Nelson, we'd better hurry."

Filthy, bloody, stinking dustrat. My only friend in the entire world. I said, "Nelson ain't coming," and knocked him back down to the ground. A hug this time.

Chapter Thirty-Four

We walked until dark, lit the flashlights, then walked until we our bodies dropped. We slept until daybreak and started walking again.

In all that monotonous walking, I found a long stick—tripped over it, more like. It felt good in my hand and was the perfect length to support myself when my legs felt ready to collapse. It also came in handy when clearing *zhu* webs out of the way. I could see them during the daytime, mostly strung far over our heads and harmless. But in the faint light of dawn, I'd wandered into several of the ropy strands; lucky for me, they'd been old and uninhabited. They were everywhere, stretching across meter-wide gaps between the sweeper trees. Often there was no web, simply random strings twisting in the air. My heart raced erratically when a sticky strand tickled my skin.

As we walked, I waved the stick from side to side before my face. When my upheld arm grew tired, I'd drop it to my side and poke the stick's tip into the ground. Layers of needles and leaves and dead things I didn't want to imagine lay between our boots and the dirt. We stepped in and out of shadows, our eyes adjusting to the gloom. In the deeper shadows, we often saw indistinct scuttling; *chongs* avoiding the light.

I'm not sure when it happened, but during that third day of walking, my mind relaxed. More than once, I caught myself deep in memories of my former life in the shallows or my business on the Hill. Dusty's voice yanked me abruptly out of my daydreams. I didn't think I'd been moving slowly, but he was far ahead of me and I jogged to catch up. He watched me approach, and when I was close, he turned and raced off through a clearing.

I followed close behind, a sudden beam of sunlight temporarily blinding me. When my vision returned, there stood my friend, every muscle of his body frozen.

Only a foot from his bent knee hovered an entirely black *chong* larger than any *chong* I'd ever seen. Rocking back and forth on stocky legs, it reached Dusty's waist. Its ridged black shell was half hidden by some woodland plants; I estimated it to be the length of two men, much larger than the redhead Nelson had zapped on the Line. I went racing toward him; the chainsaw screaming and ready.

"No, wait," he called, holding his hand up. "Look how clumsy it is."

He was right. This *chong* moved slower than the ones we'd seen on the Line, even slower than the injured redhead. It lifted one chubby leg with a slight wobble and set it tentatively down on the needle litter before raising the next.

"Dude, it's dusted out. Doesn't know where it is."

He reached his foot forward, gathering courage, and kicked the creature's hard shell. The *chong* kept walking, moving in a lazy circle, turning its back to us.

Dusty laughed and waggled his fingers at me. "Laz. Give me the saw."

"It's walking away. Leave it."

"Give." I had an idea what he was about to do, so after I put the saw in his outstretched hand, I took several steps back. The saw roared to life and Dusty whooped. When he stepped toward the retreating *chong*, the creature bent down, resting its armored head on the ground and raising its backside in the air. A noxious smell drifted out, and I coughed and gagged, then turned and jogged back the way I'd come.

Behind me, I heard the saw's chain catch with a clacking noise. Then a wet thunk, and when I looked back, a thick yellow liquid sprayed into the air. Dusty let loose a warrior cry.

"Not so scary now, are you, you *chong hundan!*" He reached down and grabbed the head of the *chong* by its motionless antennae and held it aloft in one hand, the saw still ratcheting in his other hand. Yellow goo dripped down his face. The headless creature waved its legs; they slowly stilled as the blood ran out.

The slaughter had brought a crazed expression to Dusty's face. I was used to his neural breaks, how he talked to himself and went to some bizarre places. But he seemed different from that, more unbalanced than usual, and I felt uneasy. He'd killed a creature for no reason, and somehow that didn't sit well with me.

"Careful there, Dusty," I called. "Why don't you shut off the saw? How about I take it?"

He didn't seem to hear me. Dropping the head, he faced the creature's body again and plunged the saw deep into its abdomen. Who knows how long he would have kept at it, cursing and laughing and screaming nonsense, if not for the shrill grinding that revealed the chain had come loose again.

Once the saw broke, Dusty's blood lust subsided quickly. He wandered away from the massacred body, his gaze passing over the head he'd discarded on the forest floor.

"I'm on my way. Don't start without me," he called to a phantom imagining, then walked away in a daze as though nothing had happened.

I tugged the broken saw from the *chong* carcass, yellow goo dripping from the hanging chain. Goosebumps tickled the back of my neck, and I had the uncanny feeling that someone or something was watching me. This was no neural pulse, not a tracker finding my mesh; there was no familiar pressure inside my head either. This was a physical presence, a creature that was very close.

I turned slowly, not really wanting to know, and scanned the area. Dusty was ahead of me, so I knew it wasn't him I was sensing. But there was something. My body knew it: The hairs on my arms stood up and my heart pounded. I looked up, fearful yet expecting a hidden *zhu*. Was I prey? The handle of the saw was slippery, sweat from my palms mixing with *chong* blood. I wiped down the saw with a rag and dried my hands on my pants. After glancing around one last time, I clutched the useless chainsaw in one hand, my walking stick in the other, and sprinted to catch up with Dusty.

He was just ahead of me, not so far away. I laughed at myself, at how easily I'd spooked. I wanted to talk to Dusty, see if he was feeling okay and calm my own nerves, but he was babbling to someone who wasn't there. He was graying out, not entirely dusted, and I hoped his neural break would pass quickly without a major incident. If we just kept moving, heading northwest, he could have a party between his ears and I didn't care.

But I couldn't shake the feeling that something was following us. Hunting us.

MAKING the most of the gray daylight, we moved ceaselessly forward. My throat felt dry, my mouth pasty. I realized I was thirsty, but my empty water bottle bounced uselessly inside my pack. Once I began thinking about water, I couldn't stop.

We heard faint rumblings of thunder in the distance, but they never led to rain. A constant moisture formed; drops of the fog that hovered inside the forest beaded on our skin and in our hair. I welcomed it, rubbing it over my skin to rinse away bits of web and soot, but the moisture wasn't enough to refill our empty water bottles. The constant damp was infuriating. We were uncomfortably wet from our coveralls straight through to our skin, while painfully parched on the inside. Until my jaw ached from the effort, I walked with my mouth hanging open, my tongue outstretched to catch whatever drops I could.

We mostly hiked in the deep, dark center of the forest. The thick layer of brown needles and refuse made for easy walking. Dusty's battle with the *chong* had left him feeling invincible, no longer afraid of the forest creatures. He scrambled up soft hills and raced around the massive tree trunks, but I was still wary and struggled to keep up with him.

Afraid of what hid in the shadows and unable to shake the feeling of being watched, I welcomed the rays of sunshine that sometimes sneaked through the trees. A glimmer to the east suggested a rocky area. Jutting from steep inclines, the rocks were pockets of rare daylight covered in lush plants. Though it slowed us down, I preferred climbing the boulders that broke through stands of sweepers.

"Dusty, over here," I called.

He turned, and I was relieved to see that his eyes had cleared. He was back.

"We'll lose time," he said, but he backtracked and joined me on the rocks. "There's water on the plants; look."

He was right: Droplets of fog rested on the leaves' surface.

"We could drink that, right?" I touched a fingertip to a leaf, then to my lips.

Dusty was already crouching in the plants, licking their leaves. I didn't see any *chongs*, but I still poked my walking stick between the greenery. Good thing I did, because I found a few gray, soft-bodied, slimy *chongs*. The creatures didn't seem to pose any risk, so I plucked a few leaves and licked the moisture off them.

"Lazlo, you're losing all the water doing it that way. Just bend over and lick!"

I tried Dusty's method, but it wasn't much better. The little water I swallowed only magnified my raging thirst. The drops of fog teased rather than satisfied.

And water wasn't the only thing we'd run out of. Our food supply was all but exhausted, our flashlight cells nearly dead. Our brief times walking along the boulders in the miserly sunlight had barely charged our helioscreens.

Back again in the forest, the dim light of day faded to black. Though in the light of day, Dusty claimed to no longer be afraid of *chongs*, their hard shells and skittering legs were plenty terrifying in the dark. We shared Dusty's flashlight, walking slowly as its beam weakened. When it finally flickered out, it was my turn to lead. With some half-hearted objection from Dusty, I suggested we use the bit of light we had left, not much more than what Dusty's flashlight had held, and find a spot to sleep.

Resting between three sweepers, we shared the last of the food and settled in for the night. Eventually, I heard Dusty's slow, measured breathing. The sky was rumbling again, like it had earlier in the day. Lightning flashed high above; a crack of thunder immediately followed. Hoping for rain that would penetrate to the ground, I unscrewed the lid of my water bottle and set out the bottle. Then I rifled through Dusty's pack and did the same with his bottle.

I curled on the ground beneath the tree, hugged my pack under my head, and knew nothing else until the morning.

Chapter Thirty-Five

❧

Our water bottles had collected a mouthful of water each by the time the hazy glow of morning woke me. I wet my tongue and rinsed out my pasty mouth. Dusty's bottle was in my hand before I knew it, the paltry collection of raindrops sloshing at the bottom. He was asleep, still breathing heavily through his slightly opened mouth. The thought crossed my mind. Of course it did, but despite my thirst, somehow my conscience, sounding like Ami's voice, broke through and I covered the bottle and placed it beside Dusty.

The *chong* juice had dried on the chain like a thick epoxy. I bent the chain back and forth to break it apart and scraped the dry scum off with my dirt-encrusted fingernail. When I looped the chain back around the saw, I noticed a couple of bent teeth. So far, we'd been lucky. The chain had only fallen off when we'd jammed it into something solid. I wasn't sure we should keep using the saw. If the chain flew off by itself, when it wasn't sawing through something, that wouldn't be good. I'd never seen a chain go rogue, but Kominsky had told us again and again about the worker who'd taken one in the face. I could practically see the damage; Kominsky had made sure of that.

I called up his memory in my mind and whispered his name to the forest: "Kominsky."

The old timer. My protector and mentor. Another one gone. The people I cared for, who seemed to care for me, they all left. I wasn't so much thrown away as left behind. And it didn't matter what I did. If I tried not to get attached, not care about them, somehow it still happened. And then—

Dusty was all I had left. And yesterday, it seemed like he was losing it. I watched him sleep for a minute. His skinny face was dark with dirt, his hair hard and filthy, plastered with *chong* blood and clinging *zhu* fibers. I nudged him awake.

"Hmmm? What's that?"

"Daytime. We need to get moving."

He groaned, sat up, grabbed his head. "Ow. You feel that? I think they're getting closer."

"Yeah. We'd better hurry." For a second, I felt guilty about lying. There was no pain. No PAP alarm. No tracking. But we had to find our way through this forest, and soon. We had no water, and we'd exhausted our food rations.

Dusty grabbed his water bottle and sucked it dry. "Dude, I'm starving. What we got to eat?"

"Nothing left."

"No!" He reached for my bag and rummaged through it. Empty, as I'd said. "What are we going to eat?"

I shrugged. My stomach was beyond hungry, not even growling anymore. It just hurt. "Gotta move. Now."

A day of hiking lay ahead of us, the same as yesterday and the day before. Probably the same thing tomorrow and the next day. We'd have to increase our speed, get out of the forest before we starved. Dusty had convinced himself he was feeling the tracker and was hurrying; he'd have sudden spurts of energy and take off running. I checked the compass regularly to be sure we continued heading in a northwest direction.

The steady walking soothed me. My legs were moving on their own, and I felt lightheaded. It surprised me to discover that I was growing used to the forest. I didn't feel as unnerved as before by the skittering just beyond my view. I was in a state of meditation, a rhythm of motion, watching my feet as they hammered against the thick, soft needles, hearing the gentle inner whoosh of my breathing, enjoying the movement of my legs and arms as I jogged between trees.

But I was still terrified of the *zhus*.

I saw Dusty ahead of me as though in a dream, hazy and half real. He was clawing at a tree, tearing off the bark, chewing, spitting it out.

"Dusty—what are you doing?"

Not answering me, he ran off through the trees toward some sunlight, a gap in the sweepers. I followed him, yelling his name, telling him to stop. When I caught up, he was tearing plants from the ground, cramming them into his mouth. Hours of walking, little water, nothing to eat—Dusty was glitching and I could do nothing about it. I was dizzy, my energy waning. Dusty grew dimmer and dimmer, a ghostly figure fading in and out. I barely noticed that my pack became lighter. The weight of the chainsaw was gone. The Dusty-ghost was sprinting away from me, racing toward a log. I stumbled along behind him, faint but forcing myself to stay upright.

The chainsaw kicked on, and my mind was immediately alert. Suddenly, Dusty was clear and solid. He was laughing, spinning in circles, the chainsaw screaming. Was he hallucinating? Was I?

Because I saw the same monster he did.

Chong legs. A lot of them. Way more than six. Way more

than eight. Curved at the end, pointed and sharp. They belonged to something towering. Something vast.

And then Dusty hauled back a booted foot. He kicked the thing.

The *chong* reared up, taller than two men standing one on top of the other. And then it bent in half. The back half gripped the ground for traction and the front half clutched Dusty's leg, wrapped around it up to his thigh. It dug those sharp claw feet into my friend's leg, and the scream—I will never forget it. Not as long as I live. The scream ratcheted higher and higher, louder than the chainsaw that Dusty had flown wide into the needle litter. The head of the giant *chong* latched on, chewed on Dusty's leg, and he fell backward to the ground. Releasing its hold on Dusty, the *chong* raced away, faster than any *chong* I'd seen before, faster even than a burrowing *zhu*. The hard brown shell hugged the ground and rippled away, its legs a blur, until it disappeared beneath a rotting tree.

I don't know how long I stood, struck dumb and useless by shock.

When I came back to myself, Dusty lay moaning, rolling from side to side, gripping his leg where the *chong* had clawed and bitten it. The fabric of his coveralls was ripped, shredded into thin ribbons as though a sharp blade had sliced through again and again.

I wrestled his backpack off his shoulders. "Take off your pants," I ordered.

Through shaky breaths, Dusty fumbled with the zipper on his coverall. I helped him pull the garment down to reveal his injured leg. The skin was red and flecked with blood where the claws had broken the skin. Higher up his thigh, a ring of discolored skin surrounded deeper puncture wounds. As I watched, blood began pooling in the marks. The ringed area was swelling slowly, growing in size.

Dusty glanced at his wound and vomited. "I'm gonna die, aren't I, Lazlo? This is bad, really bad." He grabbed my hand, his fingernails digging into the palm of my hand, and I imagined his nails were the creature's curved hooks. "I need dust! Where's Sid? I need some pills, something to get me out of here... AAAGH... my leg is burning... is it melting? Tell me, Lazlo. I can't look!"

I gulped at the moist air. "No Dusty, your leg isn't melting. It's right here, same as it always was."

The ring rash was spreading outward, the skin hot-looking and pulled tight. "Dude, I'm dead. It's my last day on earth. I'm so sorry, so sorry, I got us into this."

"You're hurt, yeah. But you're not dying, not today." I didn't know that to be true, but if ever there was a time to lie, this was it.

"Lazlo, the demon's got me now. Burning me from the inside out..."

He was heading into the gray zone; I was sure of it. I kind of hoped he was. Better to be a hero in fantasy land than what he was: a chew toy for a giant *chong*.

"Rajani. She was your girl."

"Yeah. She was."

"Not your fault. You are no *shashu*."

I felt a slight choking in my throat, swallowed, and said, "Yeah, I told you that when I first met you."

"You're a good one. You're my best—" His eyes rolled up in his head and he ground his teeth, moaned.

If only I'd had dust. I would have slung it like you can't believe, forced him to take it all. Or just enough that he didn't die, not like Rajani. All I knew was that I couldn't stand to see Dusty like this. So much pain. My friend was suffering, and there was nothing I could do.

It was simply a matter of time. He was going to leave me, like everyone else had left me.

I stared at Dusty, pale and feverish, begging for dust, calling for Sid. I pried his fingers off my hand.

"My fault. Shouldn't have run." He was drooling. "Water. Please, water."

I opened his pack and took out his empty water bottle, then propped his injured leg on top of the pack.

And then I left.

Chapter Thirty-Six

❧

Truthfully, I didn't know what my plan was. I didn't know where to search for water. That was all my friend had asked for, just a drink of water, yet he might as well have asked for an air-processed flat in some First City highrise. I was just as unlikely to bring that back with me.

So why had I left his side?

There wasn't much I could do for him. Nothing, in fact. I did not know what kind of *chong* had bitten him, and even if I had known, I wasn't Sid. I had no supplies to clean his wound or bandages for his leg or medicines to deaden his pain. So, what? What was there to do but sit around and watch him vomit and swell up and die?

I didn't think I could watch someone die. Not again.

If it had been the other way around, if I were the injured one and Dusty were holding the empty water bottle—but who was I kidding? Dusty would have grayed out long before this, wandered away from me, and left me to die alone. But then, I wouldn't have chased the *chong* in the first place. I never would have kicked and enraged it. What had he been thinking of? Why had he put himself in that danger?

When you think about it, I mean, what did I owe the duster? I barely knew him, right? We'd been prisoners together for less than two months. I'd never have been friends with him on the Hill. Leaving the dustrat and continuing on alone made the most sense. I mean, it was logical, if I wanted to survive. I had no food, no water. No time to sit by Dusty's side, waiting for him to die. Because he was going to die; how could he not? He couldn't survive, not after an attack like that, not out here.

Was he worth sacrificing myself for? Because that's what it would mean if I stayed. And what if we'd been wrong and Nelson actually was looking for us, trying to track us right now? Could I leave him behind? Should I?

My conscience would tell me what to do. I waited for Ami's voice to come to me. But she was silent. Nothing to say, for once. I needed to get home, fast as possible. She missed me; she was waiting for me in the shallows.

"What you are, that's up to you."

The words floated on a cloud of memory. The voice was deep and gravelly from years spent laboring in the sun and dirt, fortifying a wall that would protect strangers. It was the voice of a patriot and a soldier. Kominsky.

What did I want to be? A throwaway kid that no one loved? Or a lowlife Hill worker slinging for every bit of crypto he could get? Definitely not a *shashu* serving time in prison. I was not a double-crossing con who'd abandon his only friend to die alone in the sweeper forest.

I knew who I was.

I was Lazlo Khosravi, a *hundan* who'd made a lot of mistakes, sure. A *hundan* who was far from perfect. But I'd never betray my family.

My compass showed I was backtracking, so I adjusted course and headed northwest. I already knew there was no water behind me. I hoped to find some up ahead. Boulders loomed beyond the trees and I hurried toward them. In the open air, drizzle had broken through the fog. Some of the larger boulders had cracks and rounded divots that collected water. I climbed on top of the rocks and searched for the small basins. By painstakingly dipping my water bottle into the divots and pouring the liquid into Dusty's drops, I eventually gathered half a bottle of rain.

The entire time, I thought about Dusty lying alone and injured in the forest. I hoped he'd had a neural short and lost his connection with reality. Maybe he had dusted out and was totally unaware of what had happened. I wished for him the brief oblivion from reality. But what if he wasn't hallucinating? What if he was lying there, alone, afraid, and in pain?

I was halfway back to the grove where I'd left him, water bottle in hand, when I felt those eyes on me again. Maybe it was Ami I was imagining. Perhaps it had been her all along, ever since I set foot in this forest. Ami watching over me, guiding me. I hurried on, eager to find Dusty and help him drink the water I'd gathered.

But when I arrived at the place I thought I'd left him, he wasn't there. Remembering I'd headed in the wrong direction at first, I checked my compass. I went south for a few hundred feet, but the tree trunks made it impossible to see what lay ahead. I had to walk around each trunk, fifty feet or more each time, but I couldn't find him anywhere.

I circled back around and began yelling his name. Beyond the patter of light rain and the faint creaking of tree limbs high above my head, the forest was silent. Everything in the forest began looking the same, and I adjusted my direction again.

Dusty wasn't responding to my calls. Perhaps he had passed out from the pain? Of course, if he was in the gray zone, he wouldn't respond to me. I reached into my mind. Would I be able to throw a thought pulse to him without laying eyes on him? He couldn't be too far away. I couldn't have gotten that lost. I reached out to him with my mind. A pressure I'd never felt before pushed back against my probing. It was pliable yet impenetrable, a sort of mind membrane, a warm energy. Was that Dusty? It must be—no one else was out here. I was sure he must be alive, though I did not know where he was.

All I wanted was to see his stupid face.

The sweeper trees were closing in on me, unseen dangers behind every trunk and hiding in every shadow, and I retraced my steps. If only everything didn't look the same as everything else.

Of course there were many differences in the forest terrain: the fallen tree where the many-legged *chong* had burrowed, for example. When I finally found it, approaching from the other side, it looked different. I took a detour around it before checking my compass again, and when I turned, I knew exactly where I was—the place where the *chong* had attacked, where Dusty had collapsed. But there was no sign of him now.

"Dusty!" I yelled. "Where are you? Dusty!"

I kneeled and examined the ground, searching for clues for which direction he'd wandered. The needles were kicked around with signs of a struggle, but that had probably happened when the *chong* attacked. Had he become impatient and gone to search for water himself? That made no sense— his leg had been so swollen; he'd been in so much pain. Would he even have been able to walk? What if the *chong* had come back, crawled out from under that log and finished the job? Killed Dusty and dragged his body into its lair and eaten him?

The dead tree was only a few feet away, and I slowly

raised my head, my heart clogging my throat. I stood slowly and stepped backward carefully. Did that thing hunt by sight or smell or motion? My head buzzed with fear. Drawing a quiet, cleansing breath, I visualized the shallows, the rocking float, the flavor of a soothing tea. A thought came to me in that moment of calm—where was Dusty's pack? Surely a *chong* wouldn't have dragged that off.

And the chainsaw. I opened my eyes. Wherever Dusty had gone, he'd taken his pack and the chainsaw. He must still be alive somewhere. Had the crew found him? Had he been right that we were being tracked? I remained convinced that we were off grid. My mesh was sensitive, and I hadn't been muting beneath Ami's carpet. I would have felt the tracker. I would have felt a PAP alarm if there'd been one, if Nelson had captured his quarry.

So where was Dusty? Had he shorted out, grabbed his pack and the saw, and walked away? Had he left me behind as I'd thought about doing to him? He was gone. Vanished with all the gear.

I was alone.

That thought knocked the wind out of me as completely as one of Maduro's gut punches. I collapsed against a tree trunk and slid to the ground. Alone. In the forest. No one was looking for me. Not a soul knew I was alive. No one cared if I was dead.

I had no one. There had been no one for a long time, not really. Miz Hazel, Rajani, Kominsky, Jan, Dusty—they'd been distractions. I was alone, had been since the shallows. Only now, I finally understood what that meant.

Without others, what was the point of me? I was empty, nothing, a collection of cells and a super-charged neural mesh. Not one thing more. Invisible as I was, I might as well be dead.

No one knew I existed, so no one would notice once I was gone.

My eyes fell shut. Images were pointless. They were memories of the distant past and people I'd once loved. There was no one left to make fresh memories with.

The voice startled me. "You'd better not be a cannibal."

Chapter Thirty-Seven

✦

Accented with an archaic twang, the voice had a sing-song quality. My eyes flew open and I shouted, clumsily scrambled to my feet, and searched my pockets vainly for my multi-tool.

The thing clung to the tree, more *chong* than human. Gray scales covered its long torso, more scales over its head, soft clicking as it adjusted its foothold on the trunk ten feet away. The feet and one hand—a decidedly human hand—gripped the bark; the other held a primitive tool. It leaped off the tree and landed solidly on the ground directly in front of me, aimed the tool in my direction, a pointed tip, obviously a weapon. "Hands up," it said.

Surprise, fear, shock—all the feelings this *chong*-human hybrid aroused in me paled in comparison to my overwhelming curiosity. Unlike the *chong*s and the *zhu*s, this creature spoke, and its language sounded much like my own. It appeared to be as wary of me as I was of it, so I did as it asked and raised my hands in the air.

"Are you a cannibal?"

I stared and then shook my head.

The creature slowly lowered its weapon. "Didn't think so. I've been following you and your crazy friend for a few days."

No matter how I tried, my mouth flapped uselessly, unable to bring words over my tongue.

A snorting noise came from its head. Was the *chong* laughing at me? "Climbers and earthwalkers have at least one thing in common. Boys are useless." It reached up and pulled off its own head—and beneath the scales were a pair of unnerving eyes set into a thin face. The eyes regarded me, one blue and one green. The thin lips were set in a fierce line. "Sit."

I stumbled backward against a tree trunk and lowered my body slowly, my hands still raised so as not to startle the strange creature. Not a *chong* at all I saw now, but a young woman wearing a sort of armor made of *chong* shells. She was taller than me, maybe Dusty's height, and extremely thin, her cheekbones pressing against her skin. Her naked feet were filthy. Her hands and face were surprisingly clean and achingly pale, as though she'd not spent much time in the sun, her skin seeming even more fair when contrasted with the black of her long, unbound hair. She was unlike any female I'd ever seen, not only in appearance, but in the sturdy, natural way she held herself. Wary of me yet confident of her own strength, she looked like a solitary hunter at home among the sweepers.

"Who... who are you?"

"Ah. It speaks." Her eyes flashed. "You first."

"Now that you've caught us, do we go back to the Line or to prison?"

"You are fugitives?"

I thought about pulsing her mesh, incapacitating her and making a run for it. But she didn't look like any guard I'd ever seen. "An opportunity presented itself. Me and Dusty went for it."

"That your friend's name? The one who kills for sport?"

"He's not *shashu*. He's *hezui*."

She angled her head as if trying to hear better, and even though she didn't look like an insider, I switched from Chinglish to standard language. "He's a dustrat. An Axon user. A drug addict."

Her eyes softened, though her lips tightened. "Sorry about that. Not an excuse, though."

"Excuse?"

"I told you, I've been watching. He slaughtered a darkling beetle, took pleasure in its suffering. You didn't even eat it, and I know you're hungry. Even so, you took the life of another and wasted it!" Her eyes blazed, and the weapon pointed at me again.

"Whoa, whoa—what are you talking about—the *chong*? You're angry that Dusty killed a *chong*?"

"All souls are equal." She stated this as though it should be obvious. A common truth, like an outsider's heart stops beating between thirty-five and forty-five years.

"Did you see where Dusty went? Did he wander off somewhere?"

"I've got your murdering friend."

"You?" I scrambled to my feet. The woman allowed it. "He's not a bad person. Just loses it sometimes. How is he?"

"The centipede did a number on him. You can't be messing with creatures like that. Not that I believe the Great Ones see all," her eyes flicked skyward and back to me, "but insects deserve life too. You can't be taking their lives if you don't need them." Deciding that I posed no risk to her, she had slung her weapon over her shoulder. "Follow me."

She was fast. Running through the forest, she weaved around the tree trunks with speed and grace. She avoided the *zhu* webs with agility, bending and ducking, once even scaling the side of a tree and vaulting over the top of a low-hanging web that brought me up short.

"Wait!" I gasped, my lungs burning with each breath. Far ahead, she stopped until I jogged up to her. She was barely breathing. "How... do you... run... so fast?"

She looked surprised. "Is it fast?"

"You don't even..." I coughed, hacked up some phlegm, and spat. "I'm dying here."

"It's easier down here. I don't know."

Down here? Down where? "How much... farther?"

"A little way. He's with my people."

She set off again and left me trailing painfully behind. I still didn't know who she was.

THE NEXT BIT, well, that was something you don't see every day. Stones cropped up here and there in the distance, small and white poking through the needles. As we advanced, the amount and variety of stones multiplied: odd shapes and sizes, some round and some elongated. We were running so quickly and I was pushing myself so hard that it wasn't until I stumbled over a stone and fell that I realized it wasn't a stone at all.

The area looked like some vast *chong* killing ground. Shells or something grayish-white were strewn about, half covered in needles. I kicked at one with my foot as I slowed and it rolled out into the open.

"*Hundan!*" I recoiled, bile in my throat. "It's a human skull!" And with that, the stones resolved in my vision, became what they were, not stones or *chong* shells but bones. A vast quantity of human bones, side by side and sometimes several skeletons deep. Some white, some yellow, all covered in needles and moldering in the moist air.

The woman appeared beside me, soundless except for the gentle clicking of her armor. She reached her hand to me and hauled me effortlessly to my feet. "Yes." Serene, she seemed comfortable, at home even. "These are my people."

"Your—your people?"

Standing together surrounded by the skeletons of I couldn't imagine how many hundreds of humans, my skin went cold. I remembered the question she'd asked me. Was I a cannibal? She'd asked if I ate human flesh. Did she?

I jumped away from her, tripped over a bone, and held up my walking stick—because I had nothing else. What was I going to do, jab her with it?

She cocked her head and regarded me, her long hair falling darkly over one side of her face. "You're no cannibal. You're too afraid of remains."

"Remains? These are dead bodies! Dead people!"

"No, they're skeletons. The beetles and centipedes stripped the bones clean long ago. These are the bones of climbers a generation ago. Their spirits have been gone for maybe a hundred years. The bodies too."

I spun around, searching for other humans clothed in *chong* shells and speaking some weirdly accented American. Where was I? We'd run so quickly through the forest—she'd known instinctively where she was going—I hadn't looked at my compass since I'd lost Dusty. Were there more like her? Had she lured me here, and for what purpose? To feed me to the rest of her strange cult?

I jabbed the stick in her direction. "Stay away from me! I won't let you eat me!"

"Don't be ridiculous." Her eyes were solemn. "This is where the bones of my people rest. When our lives are over, we feed the Great Ones. We are not cannibals. We escaped long ago to save ourselves from your people."

"My people?" I laughed bitterly. "I have no people."

In an instant, I was on the float again. It had been difficult without Appei, but somehow Ami had kept food on our table. She was always sewing; her needle moving in and out of multicolored fabrics, mending pants for someone's husband, letting out a dress for someone's daughter. My eyes opened in the early light to the vision of Ami bent over the mending and they closed in the evening as she sat beside a flickering candle, her eyes straining to see.

One morning I woke to find her asleep across the table, the candle burned out beside her. She didn't rise to make me breakfast, and she slept through lunch. By dinnertime, I was hungry, but there was nothing to eat. Still, she slept. I lifted her body and dragged her to the bed. She was a small woman, and I was my father's son, stronger than I looked. I curled my body around her and fell asleep.

She didn't wake up the next morning. Or the morning after that.

I don't know who called the authorities. Maybe someone had come looking for their mending. They dragged me away from Ami. How I screamed and fought to stay with her, but still they stole me away.

Ami had gone silent. I'd always known, but my refusing to accept the fact that she'd died all those years ago didn't make it any less real. Time to stop lying to myself.

I dropped my arm, the useless stick hanging from my hand. "I'm alone."

She stood silent and still, her eyes probing my face. "So am I." She jerked her head, meaning that I should follow. "Watch your footing. They'll pile up as we walk farther in."

I walked behind her, my boots settling into each of the impressions her feet made. We were moving carefully, stepping gingerly between skeletons. She seemed to have come this way often enough to determine the best path forward. Because I was looking down and watching her feet, I didn't see the macabre fence until we passed it. Someone had raked the needles flat and excavated the skulls and bones around a grove of the biggest sweepers I'd ever seen. A terrifying dry stack of human remains encircled the giant, *chong*-hiding trees.

"What is this?" I gasped out.

"The Great Ones," she said. "Where it all began."

"Where are your people? Why do they leave their dead out here like this?"

She looked up, and I followed her gaze. Her eyes turned glassy; they looked about to spill. Then she shook her head and said, "I have no people." Forcing a smile, she motioned to me. "Your friend is over here."

Chapter Thirty-Eight

✦

A primitive lean-to of tree limbs and plant debris huddled against the trunk of a sweeper. I could see Dusty inside, stripped to his underwear and sleeping on an elevated structure beneath the green roof. The woman went inside and squatted beside him, and then closed her eyes and placed her fingers against Dusty's throat.

"His heart is still beating rapidly. Centipede toxin will do that." She had packed green leaves into his thigh wound and removed them as she spoke. Her hands moved quickly, her fingers slender and sure. Grabbing a roughly carved wooden bowl from the ground, she stood and walked away.

"Wait! Where are you going?"

"Poultice. Your friend needs one."

"I don't understand."

She called back over her shoulder. "Don't worry. He's not dying."

Everything in me wanted to hug her; she was so certain that Dusty would live. She knew things I did not, and for some unknown reason, I trusted her.

A low moan came from within the lean-to as Dusty woke. He gave me a weak smile. "Hey dude."

Tears welled in my eyes, but I swallowed them back down. I handed him his bottle and said, "Water."

"Thanks." He guzzled it, then closed his eyes and shuddered. "I think the pain stops when you're dead." He exhaled shakily, blinked his eyes open. "That girl. Freaky, huh?"

"Yeah."

We grinned stupidly at each other. Neither of us had seen a woman in a while.

Dusty groaned and struggled against the bed. "Do you feel that Lazlo? They're coming! Do you feel it?"

"No. Nothing." I took his hand and squeezed. "You're probably dusting, or maybe it's something from the *chong* bite."

"Got to go. Now. Run!" Dusty gritted his teeth and cursed.

The woman was suddenly back and elbowed me out of her way. "What's happening? Where's the pain?"

And then it hit me, hard. Out of nowhere, the pain brought me to my knees. I reached for my mind carpet and wrapped it tightly around, but the signal was so fierce, so close, traces got through to my mesh. Dusty's lips moved, and though I couldn't hear his voice, I knew what he was saying: We need to run. He struggled to his feet, swaying on unsure legs, falling back to the ground.

I hauled him up and wrapped an arm around his waist. He leaned heavily into me. We staggered forward like some kids running a three-legged race.

She yanked Dusty away from me and shoved him roughly back to the bed. "He's injured. What are you two doing?"

The carpet fell away from my mind. "They're coming," I forced through clenched teeth. "Sending an alarm to our brains... incapacitating us. They'll be here in minutes... drag us back to prison. Or... worse."

Her face went hard. She became a *chong* again, rapidly fastening the helmet to her head and gripping her weapon tightly in a warrior fist. She disappeared silently into the forest.

———

THE PULSING PAIN STOPPED SUDDENLY. A movement at the edge of vision caught my eye, and a yellow uniform marched into view, stopped in front of the lean-to, and crouched by the opening.

"There you are. Found you," said Jan Oh, resting the PAP tracker on his knee.

"Where are the rest of them?" I asked.

"Who? Nelson's crew?" Jan scoffed. "Those cowards aren't coming. They took one look at the Line break and figured you'd all died. But your gear was gone, so I figured you'd done a runner."

"And Nelson just gave you his tracker?" I'd never known Nelson to let anyone touch the PAP tracker. The man slept with it under his head or shoved down his pants, I was sure of it. He'd surely never give it away and then stay behind with the crew, unarmed.

Jan winked at me. "Let's say something in his mind encouraged him to entrust it to me."

"Back away, slowly." The woman had returned and was pointing her weapon at Jan.

In his unflappable way, Jan Oh took in the woman's *chong* helmet and armor. "Now I've seen everything."

He raised his hands and stepped slowly away from the lean-to. He relaxed his eyes a moment, and I knew he was sending her a thought pulse. I sensed it, just as I'd sensed there'd been something, or as it turned out, someone, watching me in the forest.

Unphased by Jan's efforts, the woman's resolve didn't waver.

"No reaction. Interesting," he said. "You have no neural mesh, do you? Uh, Lazlo? Care to help me here?"

I nodded at the woman. She scowled at me, frowned at Jan, and then warily dropped her arm.

"You know about thought pulses?" I asked Jan.

"You think you're the only one who can seed a thought, Lazlo?" He chuckled. "Wait until you figure out what else you can do with that mesh in your head."

I'm ashamed to say my mouth dropped open. "You know?"

"I had a feeling. You were smart. Never pulsed me once, did you? I wasn't entirely sure, though. Not until the mudslide. It wasn't me saved the crew. Don't care about any of them. Just my *zhong shi de peng you*. And I can't sense him anymore."

In my month on the Line, that was the most I'd ever heard Jan say.

I said, "You know he's dead."

He nodded.

"It wasn't us," said Dusty. "We'd never hurt him. You know that, right? It was one of those bombs—"

"Calm down, Dusty," I said. The smallest flicker passed across Jan's face, and he was placid again. "He knows."

Then I said, "Why'd you follow us?"

Jan's gaze went to Dusty, lying injured in the shelter, then back to me. "Kominsky would have wanted it."

Dusty said, "Will you take me back?"

I stared at Dusty. "We talked about this. We aren't going back, the added time—"

"You can't go back, Lazlo. Just you. Me? It's only two

years. In prison or on the Hill? What difference does it make? I'm a dustrat, Lazlo. Always will be."

"No. You can change," I said.

Dusty shook his head. Wouldn't look at me. "It's what I am."

He was telling the truth, his truth. Something in his insider's life had broken him badly. Chances were, he didn't remember what had broken him. And that was how he wanted it.

"No." I looked at Jan. "You're not going back, are you? They'll say you ran, give you a longer sentence. We'll keep going, get clear of the sweepers, and be free—"

Jan watched me sadly. "Lazlo, you know my time is ending. My generation is going silent. I can feel the weight in my heart and in my lungs. I've had longer than most because I was an insider, but I've aged quickly since coming to the Line. My faithful friend is gone, and once Dusty is fit to travel, I'll take him back. Then, I'm done."

Dusty would return to the Line and ultimately Coulee with Jan. They'd made their choice, so I made mine. "I'm never going back to prison. I'll continue on alone."

She'd stood so quietly I'd nearly forgotten she was there. Her soft, lilting voice broke the silence. "I'll go with you."

The Present

Her long fingers wipe the tears from my face and I glance up. Those mismatched eyes watch me. Still serious and unafraid, but something else now too.

She rocks back on her bare heels and stands. She reaches out a hand to help me up, but I ignore it and stand on my own. I clear my throat, look at my hands, look at the ground where her people lie, look anywhere but at her. I'm tired, embarrassed, and relieved.

"You survived," she says. "And you're free."

She places stones on a mound she calls a cairn. Stretching her hands to either side, she tilts her head back and chants something that sounds like a prayer. And yeah, I think. That's the right thing to do when people die. That's what I never gave my mother.

Appei's face fills my memory as I try to remember how to do it. Facing east, I recite the prayers from my childhood. When I kneel, I pray for Kominsky, for Rajani. I pray for Appei. And then, I pray for Ami.

I talk to the heavens for a long time before I stand. Our eyes meet. She knows me.

She smiles and takes my hand. "Ready?"

"For what?"

"I'm going to the ocean. Or have you got other plans?"

We leave her people and my past in the boneyard. All my guilt and untruths lie buried there now. She's left something behind too. She'll tell me when she's ready. It's a long walk to the shallows.